THE
DARKSLAYER

VOLUME ONE

CRAIG HALLORAN

ROBYNN !
YOU
BROOL !

CRAIG
HALLORAN

CONTENTS

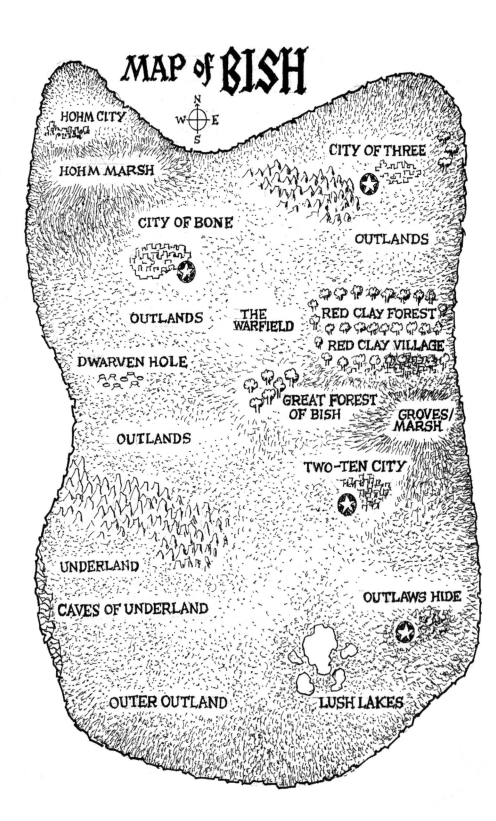

MAP of BISH

N W E S

HOHM CITY

HOHM MARSH

CITY OF THREE

CITY OF BONE

OUTLANDS

OUTLANDS

THE WARFIELD

RED CLAY FOREST

RED CLAY VILLAGE

DWARVEN HOLE

GREAT FOREST OF BISH

GROVES/ MARSH

OUTLANDS

TWO-TEN CITY

UNDERLAND

CAVES OF UNDERLAND

OUTLAWS HIDE

OUTER OUTLAND

LUSH LAKES

THE DARKSLAYER

VOLUME ONE

CHAPTER I

BISH AND BONE

The City of Bone was home to the wildest, wickedest, and most ruthless men and women of the world of Bish. Many factors were at the root of the city's problems, but it was mainly that the human inhabitants in the City of Bone were an undeniable mess. It was the largest city of the world with well over one hundred thousand citizens, who were kept under control by its so-called rulers by means of intimidation, torture, and death.

The ruling class, who called themselves the Royals, managed to keep order with unjust trials and public hangings as well as several forms of public humiliation. Despite these efforts, things were often tumultuous and out of control, as the massive city of unrivaled temptation was too much for its feebleminded people to handle. A very good man could lose his sense of wellbeing as quickly as blowing out a candle, while his remaining goodness drifted away forever like a wisp of smoke.

It was a dreaded place for the common man and woman who wanted to live a simple life rather than risk all in the unprotected lands beyond the great walls of the City of Bone. The crowded streets were filled with liars, alley trolls, murderers, thieves, slavers, politicians, and evil incarnate. It was the home of all the world's greatest dangers; at least that is what all natural-born citizens in the City of Bone thought, but that was only because most of its human inhabitants had never left the city, and so, according to them, nothing outside of its walls could possibly be worse. They had all long since assumed that just living in that great city made them tough enough to survive anywhere else if they had to. By their own unmerited account, a day in the City of Bone was like a month in the dangerous Outlands, which was all the land outside of the city's massive walls. Of course the majority of the population within the City of Bone were poor, decrepit, and desperate, with nothing better to do than gripe all day about surviving. And yet, the City of Bone was the star city of the tiny world called Bish.

Compared to the City of Bone, the rest of the world of Bish was another matter entirely. Bish contained other races, as well as other cities with the same problems as the City of Bone. The truth was that the City of Bone meant no more to the rest of the world than the world meant to the City of Bone. The people of other cities and races didn't really care about much at all; they were mainly selfish in some shape or form, and had their own survival to be concerned about. On Bish you had only two main things to worry about: the overbearing humans and their even more overbearing rivals, the underlings. The underlings did not live in cities above the ground, though; instead, they lived in small cities and majestic caves below Bish's surface. Underlings, unlike humans, were an entirely evil race, whereas humans and other races, for the most part, contained both good and evil. The underlings, though not outwardly at war with humans at this time, hated humans more than any other race on Bish. Humans always had the greater population, but the underlings had the greater lifespan. The underlings were also more patient, and there was often apprehension on Bish about the threat of all-out war. At this time in particular, the underlings had lost patience, not with all humans but with one specific individual who had singlehand-edly been causing irreparable damage to the underling population. That one human was, at this time, in the wonderfully wicked City of Bone. He was the one that the underlings, as well as many others on Bish, called the Darkslayer.

———

A single candle-lit lantern illuminated the large man imprisoned in the gloom of a damp dungeon cell below the restless City of Bone. Rats the size of cats scurried about on the moldy stone floors, feasting on any leftover scraps or excrement that would fill them. Even the leftover bones of long past occupants were consumed if the rats had no other option. The lone man chained to the wall of the cell was snoring loudly, his deep rumblings keeping the hungry rats at bay. Long, stringy locks of sweaty blonde hair hung over his snoring face. Dirty, ragged clothes still covered most of his freshly beaten body. The man had slept through his beating, stunning the city guards so that they decided to hang him in his cell until he came around, to assure themselves that he had felt something.

The guards did not realize the significance of this man, nor did they care. Named Venir, the man seemed at peace as if his conscience was clear, whatever crimes he had committed. But killers have no con-science, especially in his case. For Venir was more than just a common killer. He had unknowingly been serving the greater good of Bish for some time. It was Venir who the underlings called the scourge of their kind. It was Venir who had decimated their ranks, time after time, and it was Venir they wanted dead. But Venir was in this situation for an entirely different reason, and the underlings did not realize who this man was, or why he was hanging in a small dungeon beneath the City of Bone. No, the name of Venir meant nothing to the underlings, for they called this human by a different name. With great hatred and reverence, they called him the Darkslayer.

Th events that brought him to the dungeon occurred one night in the city while the two moons cast shadows on the city structures, adding a strange red hue to the colorful flowers and curtains in the apartment windows above. Venir, the warrior, and Melegal, the thief, decided that this particular night had a good feeling to it. The alleys in the City of Bone seemed less smelly and the puddles of urine fewer than usual. The screams of pleasure and laughter seemed to outweigh the screams of terror that normally filled nights in the City of Bone. It was a hot and dry evening, and many strolled about among the shadows and brilliant banners of the Royal's houses that marked their districts.

It was good to be home in the city again, thought Venir. The brawny warrior was strutting the streets with a broad grin on his handsome face. His long blonde hair was blowing in the breezy night air, and he kept having to brush it back from his blazing blue eyes. Venir stood out among a crowd, and if you did not see him, you certainly heard him, for that is the way he liked to unwind and have fun. He had been hunting in the Outlands for several weeks and was glad to be back among the pleasures of the big city. He was looking forward to being home and relaxing among the human population, enjoying some good grog and playful debauchery.

Venir and his old buddy, Melegal, had lived a long time together, though not always, in the city they recognized as home. More reserved and less noticeable than his bulky comrade, Melegal liked to maintain a low profile. In the wealthier districts of the crowded city, the two adventurers enjoyed skimming from the Royals. Skimming was one of their less risky and more successful pastimes. And venturing where they weren't normally welcome seemed to draw the two men like raindrops to a river. Venir was currently posing as a noble warrior, and Melegal as his wealthy comrade, claiming to hale from the City of Three in order to get into a noble tavern, the

Chimera, on this night. They had performed this stunt a dozen times over the years, and the profits they made had grown along with their experience. As the evening drew into night, and the alcohol battered better judgment, Venir and Melegal knew they were in for another profitable venture at the expense of the city's self-appointed leaders.

The Chimera, however, was not just another tavern with typical occupants in the upper districts. The Chimera was known for its low-key discretion, as it drew some of the City of Bone's upper class Royals, who oft times enjoyed a seedier sort of lifestyle away from the proper manners of higher society. The sweet, expensive perfume that filled the air came from the gorgeous, sweaty bodies of the most beautiful and expensive women in the town. This was a den where many, particularly young ones, liked to sow their Royal oats from time to time, as well as having fun at the expense of the common folk. The Royal class had two types of men, the good and the bad. The good ones would never be caught in the Chimera, but the bad ones came and went shamelessly whenever and wherever they wished, and none held them accountable for any indecent acts they committed. "Do as they say or die in the dungeons," the poor store-keepers would say. "Do as they say or disappear," the commoners would warn. But Venir and Melegal could not have cared less what anyone had to say. They had been this way since their childhood.

Venir and Melegal settled quickly and without suspicion into the accommodating atmosphere, and their spirits rose high into the night. They gambled with the girls and related exploits to the locals, and it wasn't long before these two, allegedly from the City of Three, were the talk of the tavern. And then, while Venir and Melegal were throwing back some dark grog and making new acquaintances, a cocky young warrior named Tonio introduced himself to Venir, and made him a challenge.

"For the honor of the City of Bone, I challenge the proud warrior from the City of Three to a quick fence!"

The quick fence was one of many common tavern displays of skill and bravado that were a long-standing tradition of the humans in the City of Bone and other Bish cities. Younger men often challenged one another to impress a woman or shame a friend. The greatest dangers a man usually faced in such bouts were bruised bones or broken pride.

Venir had no such worries. "I accept on behalf of the City of Three!" he shouted.

Venir and Melegal smiled wryly at one another as people quickly gathered round, cleared an area for the two participants to enter, and then encircled the two warriors.

The crowd started roaring, chanting, placing bets, and ordering more drinks.

The head barkeep, Sam, was the referee of the quick fence. He was an older, heavily set man who was clearly a veteran of the city guard, judging by the distinct tattoo on his right forearm. Calmly he strode between the two opponents and placed a chest-high, heavy, wrought-iron candle stand between them. With his cigar he lit the thick, white, foot-high candle, and placed it on the spike of the candle stand to prevent it from falling off.

The warriors then faced off, each a sword's length from the candle.

The crowd grew silent as the barkeep stepped back, raised his hands high, and blew a giant smoke ring into the air.

"Best of three!" he announced.

The two participants squared off, hands on their sheathed swords. The young Tonio tightly gripped his long, fine sword with its jewel-encrusted hilt. Calmly, Venir gripped his hefty, not-so-fancy broadsword. The women swooned with excitement, loudly whispering their preferences: either the rugged good-looking warrior or the younger, taller Royal. Their fantasies became clear in the air in the moments before Tonio spoke.

"I hope you've got a lot of money, old man."

There was some snickering. Venir didn't move, but the excitement of the contest blazed in his eyes. He focused on the candle's burning light.

"Go!" shouted the barkeep.

Venir yanked his sword and just missed the candle before it fell at the mercy of his opponent's blade.

"Ton-ee-oo," the crowd cheered, "Ton-ee-oo!" Tonio lifted his arms high in victory, thrusting his sword in the air in unison.

Venir handed his sword to the barkeep, who inspected it, then wiped the blade down and returned it to the warrior. Venir sheathed his sword while Melegal raised the betting odds with the excited crowd. Next, Tonio's blade was inspected and then wiped down, and Tonio calmed himself and got ready for the next signal. Venir prepared himself as the barkeep replaced the candle with a new one and lit it. The crowd quieted as the barkeep raised his hand.

"Go!"

Blades licked out quicker than the alcohol-glazed eyes could see. The candlestick fell to the floor. The crowd looked about, confused, not too sure who had made the cut. They began to mutter, most saying that Tonio had won.

"Hold, hold!" shouted the barkeep at the top of his lungs. "I must check the blades!"

The contestants surrendered their blades, one at a time. The barkeep first inspected the sword of Tonio with a keen, smoke-reddened eye. Then he wiped it down, returned it, and checked the broad blade of Venir. His inspection revealed a small residue of white candle wax at the tip of the blade.

"The warrior from the City of Three is the victor!" declared the barkeep. The crowd booed and hissed. Then there were more shouts of encouragement to the Royal favorite, while other locals complimented the warrior from the City of Three with kind words ranging from "son of a trollop" to "inbred cattle molester", some of which even Venir didn't recognize. He felt flattered.

While the barkeep placed the last candle, Melegal continued placing and accepting bets, and the two contestants prepared for the final round.

"Luck," sneered Tonio. "I haven't been beaten in two years and I'm not about to end my streak with someone like you. I'm the best and you won't ever beat me again."

Venir seemed unperturbed. "For Bone!" he shouted to his rude fans, forgetting his disguise in the excitement.

"Bone. . . Bone. . . Bone . . ." they chanted.

Venir eyed the flame. Tonio gripped his blade as the sweat beaded heavily on his forehead. The barkeep stepped back and raised his arms high. The locals fell silent.

"Go!"

The thick white candle hit the floor. It lay there quietly, still burning. Tonio looked at the candle in amazement, and the crowd shared his astonishment. His sword was still half in its sheath. He looked across at his opponent.

Venir stood there with his arms crossed over his chest, smirking back at him. "Looks like you lost your streak. Guess you'll have to start a new one now, young man!" he laughed.

Melegal was collecting money, and the wary barkeep was looking dumbly at Venir, while the crowd cursed their losses. Tonio stormed away, fuming and pouting.

The crowd quickly went back to the business of drinking, while Tonio's buddies gathered at their preferred table and offered him words of sympathy.

"Did you have to draw that fast?" questioned Melegal quietly.

"He's a such cocky little baby. I wanted to humble him. Who knows, maybe it'll do him some good."

"I doubt it. Not those Royal types, they're all rotten to the core!"

"Yep, so why pass up an opportunity like that? Anyway, how'd we do?"

"Better than usual. These guys have deeper pockets than the crowds we're used to. Let's get a couple of drinks and then get out of here. I'm leery of the Royals and the city patrol." The two companions grabbed a table and ordered a few more rounds of grog and ale.

The room got smokier as the evening wore on. The tavern was full of drunkenness, laughter, arguing, broken pottery, and the occasional whiff of vomit. The two men were starting to feel at home again, but Melegal was still a little edgy about being in such a wealthy part of town. Finally, however, not recognizing anyone who could possibly identify them, he began to loosen up. Venir was loud and rowdy, racing other men in drinking contests, buying escort women drinks, and even buying a drink for a thirsty-looking dog. Luckily, people didn't seem to mind, seeing that he was buying drinks for them all.

Something was up though, Melegal noticed. The younger nobles had further isolated themselves from the crowd. The Royals of Bone would never lose graciously to Royals from another city. But something more menacing seemed to be agitating the Royal Tonio, as if the young warrior was being set up by others. Melegal's thought was broken as two voluptuous ladies of the night pressed their full bodies into his face with offers of pleasure beyond even his own imagination. It didn't take long for them to titillate Melegal into accepting their irresistible wares.

Then the unwanted happened.

Tailed by a small pack of encouraging friends, Tonio stormed towards Venir. The pack of pampered young men in colorful and expensive clothes gathered around Venir's busy table.

"Hey, Tonio," suggested one shifty warrior of a different Royal family, "challenge him to a real man's game! The strength test!" This re-energized the deadened, late-night atmosphere. All the young men and tavern dwellers let out a roar of encouragement.

"What do you say?" demanded Tonio. "Care to put your money on a real challenge?"

"I don't know, boy, I'd be afraid I might end another of your streaks!" slurred Venir.

"Ooh!" The crowd liked it.

Tonio tore off his leather jerkin with its gleaming studs. "Let's see what you say after you eat the floor, mongrel!"

"Let's go, then, you double-cur-eating momma's boy!" Venir answered, pointing drunkenly at one of Tonio's colleagues whom he thought was Tonio, who said "Yeah," with a wink to the crowd.

The crowd was so excited that Melegal had trouble taking the bets, but the bets were huge, and Melegal was salivating. The roars rose to an almost deafening crescendo as the two big men squared off.

The crowd sized them up as they stood chest to chest. Tonio stood about six-and-a-half feet tall, well groomed and powerfully athletic, glaring down at Venir's six-foot stature, and breathing heavily onto his balding blonde head. In Venir the crowd saw an older man, thirty-something years of age, wearing a unique, heavily-hooded smock with white wolf-fur shoulders over attire that was more typical of a man from the City of Three. Although the hooded smock made Venir's shoulders appear inhumanly large, the two warriors still looked mismatched to the onlookers. The consensus in the room was heavily in favor of Tonio.

Tonio was sneering. "You're going down. I'm the best at this and you're going down hard!" he growled.

"No kicking, biting, spitting, head butting, or tripping!" the head barkeep announced loudly. "Your hands must be locked on the other's upper arms at all times. Whoever forces his opponent on his back, wins!"

Venir readied himself by removing his hooded smock, exposing his bare arms. The spectators let out a slight sigh of amazement.

"Take up your starting positions!"

They faced each other to lock arms. The younger warrior looked slightly surprised when he had trouble gripping onto the giant arms of Venir. Even Tonio's large hands could not get a solid hold on Venir's smooth, gorilla-sized arms. The muscle wouldn't even give way to a squeeze. Venir locked onto Tonio's powerful, unscarred arms, gripping right below the biceps, while Melegal started taking bets.

"Are you ready?"

Both contestants nodded as they stared at one another in anticipation.

"Last chance to save some money, boy," said Venir dryly.

"Never!" Tonio replied.

"We'll see!" Venir said with a menacing grin.

The barkeep gave the signal.

Tonio made the first move. With a terrific upward tug of Venir's arms, he drew Venir close and quickly tried to drive him off balance, forcing him back a full step.

The crowd whooped and roared, thrilled at the two men finally going head to head.

Tonio began twisting and jerking as he tried to shake Venir left or right to get him off balance. Venir knew all these basic moves, but they were good moves and well executed, so he grunted and shuffled, allowing Tonio to lead the dance.

Tonio was driving him back. The crowd screamed. The young warrior's friends, full of fire and liquor, chanted obscenities and not-so-pleasantries to Venir, and to Melegal as well.

Tonio was looking good, and Melegal kept up the betting for another ten seconds.

Then the time was up for the charade. Venir took the offensive, his large hands suddenly squeezing so hard that the blood almost stopped flowing into Tonio's arms. As surprise overcame his opponent, Venir half jerked the young warrior's arms out of their sockets. Tonio began to bite his lip as Venir's squeeze deepened further.

The younger warrior tried to no avail to pull away, but pride and anger kept him in the contest. To Venir's surprise, Tonio's natural athleticism kept him in the game as he fought back. But Tonio began to realize that he didn't have the strength to match Venir's might, yet could not pull free of the older man's grip. The crowd was going wild.

The match was taking longer than Melegal had anticipated. Both Venir and Tonio were getting winded after all their drinking, but they short-stepped back and forth with all their might. Tonio was weakening. In desperation, he head butted Venir square in the nose. Blood trickled down the older warrior's face, its redness quickly covering his chin and dripping to the floor. The sight of blood drove the men and women into such frenzy that the head barkeep stood atop the bar with a large oaken club in his hand.

Venir growled and snarled, half man, half bull warrior. With arms locked on Tonio like a vice, he drew the young man in close.

"Down you go!" he roared through blood-splattered lips.

Venir crossed his exhausted opponent's arms and pulled him in tight, turned his hip under the man and, impossibly, lifted the young warrior's arms and body over his own head. A monstrous crack exploded from Tonio followed by a massive release of air as Venir smashed him, back-first, into the hardened oak floor.

Silence filled the room. The crowd was stunned by the sudden and unexpected ending to the battle, executed with a move none had seen before. It was a contest that would be remembered for a long time in the Chimera.

Tonio was still breathing, but out cold. Lifting him to carry him out, they discovered that it was the hard oak floor that had cracked, not the warrior's back.

Melegal hastily collected all the money from the hapless audience. While Tonio's companions carried the young man out the back of the Chimera in a crumpled heap, Venir and Melegal decided to down a few victory drinks.

It was well into the morning when the two companions made their way out. Several of Tonio's fellow warriors scowled and made feeble excuses for their leader, saying he had been too drunk, and other such excuses. When Venir and Melegal left with some ladies in tow, a couple of suspicious-looking Royal warriors caught up to them outside, congratulated Venir on an awesome feat, and expressed their appreciation for his thwarting of the overbearing young Royal. Venir, whose pride hurt more than his nose, felt embarrassed that the battle had lasted so long.

"Gee Venir," Melegal finally added after the Royals had left them alone. "It almost looked like you weren't in control of that whole bout. It could have cost us." But Melegal wasn't complaining as much as normal, due to the comforts of the ladies in the nooks of his arms.

"That kid surprised me, is all I can say. I have a broken nose to show for it. But don't worry, Me, I won't be so careless next time."

"Don't worry, big boy," added one of the blondes that hung onto Venir's bruised arms. "We'll take care of you."

As they all laughed and headed back to the apartment of the two adventurers, somewhere in the shadows, someone from the Chimera took note of the big warrior's whereabouts.

CHAPTER 2

CHAIN LASH

It was raining heavily in the City of Bone. A few days had passed since Venir's careless pride had cost him a broken nose in the Chimera. Right now he was drunk, and well beyond his ability to exercise good judgment, which was never one of his finer points to begin with. He often rushed headlong into adventures of all sorts with fear far from his mind, and would seldom hesitate to do something foolish as long as he felt it would be fun. Normally, Melegal kept his foolhardy friend on the right track, but even Melegal needed a break from his brutish friend from time to time. And so tonight, Venir was without Melegal.

The grinning warrior walked through the rain, whistling a tune he had heard somewhere earlier in the dreary day. He had decided to go back to the Chimera to get a few more drinks, and maybe bump into some of those people he thought he'd impressed a few nights earlier. However, in his alcohol-induced state it escaped his thoughts that he had disguised himself as a Royal last time. His current appearance was that of a commoner, a very large, poorly clothed one to boot, entering into a place where he didn't belong, with neither a plan nor a care. Venir wanted some more of that premium dark grog, and maybe a bottle for the road. More than likely someone would want to buy him a bottle, he thought, laughing out loud. He wouldn't stay too long. He would shake some hands and soon be out of there, without any trouble.

Soaking wet, and wearing a heavy black cloak and muddied boots, Venir strolled in. He could not have been more out of place if he'd had a dead cat strapped to his head. There were only a handful of Royal types in the room, one of whom clearly recognized him from the last time. Venir was too drunk to notice the displeasure of certain patrons at his appearance. Oblivious, he went up to the bar and barked out an order for some of that dandy grog. The same pock-marked head barkeep prepared his grog, and signaled silently to another Royal patron, sitting well back behind Venir. Venir didn't seem to notice. It was not long before that particular patron, a Royal, disappeared into the back of the tavern.

"Thanks, Sam," Venir muttered almost inaudibly, tossing him a large silver coin that more than covered his tab.

"No problem, Mister," Sam replied, sweat beading his brow. Venir stared him in the eyes and drained his glass. Something didn't seem quite right, but the grog went down just fine.

"That was good," Venir grinned. "How about another? Two!"

After another couple of whiskies as well as several ales, Sam offered Venir one more small glass of grog, courtesy of a shapely red-head he'd failed to notice at the opposite end of the bar. Flattered, Venir turned to the other patrons and toasted her, roaring his drunken thanks and describing her comely body in a booming voice that all could hear. Then he shot back the grog and slammed the glass down onto the bar. There was a low, wicked chuckle from somewhere in the room.

The grog had tasted different this time, Venir noticed—more bitter, but certainly intoxicating. Beginning to realize that this wasn't the same dandy grog, his brows buckled in anger, but when the floor suddenly smashed him full in the face, he didn't feel a thing.

He awoke disoriented, chained, and hanging from a wall in a small, smelly cell. His angry grunt aggravated the throbbing in his head, and awakened the unkempt, heavyset young guard. The guard got up from his chair, scratched his unshaven chin, and looked through the bars at Venir.

"Finally got yer hide, didn't they, tough guy?" the guard asked, spitting tobacco through the cell bars, though it didn't reach Venir.

Venir uttered a faint laugh. Offended, the guard unlocked the cell, swung back its barred door, strode up to Venir, and spat thick dark tobacco juice full in his face.

"What d'ya think of that, tough guy?"

"I think," Venir replied almost politely, "you'll be the first to die."

The guard slammed his fat fist straight into Venir's rock-hard stomach, then winced in pain. A little panicked and unsure of himself now, the young guard quickly left the cell and locked it. Holding his injured wrist, he skittered down the hall to notify the warden that the prisoner was awake.

Venir checked out his all-too-familiar surroundings. He had been here and in similar city dungeons, for one reason or another, but had always found a way out, or an associate who might post bail. The only unfamiliar detail was the chubby city guard. The young rookie was fresh meat and he probably wouldn't kill him, Venir thought to himself, but just damage him severely. He inspected the chains that bound him. They were rusted and breakable, and the cell door could probably be knocked off its hinges with one mighty kick, for its better days had passed. But he figured he'd wait until he knew why he was in here this time; and he really needed to know who had drugged his grog. That had really ticked him off. It was embarrassing to have been duped again so easily at the Chimera. To make matters worse, his nose was aching again and the rest of his body was now bruised to match. But it could have been worse: nothing felt broken, not even a rib. He was lucky all he had was a headache this time. But who would have the nerve, he asked himself. It must have been the Royals he'd crossed once too often.

Many hours passed before his thoughts were interrupted by several sets of footsteps coming along the dungeon hall. Four figures strode into full view at the cell door: the rookie guard, a warden he recognized well, a familiar young brown-haired warrior, and a much older, rich and powerful-looking man. The last two were both over six feet and looked alike, obviously father and son. They stood out as upper-class Royals, and their appearance in the dungeon surprised him, though he didn't show it.

"It hasn't taken you long to wind up here again, I see," announced the ugly warden, trying to impress his guests.

Venir didn't reply.

"You've been brought in for assault of a Royal and theft," the warden continued, "and threatening a city guard. What do you say to these charges?"

"It's bullcrap! I'm here because I beat that loudmouthed little braggart in the quick fence and strength test, and embarrassed him in front of his rich little buddies."

"That's not true!" screamed the young warrior, reddening as he gripped his fancy long sword as if about to pull it out and use it. "Look, Dad! I broke his nose when he tried to challenge me. Look!"

Venir winced. "Did you tell your daddy how much money you lost, boy?" he goaded. "Quite a bit, I recall!"

"Lying crook!" whined the young man. "You attacked me from behind and stole my money!"

"You mean your daddy's money? And how would you have seen me attacking you from behind?" Venir was laughing aloud now.

"He's a liar, father! He didn't beat me! He's a thief! Open the gate! Open it! I'll tear this bum to pieces. You scum! You'll rot in this cell or die by my sword!"

His father cut him off with a quick backhand to his face. Silenced, the dejected Tonio continued to fume. It didn't help that Venir was laughing and making mocking faces at Tonio. He even stuck out his tongue, making a funny "phlllyt" sound. The young warrior stormed from the room, wailing obscenities.

When Tonio was out of shouting distance, his father haughtily ordered the warden not to feed the prisoner for two days and to give him ten lashes twice a day. The father cast Venir one last look of pity. "What a waste of a man. At least if you were a Royal, you might not have to die for such a meaningless crime." Then he left.

"Unless you're lucky enough to die within a week," the warden told Venir, "you'll be calling this dungeon home for most of your life. A crime against a Royal means you don't get a trial. You messed with the wrong people. They've got the money and power to make you pay."

"I can leave when I choose," Venir assured him, "and nobody can do anything about it."

"Yeah, right!" said the warden. The guards left Venir hanging alone in his cell.

This situation was new to Venir. He had never been brought up on charges more serious than public intoxication, damage to public property, provocative speeches, or skimming, and never by a Royal. Mostly he stayed just a few days in jail. But this time Royals had it in for him, and he actually felt uncertain about his future in the City of Bone.

The Royals were the elite rulers of the City, and the less wealthy had no rights over them. If a Royal accused you, you were guilty. You either paid a penalty, were killed, or spent years—decades, even—in the dungeons. To survive, the best the lesser classes could do was steer clear of the Royals or do as they said, in what usually amounted to a form of slavery.

As bad as that may seem, it was easy to avoid such troubles, because the Royals made up less than ten percent of the population of the City of Bone, and if a Royal accused you, it was easy to hide in such a big city. In addition, the city guard was incapable of enforcing all the frivolous accusations of the Royals. There was too much crime and not enough manpower. Several areas were not even patrolled, and these were the areas Venir frequented. He was safe in the dark local areas, and he knew that the guards there only pursued criminals after large numbers of major offenses. And anyway, major crimes were more lucrative for the city guards.

So how had Venir been caught? After some hard thinking and remembering his encounter with Tonio several days ago, it finally dawned on him. What an ego he must have, thought Venir, to go to all this trouble to get me back.

Venir realized it was his own fault he had been drugged, and blamed himself for returning to the same establishment too soon, too drunk, and without Melegal. This was a no-no in their business. A rich, smart, and vengeful man could easily pay a spotter to alert him when a foe was around, and the spotter could have been anyone within a quarter mile of the establishment. He should have known this little warrior would have it in for him, but Venir had got a little too cocky and stupid. Unlike most people in the City of Bone, Venir never felt in danger there. He was too weathered by his ventures in the Outlands, and had seen horrors such as the common people had never heard of. Besides, dark grog can make a red-blooded man feel invincible, and in Venir's case, it worked every time.

So here he was in a dank gray cell, hanging in chains, feeling hungry, foolish, and hung-over. A slow hour or so passed before he heard a scratchy voice from somewhere diagonally to his right.

"Hey, big Vee. What's up?"

It was Melegal. Venir was not surprised. He had long gotten over his amazement at Melegal's way of appearing out of nowhere.

"Nothing, just hanging," he replied sourly.

Melagal explained that as soon as he'd found out Venir was in the city dungeon, he had promptly had himself thrown in as well, for calling a city guardsman a "big, ugly, cow-loving orc-face". Apparently, Melegal had already escaped his first cell and managed to sneak into the one he now occupied.

Melegal wanted to make sure Venir got out of jail; he needed him around for protection and profit. This was their relationship, and it worked for both men. Melegal had been raised from birth in the City of Bone and he knew its history well. The two had met as children in one of its many orphanages, and Venir had liked Melegal, though most did not. The orphanage offered the adventuresome boys few comforts or choices, for their days were filled with hard labor performed beneath the City of Bone. Months would sometimes pass before they caught even a glimpse of sunlight. Many hopeless and pain-filled years passed for the two young boys before they grew bold enough to escape and live on their own in the City of Bone. Once they found freedom, they never looked back or reflected on their past. The pair managed just fine despite their young age. But eventually Melegal had branched out to test his own skills within the City, while Venir, who had been born in the Outlands, headed out to the land he knew best.

Venir looked across at Melegal, thinking how funny it was that this gaunt, average-sized man with his unhealthy complexion always looked exactly the same. He had an unfriendly, though not uncomely, demeanor, a not-so-freshly-shaven face, and sharp features with gray eyes. He had looked forty-five years old when Venir was twenty, yet they were about the same age , as far as they knew. Melegal was still wearing his drab gray rags, and even had on the annoyingly floppy black cloth hat he always wore, hanging like a dead leaf down the right side of his head. Why it was so special to his friend, Venir did not know.

Their friendship had begun as young boys in the orphanage, the day some older bullies snatched a similar hat from Melegal. Venir, the new and well-intentioned defender of the weak, whipped the bullies soundly and took back the hat for Melegal. They had been friends ever since. Men always hated Melegal's hat, but women, for some reason, liked and commented on it. Venir never understood the importance of the hat, but found it funny when Melegal explained that it made him look 'distinguished'.

Melegal was a great friend and a most capable ally. His greatest skill was thieving. He could pick locks, pockets, and traps with ease. He could squeeze like a contortionist into crevices and through bars. He was unnoticeable by day and invisible in the dark, and he just loved to steal and skim. He was born to it. He was born to blow it all too, for he and Venir shared the same passion for grog, ale, and women.

"So, do you want to get out of this one," asked Melegal, unlocking Venir's cell and walking in, "or shall I sneak you out again? May I unchain you, Mr. Stupido?" he mocked.

"Just get me some food and drink, Melegal."

"Oh no, no," piped Melegal. "They specifically said you're not to eat for two days. Sorry, but rules are rules here in the palisades."

Venir knew the thief was mad at him for his blunder, because it would cost him business while he wasn't on the streets. Venir was his bodyguard, so to speak. In turn, Melegal felt he had to come to jail to protect him and maybe help him escape.

Venir knew Melegal wanted him to admit his mistake before he fed Venir. The thief always played these games, but had never got Venir to acknowledge any mistake. And Melegal was always too greedy and impatient for the next business transaction to regain his lost profit. He soon disappeared, and reappeared minutes later with a nice plate of fruit and meat jerky.

Venir didn't even acknowledge it.

The minutes became hours. Finally, two familiar guards entered, carrying a whip.

The city warden was a big, cruel-looking man with merciless eyes, while the chubby new recruit was dedicated to duty and appeared as nervous as he was excited to witness his first lashing.

"On yer feet, dirt!" snarled the big whip-wielding warden. "Time for yer beating."

"I'm sorry, my current situation doesn't allow my feet to touch ground," mocked the hanging prisoner.

"Ew, that will cost ya an extra ten, smart aleck. I'm gonna enjoy this," said the warden with a sinister smile.

The new guard seemed impressed by his mentor's show of machismo, and gave an approving nod. It was a bonding moment between student and teacher.

The two guards unlocked, unchained, and half-dragged Venir to the lashing area at the back of the little dungeon. Together they connected Venir's metal wrist cuffs to a pair of hanging chains, each two feet long and half an inch thick, attached to a thick steel ring mounted on the ceiling eight feet above.

"Spread yer legs!" said the torturer to Venir's back, as he kicked his legs into a wide straddle and shackled them to similar rings in the floor.

He looks like a big X, thought Melegal, who had entirely escaped the city guards' attention by feigning sleep in the other cell. The young guard checked that Venir's chains were tight while the other walked him through the steps. All secure, they were ready to start whipping.

"I'll do the first fifteen," said the ugly torturer, "and you finish the last five. Well, maybe seven. It'll be good training for you. Now, pay attention. You don't have to hit hard to make it hurt. Just watch the ol' expert; I've done this a thousand times." He snapped the whip with a crack that echoed through the stale air. The young man nodded, wide-eyed, as the warden reached to rip off Venir's shirt.

Suddenly, the door burst open. Tonio strode in, and pushed in front of the two guardsman. He began screaming obscenities at Venir's back, consumed with rage. Venir merely rolled his eyes slowly toward the ceiling.

"Hand over the whip!" Tonio screamed at the warden.

"Don't you give me orders!" the warden growled. "That's my job."

"You want to lose favor with a high-ranking Royal, do you?" raged Tonio. "I could have you demoted, and you know it!"

The grizzled warden stood his ground, looking for a moment like he might turn the whip on Tonio. But Tonio stepped up to him. "If you even think of using that whip on me, I'll flay the skin off your back, and do the same to your family, while the fat farm boy over there digs your grave and dumps you in it." The warden held Tonio's gaze while fire burned in both men's eyes. But the veteran of the dungeon was no match for a highly trained young warrior like Tonio. At last, he held out the whip.

"Remove his clothing to the waist!" Tonio ordered.

"Do as he says," the warden told his younger counterpart.

"I'm gonna scar every inch of his filthy back," Tonio ranted, "and make him scream for mercy! I may even break his big nose again!"

The chubby rookie ripped Venir's shirt down to the waist in a few tugs, exposing Venir's upper body. Then he stumbled back in confusion, staring. Clearly imprinted between the prisoner's knotted shoulders, over the bullish, thickly layered muscles of his gigantic, scarred back, was a large black V.

"Let me flay that stupid tattoo off your back, dog!" Tonio roared.

Venir appeared subdued, his head drooped, yet his breathing was growing heavier, and the room almost seemed to brighten. Unnoticed, his eyes appraised the rusty shackles around his ankles.

Tonio drew back the whip. The rookie guard hastily stepped back again while the warden grinned. A dark anticipation filled the air.

There was a loud crack as the whip came down in the middle of the V spanning Venir's broad back.

A snarl ripped from Venir's parched lips, and with a mighty yank he wrenched the metal loop out of the stone ceiling, then twisted, heaving one leg from its shackle on the floor. A loud ringing followed as he ripped the chain clean from his left wrist cuff. A full two feet of heavy chain now hung like a weapon in his hand.

On a foolish instinct, the warden charged him.

With a loud crunch Venir shattered the man's jaw with his knuckled fist, dropping him to the cobbled floor. He was out cold. Venir then turned on the startled Tonio, who dropped the whip and went for his sword. It was only half out of its sheath when the thick chain smote the Royal warrior's hand, breaking several bones. Tonio screamed and cursed in agony.

Venir's face was pure contempt. Tonio grabbed for the whip with his other hand, but Venir whipped the chain across Tonio's shoulders, imprinting a memory of pain that would last the young warrior his lifetime.

Despite his agony, the tough young Tonio stood straight up and prepared to defend himself. For the first time he got a good look at his opponent. This was not the warrior from the City of Three that he had faced in the Chimera. This was an entirely different being, a six-foot giant of brawn, scars, and anger, rampant as the legendary Minotaur. The iron-blue eyes held no mercy and the jaw of granite had no words. He appeared almost inhuman, filled with doom and fury, but endowed with some primal ability to survive and punish all enemies.

"You're nothing but a street dog!" cried the young warrior, too arrogant to realize his danger. "That's all you'll ever be!"

Venir snapped the chain off his right cuff and tossed it to the floor. He then closed in on Tonio, who punched him in the jaw with a smack that drew blood. Venir spat out the blood, blocked Tonio's next punch, and countered with a right uppercut to the belly. Tonio fell to his knees, winded, but stood up again. Venir then shattered his ribs with his knuckled hands, and Tonio fell to the floor like a sack.

Shockingly, Tonio somehow rose to his feet again and tried to swear at Venir, but only produced a bloodied spittle that ran down his chin. Venir then blackened his eye, broke his nose, and shattered his loudmouth jaw for good measure, leaving him out cold, bleeding heavily.

Then Venir noticed the trembling rookie guard, who was holding out his set of keys with his eyes shut, so he didn't see the knock-out punch coming. Venir cast around for other guards, but saw and heard none.

Despite all the violence, barely a minute had passed since the whip had lashed Venir's back. The constant rumblings from the streets above had muffled the chaos from those who might have been close enough to hear.

Venir now looked about for Melegal. He was gone, and only a small red apple was left behind in his cell. With the keys and the apple, Venir sneaked out of the old dungeon.

It was dusk outside the small compound as Venir made his way deep into the city, stole a shirt from a merchant stand, and headed back to his stamping ground, the Knuckled Talon Tavern. There he came upon Melegal, who already had his grog and ale ready.

The gray one sipped at his grog. "So, the new guard seemed to recognize ya."

"He didn't look familiar. I may have met him some time somewhere on the outskirts of the city. There are still normal people out there, you know. Where do you think all our food comes from?"

"Smart kid, taking a shot on the jaw to save his job," commented

Melegal. "Might even get him a promotion."

"Gee, Me, thanks for the help." Venir's once snarling lips now formed a handsome smile. "But you could at least have stolen the whip!"

"Oh, I thought you farm boys enjoyed that sort of thing. Why end your fun? Besides, I thought you were looking a little homesick."

"You're sick in the head, Melegal."

"Well, who'd notice better than you!" Melegal retorted.

Both men laughed hard and loud, and Venir sucked down his drinks and ordered another round.

"Well, big Vee, I don't know what you get up to outside the City of Bone, but you seem better known in the Outlands than here. We keep coming across people in Bone that think they know you. I see recognition, respect, and even fear in their eyes. I'm getting curious. You've changed since I last crossed the Outlands with you, and you spend so much time out there these days. One day I might even follow you there again."

"You wouldn't want to. There's no easy pickings in the Outlands!"

"I hear stories, you know. Most of the good ones mention the Darkslayer. Do you ever come across the Darkslayer?"

Melegal was laughing now. He knew his big friend well enough to know it was he, but not how he had become the Darkslayer, although he had his suspicions. But Venir's secret was safe with him, because the Darkslayer didn't play inside the City of Bone. Venir would never let on, however, and that was just as well. It was one of many things that were still a mystery to his good friend Melegal.

"Quit patronizing me and drink your grog, girlie boy!"

And so they passed another blurry but companionable night in the City of Bone. It had been just another day in the park for the Darkslayer.

CHAPTER 3

UNDERLINGS, CHONGO AND VENGEANCE

A couple of days had passed without incident since leaving the dungeon, when Venir woke to the sound of pounding rain. He was in the little apartment he shared with Melegal during his stays in the City of Bone. On the top floor of a dingy four-storey apartment building, it was just adequate for the two full-grown men to live comfortably enough in such a miserable city. The candles mounted on the walls were unlit, but the lantern glowed, and there was a hint of light at the small window where the rain pounded heavily. Melegal's bed was empty, but Venir observed his roommate conducting a rigorous routine of calisthenics beside the woodstove, on which some tealeaves were warming.

"Morning," yawned Venir.

"Crap!" replied Melegal, with his feet behind his head on the old oak floor. "It's almost noon."

Venir turned to the single window by his bed and peered deeply through the rain.

"Crap! It's just gone dawn."

"No fooling you, big Vee."

Venir got up and went to the water basin beside the wood-stove. He rinsed his face, washed out his cottonmouth, then spit into a large metal pipe between the woodstove and the basin. The indoor waste shoot was the reason they had chosen the top apartment; so they would not have to listen to any other occupants spit, wash, and urinate into the spout above, down into the nasty sewers below. Indoor plumbing was one of the marvels of the City of Bone, rumored to be the only city with such advanced technology. In truth, this ancient city was almost the only one with buildings over two stories high. The humans that built the City of Bone had been creatures of comfort as well as the most advanced race on the world of Bish. But, over the centuries, even they had forgotten most of what they had done, and why. For the City of Bone had been burned down more than once in its long life and rebuilt on the bones of its dead. That was how it had acquired its current name. And, very likely, it would burn down again.

Venir sat down beside the skinny thief and began duplicating his calisthenics. After about thirty minutes Melegal finished and went to pour some tea. Venir, in his loose sleeping shorts, was still on the floor with his legs behind his head. Melegal could not hide his amazement.

"How'd you get your legs over those monstrous shoulders?"

"Don't know," he replied, flopping them back to the floor.

Melegal watched Venir's massive muscles bulge with every movement. At one point Venir took a deep breath and stood like a statue for a full minute with every muscle in his body flexed. He looked like a great oak whose roots and sinews were about to burst free.

"Ahh!" the large warrior exhaled finally. And then, "How 'bout some tea, little buddy?"

"Here." Melegal poured and passed it. "So, what's the agenda for the day? Are you planning to stick around a bit longer, or head out already?"

"It's that time again, it seems. Besides, after that last run-in, I'd better be going. You gonna come this time, or chicken out again?"

"After all that money we just made, would I rush off and risk dying again?" Melegal frowned. "You get me into one life-threatening mess after another. It's insane! You're insane. I like the easy life inside the walls."

"Ah, bullcrap. You get bored outta your mind when I'm gone. Besides, you like it on the edge with me. And I always keep you safe, you know that."

Venir opened the closet and extracted an abnormally large leather sack, which landed on his bed with a clank.

"Pulling out the artillery," Melegal said dourly. "So you are getting ready to go." His eyes were on the giant sack as Venir reached inside it and pulled out a great round shield, three feet wide. It was a simple design, a grid of worn iron bands welded over a body of dark gray metal unknown in the City of Bone. Neither Melegal nor Venir had any idea what metal it was. Although the shield was rather grim and heavy looking, Venir flipped it around with ease. It fit his frame like a glove. Then he pulled out a colossal battle axe. "Brool," he whispered lovingly.

"You would have a name for the nasty thing," grimaced the thief.

"All good friends have names!" Venir smiled, swinging the axe like a toy. Brool was a four-foot double-bladed battle axe, with an iron-tipped dark oak handle. A serrated spike at the top made the weapon almost five feet in length. Long enough to impale two of me, Melegal thought to himself. The blades were of the same metal as the shield, and were currently whirling around Venir's body like black lightening. The eyes of the skinny thief followed the fluid movements with a silent shudder. Brool was an oddly designed weapon; bigger than a battle axe, yet smaller than a great war axe. Venir always said it was a hand-and-a-half axe. Certainly, there was no other like it on all the world of Bish. Remarkably, Venir often fought one-handed with it, but he could deal out even more damage two-handed. It was a terrible thing to face Brool in his hands.

"So, why have you decided to head out this time?"

"There's word of some trouble in the southern provinces where I spend a good bit of time. I believe I could help by hiring out my special services. The caravan officials say the battles on the trails are increasing." Sweating now, he put down his weapon, and fetched the final object out of the bag.

"Helm," he said, placing a matching gray helmet over his great skull and buckling the leather chinstrap. The helmet was banded with iron like the shield, with a serrated spike on top like Brool's, only smaller. It covered Venir's face fully, but for two eye slits.

It was a menacing sight, and an eeriness settled over the small apartment. Here was the figure that the Outlanders—the farmers and villagers—all hailed as the Darkslayer.

Melegal hesitated, uncomfortable. Then he tossed his head. "Where'd you find that ugly getup? And anyway, you're still in your sleeping shorts."

The warrior seemed in a semi-trance, only half noticing the words. "Huh? Oh." he replied, "Guess I do look kinda silly, don't I?"

"Yep. You do."

"The underlings won't think so, Me, when Brool and I get a fix on them. I'm itching for it."

Venir's broad smile made Melegal shake his head. "Think they're the ones causing trouble on the caravan trails?"

"They're always causing trouble, little boogers," he retorted. "I hate 'em. But in this case I don't think it's them. Some brave bandits that got organized, more likely. But the underlings have been seen a lot more than usual in the Outlands these days. The smaller farms seem to be suffering, and the villagers don't stand a chance. Lots of people showing up dead or disappearing. It's a shame."

"Well, they say the Darkslayer has their number. At least that's what I've heard," Melegal added with a straight face.

"Darn right!" Venir gave the air a two-handed chop with the axe, and Melegal leapt back. "Watch it with that thing, will you? You could put a dragon's eye out."

"Sorry, Me," he grinned. He shoved the armaments back into the sack, and then began pulling on his clothes.

"Why not tag along on this one? It's been a while, and you're getting rusty. These city walls make you soft, Melegal. Even though you've got it all under control here, there's bound to be a day when the walls come down. You might not be ready."

Melegal was at the mirror arranging his beloved floppy grey hat. "I've got it better now than ever. Why give it up to risk my neck with you? There's no comfort outside these walls. It's as nutty as Bone! What's to gain? I have money, privacy, and a nice place to live. I'm going to enjoy it while it lasts. And the women are a lot easier here too. Out there they usually have three eyes, hairy backs, and fangs. I'll pass!"

"No need to be nasty. Besides, I recall you liking those little hairy lycan gals from time to time," Venir laughed.

"No more of those, Venir. That about did me in. Who'd have thought she'd kill half the women I even looked at for no reason. I don't want to take the chance of running into her again. My guess is she's still around."

"Fair point." Venir pulled on his long leather boots. "Look, I'd like to stay, but I get restless here too long," he said, attaching a large belt pouch over his thick brown woolen shirt and matching long-shorts.

Melegal looked at him ruefully. "I'll walk you to the stables, then I can check on Quickster. If Georgio isn't doing his job I'm gonna kick his fat butt. Hey, in a couple more years you can take Quickster with you. Then you won't need me anymore."

"If you say so. But how about first heading down to the market with me? Gotta load up with supplies before I get outta this stinking city."

Venir tossed the remainder of his belongings into another sack while Melegal activated his homemade traps to keep out intruders. As the two adventurers went out the door slammed shut behind them, and the thief picked the lock shut with a razor-thin self-made key. The lock tumbled quietly into place several times.

"Is that necessary? Nobody's gonna break in before you get back," Venir said, scratching his head.

"I'm trying to not go soft. Being prepared, like you were lecturing. Now let's get you outta here," he laughed. "You're attracting flies!"

The two companions headed down the four flights of steps, through the empty Drunken Octopus on the ground floor, and out of the tavern door into the malodorous city streets.

Southwest of the City of Bone was the Underland, home of the underlings. It was a catacomb of caves that began in a vast mountain range and went down as far as the mountains were high, or perhaps further. Aside from the underlings, only a few people of Bish knew much about the Underland, for only a few had ever been bold enough to venture into the belly of those evil mountains. And, mostly, those who went in didn't come out; the countless captives never escaped and were rarely released. Their ghoulish tales had helped fuel the fear of the underlings, and the horrors they spoke of swept through the lands of Bish like the wind itself. Hence, no one ventured near the mouths of the Underland.

For underlings, the Underland could be reached through the

many hundreds of cave entrances, large and small, that sat like open mouths at the base of the mountain range with no name. There were stories of monsters and treasure and lost cities in those mountains, but only the icy winds knew for sure. Whatever lived in the mountains stayed there, and everyone preferred it that way.

The caves that led down into the Underland sloped steeply downwards, and the light disappeared with every step. The entrances were never guarded, for there was no need. Anyone who was not an underling would quickly be lost in the catacombs. The black walls were slick and shiny when lit, and the dripping of water echoed endlessly through the damp caverns. The black tunnels contained no light or life, but, if one ventured deep enough, a faint blue glow would begin to outline the cave walls. This was called the underlight, and its source was said to be the magic from deep below Bish itself, although the true source was most likely the powerful underling magi that ruled the Underland. The underlight had arisen from ancient spells cast centuries ago in another time, for which even the underlings did not know if they were responsible. This day, deep beneath the mountains, many leagues west of the southern humanoid settlement of Two-Ten City, the underlight illuminated a disturbing scene.

Side by side before a thick pool of blood, two robed figures were passionately contemplating a fresh project. Unlike ordinary underlings, they radiated a magical power. The magi pair wore dark robes laced with intricate inlaid patterns and lined in a subdued silver. Only their hands and heads protruded, and they seemed to float above the damp cave floor. Their thick black hair was short and wiry above the ears. Like all underlings, their physical frames were humanoid, only more lithe than their hated human rivals. Their ashen skin was covered with a fine, silky fur like that of rats, and their hands ended in long, thick black nails filed into points. Only the eyes and faces distinguished one underling from another. Their eyes could be any color on Bish, and their heads could be round or thin, large or small. But they all had an evil countenance and gray, razor-sharp teeth.

"What a work of art!" said one of the magi in a weasel-like voice, his gold eyes coolly surveying the dozens of lacerations and scalpel-like wounds on three humans suspended against the dark, wet cavern wall. "Master Sinway will like this one."

"It's one of our best yet, Verbard," agreed the taller brother, his silver eyes sparkling as he stared proudly at the humans. They hung limply, but the underlight revealed that they still breathed. He raised a glowing index finger and ran it through the freshly smeared blood on the leg of the middle human, then jabbed suddenly into a deep laceration on the thigh.

"Aaa!" the man howled. Lord Catten chuckled, boring until he hit bone, as the poor man writhed in his chains.

"Wonderful sounds they make, don't they?" Lord Verbard commented.

"Like music," Catten answered, studying the man's face. "Did that hurt, Mister Human? Was that a sound of pleasure or pain?"

"Curse you!" the man croaked. His strength was waning as the blood gushed freely from the agitated wound, and his eyes began to roll upward.

"Are you going to sleep on me?!" he demanded, turning from the dying man. "Verbard, we cannot allow him to sleep again. It's the ninth time today. I will not be treated like this by my guests."

"And we can't have them sleeping when Master Sinway arrives." Verbard looked concerned for a moment, then brightened. "Let's cut off their eyelids."

It was mid morning when Venir and Melegal reached the stables. Melegal had used his haggling ability to perfection and Venir was stocked up with plenty of dried meat, fruit, and water for the journey south. It was a long walk to where the stables were located on the southern wall of the City of Bone.

"I hate long walks in daylight like this," the thief whined. "It must be three miles to the darn stables. You need to find a new stable closer to the Drunken Octopus."

"Quit crying, we're almost there. Besides, you'll be happy to see me go."

"Sure will!"

The back alleys of the massive city remained gloomy even in daylight. Most of the city wasn't safe even on the brightest days on Bish. Only main streets offered some safety. The two companions always took shortcuts, however, leaving a confusing trail in case of oncoming pursuers or robbers. Melegal always led Venir along a different route through the dank alleyways, and the big warrior moved like a giant ghost with his gray shadow ahead of him.

"Do you think that Royal boy learned his lesson?" Melegal wondered out loud, "Or do you think he'd have the gall to come after you again?" His voice appeared to come out of nowhere. "I mean, the beating you gave him, it should have scared the life outta him."

Venir gave him a strange look. "Are you worried about that Royal brat, Tonio? If he comes after me again he'll die."

"Well, I've discovered he's from a very high Royal house," he said, a bit sheepishly. "They don't like scum like us screwing with their own. They can be vengeful," Melegal added.

"I'm sure we put an end to it. Besides, he shouldn't be able to walk or talk for days."

"If you say so," the thief shrugged, oblivious to the invisible eyes watching.

It took no more than ten minutes on their fleet city feet to reach the open place where a large cobblestone street took over from the alleys. A market was abuzz and the streets were alive with trading, soliciting, and stealing amid shouts of joy and suffering. Not far from the cobbled road loomed the great southern gate, smaller than the northern gate but almost five stories high. The mighty portcullis of woven steel was shut, and traffic was directed in and out through a smaller gate to the left of it, by a squad of city guards. This gate controlled the passage of all vehicles and pedestrians in and out of the southern part of the city.

The wall surrounding the City of Bone was a sight to behold. It stood three stories high, made of stones so large that none knew where they had come from nor cared to know. The story of the old seers was that giants had built and occupied the City of Bone, but there was no evidence to support such a tale. On top of the huge stone walls stood many battle towers, with dozens of heavily armed guards posted in pairs, evenly spaced as far as the eye could see.

"Fun job," Melegal observed. "Let's get you to the stables and outta my hair."

Along the wall, about four hundred yards east of the main gate, they came to a dozen large wood-framed barns laid out in two rows, each some twenty feet high and a hundred yards long. The two companions headed toward the barn furthest from the gate. The smell of hay and manure was strong as they stepped through a small, nondescript door in the middle of the barn used by the stable hands. Hundreds of stables lined the walls, and the sounds of stabled beasts rose to the rafters, most belonging to the militia and the Royals of the City of Bone. An open roof cast light on several well-bred horses at the northern end, being tended by various stable hands that were busy about their chores.

The two turned toward the southern end, which was quiet and mostly empty except for a curly-headed boy seated on a stool, buffing his shoes with a horse brush. Seeing the two coming his way, the young fellow squinted, then jumped up and began running and hopping toward them, trying to put his shoe back on.

"Venir!" he yelled, running up to give the lumbering warrior a two-armed wrap around the waist.

"Georgio." Venir smiled and patted him on the head, trying to pry his arms off. "Easy, big fella. You're getting stronger every day, I see."

Georgio released him and beamed. "I want to be strong like you, Vee. The strongest man in the world. I moved five hundred hay bails last week. Taking care of Chongo is a lot of work. Didn't think you were ever gonna come by."

The curly-haired teenager started skipping and motioning Venir to follow, but Melegal grabbed his arm. "What about my mount?" he hissed. "I hope you haven't been neglecting him!"

"Aw, let me go, Me." He jerked his arm away. "Your stinky donkey's just fine. All he ever does is sleep and crap everywhere."

"Don't smart mouth me," the thief pointed in his face.

"Enough, you two. Man, can't you guys get along? You know Georgio always takes care of Quickster, Me."

"Not last time he didn't. Quickster was sick 'cause of him."

"That wasn't my fault, Vee. That dumb donkey started eating from the waste bins when I was trying to walk him."

"He's not a donkey. He's a pony!"

"A pony that looks like a donkey and eats poop!" Georgio backed away as Melegal lunged to smack him. The hefty teen moved with speed that belied his formidable girth. Melegal started in pursuit but Venir obstructed him. "Let it go. I'm sure he's fine this time."

"He better be or I'll bust Georgio's butt."

Melegal followed Georgio along the passage with Venir behind. After about thirty yards Georgio stopped at a stable and mumbled in low tones. It was oddly quiet, Venir suddenly realized. Chongo usually went wild at the voice of his master. Something was amiss. The reason began to dawn on him...

"Don't move!" rasped a harsh voice from behind.

Venir stopped. Ahead of him, Melegal whirled about and saw a familiar figure behind Venir, and a curious look on Venir's face.

"Tonio," Venir muttered, turning slowly to face his adversary.

With some surprise he noticed that Tonio's jaw had recovered, and his hands were healed. The hands were now wrapped eagerly about a double-triggered crossbow, and two thick bolts pointed dead at Venir's head. Venir began lowering his two sacks slowly to the ground.

"Keep those sacks up! You too, thief!" Venir stopped moving.

"Can't believe I'm better, can you? You should have killed me. Because I'm a Royal, with the best healing at my disposal. Too bad your poor hide won't get any such treatment. Because I've got you now. Nobody messes with me. Nobody!" He motioned with the crossbow for the two men to back up.

"I have a stable set up for the two of you. We're going to have a little meeting in it. Hey, fat boy back there, stop fidgeting!"

"Do as he says, Georgio," said Venir, stepping slowly back until he and Melegal were side by side with Georgio. Tonio kept both men in his crossbows sights. Tonio was sweating, Venir noticed, and his eyes seemed dilated.

"Don't stop, you two! Boy, go open that empty stable."

Georgio swung open the empty stable gate, and carefully positioned himself behind it, while Tonio was focused on the men.

Venir and Melegal moved back to the next stable and stopped again.

"I said don't stop!" Tonio yelled. "Are you deaf? Keep moving!" He was one stable behind Venir and Melegal. They stood motionless, ten paces away, watching his finger on the trigger.

"Fine!" he shouted, "You can die right there!" Taking aim, the young warrior hesitated momentarily as Venir gazed dead into his eyes with a mysterious smile. Growling in disgust he took aim again, when a massive lion-like paw reached at his face. A burst of snarls and barks followed as another clawed paw reached for his head and thrust him into the stable gate.

"Aagh!" Tonio wailed as two massive dog heads snapped and tore at him. He managed to shoot his two bolts but Venir was already well out of harm's way.

His face gashed and bleeding, Tonio screamed and fought for his life. But the beasts kept pulling at him, pinning his body against the gate with their giant paws. Panicking, Tonio got just a glimpse of a massive pair of jaws as they bit down, gripping his head tight, while another set of teeth sank into his neck. The resounding crunch sent a flock of doves from the rafters in a plume of white and grey. Outside the stables few noticed their flight, for it was nothing extraordinary to a commoner's eye, but one person noticed the uniqueness of the event. Tonio's body went limp, and the two dog heads shook the corpse a couple of times and then dropped it to the stable floor like a discarded toy.

Venir pulled Tonio's broken body out of the way and swung the door open.

Chongo bounded out, his two tails wagging excitedly, and both monstrous, bloodied heads licked the warrior like a happy puppy, while Venir labored under his affections. The size of a small horse, the two-headed Bull Mastiff was one of only a handful on the world of Bish. The shaggy red-brown coat shone in the open light as Venir tried to calm him. Chongo had been nearly impossible to tame as a mount. Finally the beast sat, both heads eye to eye with Venir's, tails still flailing.

"Good boy, Chongo. Good boy." Venir scratched his ears and looked about for Melegal and Georgio.

Georgio was still squatting behind the gate, staring at the cross-bow bolt imbedded in it. Venir signaled the boy over. Melegal, with a foul look on his face, was leading a shaggy, dark gray quick-pony out of another stable.

"See what you've done!" blurted Melegal. "The city guard's gonna be all over our rears. The Royals will have a price on our head so high we'll never be able to come back. They'll be hunting us nonstop. I'm gonna have to go with you. I knew this would happen, I bloody knew it! I told you we shoulda been worried!" He carried on cursing under his breath, glaring at Venir. "Now what?"

"Be silent!" hissed Venir, looking about warily to see if anyone was around.

Venir held two fingers to his chest, paused, and then held up one. Melegal repeated the signs back to him, and handed Georgio the reigns of his pony. With a parting glare, he shook his head and disappeared.

"Where's . . ."

Venir stopped Georgio with a tug on the ear. His memory jogged, Georgio rapidly began harnessing and loading the beasts for travel. Moving quickly, they made their way to another stable. Georgio stepped in and pulled an old rake off the wall. Then he reached it high above the rafters and yanked at something. An angled wooden walkway dropped down at the back of the stable, and opened into a deep passage that led southwards. The mysterious passage had been revealed to them by an old stable hand. The old man said he had seen it used only used once when he was a boy. Apparently it had become another forgotten secret among a thousand others in the great City of Bone.

Venir led the two mounts along it into the passage, and signaled to Georgio. The boy closed the hidden passageway and used the rake to cover the secret way with hay, manure, and dirt. Finished, he made his way to the pedestrian lane at the southern gate and out of the city.

Venir traveled underground steadily for about a mile without light. It was straight, and he'd traveled it a dozen times. The passageway was large and slightly sloped. After half a mile they crossed over an iron grate, with the sound of water running far below. Venir always assumed it was a large storm drain, but wondered if that was its only purpose. From there the passage began sloping upward and finally came to a dead end. There he waited. About fifteen minutes later the dead end opened up and scattered daylight poured in. They were inside a small cave. Georgio's big pie head appeared.

"Good job, Georgio. Now, help me saddle Chongo. I'll keep him calm while you hook it up."

The tubby teen closed off the secret passage and took the large saddle from Venir's shoulder. Venir sat Chongo down, talking to him and scratching his head while the dog-beast growled in protest as Georgio saddled him. Venir kept him calm long enough for the boy to finish the last buckle. Then Chongo leapt onto all fours and turned on the boy, barking. Georgio backed away helplessly.

"Heel!" Chongo complied, lowering his heads in submission to Venir's command. Venir loaded his two large sacks and emerged from the cave while the boy saddled the quick-pony.

The two noon suns were hot over the dry, open land. The City of Bone's southern wall stood like a blackened monolith barely a mile away. Yet already the Outlands loomed huge and dreadful.

Venir smiled, enjoying the moment. The air was fresh and pure, the sunlight hot on his face. Around the southern gate, several groups of nomads were clustered near the walls for protection from the harsh Outlands. They lived outside because they were not always welcome in the City of Bone. The main southward caravan trail was busy with comings and goings and all types of trade. Heavy clouds of dust from beasts of burden obscured the figures with their carts and wagons.

Georgio rode up beside Venir and Chongo, and together they set off.

"Where to?"

"I'm taking you home. Melegal will meet us in a couple of hours.

You'll be safe; the city guards don't come out more than a day's ride."

The dog swayed with a fluid, cat-like gait, tongues hanging out in the heat, ears and eyes all alert.

"Why didn't Chongo bark when you showed up?"

"Sensed danger, I guess. He's good-natured. Doesn't like bad people. I think he can sense evil."

"How come Me has this dumb pony? Why can't he have a real horse or something?"

"I told you before." Venir looked annoyed. "Quick ponies move just as fast but they carry like a pack mule. Melegal likes lots of stuff. Plus, it didn't cost anything."

"Well, Quickster's a stupid name. He should be called Poopeater."

"Enough!"

The land south of the city was mostly red clay, dirt, and rocks, with little vegetation. It was fairly flat and easy to travel, except for the constant burning of the suns. The Outlands offered little comfort to those who were ill prepared. Not much was to be encountered between cities or villages, except in the cool of the evening. Bandits knew the pickings on the trails were slimmer at night, but that was when they came. During the day the dreaded, blistering heat of the suns helped to protect travelers. Day or night, you could never get comfortable.

The two hadn't traveled far when they came upon a dry well with sparse vegetation. Tall lean cacti were abundant. Venir found a nice round cactus, lopped off the top, and started pulling out the watery pulp and feeding it to Chongo. Georgio did the same for Quickster. In the distance, the City of Bone hovered like a mirage, wavering in the sunlight like a ghostly castle. Venir stared intently towards it, watching for any hint of activity coming their way. Georgio, sweating profusely, helped himself to some fresh water from Venir's waterskin.

Venir went to one of his large sacks and pulled out two beige cotton cowls. "Put this on your head. It'll keep you from frying." They each put one on. It had been over an hour and Melegal was nowhere in sight.

"Bloody thief's gonna be late," muttered Venir. "Told him he was getting rusty."

"Rusty? I've been here two full minutes. Trying to decide whether to kill you."

Venir whirled around, grinning. The thief was dressed in earthy tones that matched the drab landscape. "Well, maybe I was wrong. Any news?"

"There was a stir as I left the stables. The higher city patrol along with some Royals, I believe. I thought I saw a familiar face from the Chimera, but I recognized no one else. But you can bet your ears they'll be looking for us for a long time coming. He wasn't alone, I'm sure. Good-bye nice apartment. Good-bye easy life."

"Who could've seen us? I know Tonio's father knows what I look like, and a few guards too, but I seriously doubt . . ."

"You know as well as I not a man in all of Bone can hide forever when he's on the list. All you can hope is we don't make the list. But now that Chongo's turned one of their own into a chew toy, I don't see any hope!"

Venir kept his own discomforting thoughts to himself.

"I don't understand why that Royal brat Tonio even conceived of coming after you," the thief went on. "Usually they get their dirty work done for them. It was insane!"

"Maybe we became pawns in something bigger, Me. The Royals like doing one another in."

"My gut's telling me the same," Melegal returned. "That's why I gotta get my happy arse out of Bone!"

"One way or the other, they were coming after us. So don't sweat it. At least we didn't get cornered in the city. We'll hole up in the Two-Ten City. We'll be okay there; they hate Bone." Venir tried to sound positive.

The thief shook his head in resignation. "So what then? Are we taking fat boy home, then heading south for adventure?"

"Well, I guess you're coming after all!"

"Why not? I've nothing to live for anymore, might as well die trying to live."

"Who're you calling fat boy?" Georgio pouted.

"You!" the two said, and laughed. They loaded up and the boy hopped onto Chongo's back behind Venir.

Despite their quick pace, it was a long, hot day's ride to Georgio's home village, which hosted some of the best farmland on Bish. It was just growing dusk when the small party finally stopped, just inside the shady northern edge of the Red Clay Forest.

CHAPTER 4

THE RED CLAY FOREST

Infinity was not always the best place to be. Although it was considered heavenly, it was sometimes quite hellish. Anything imaginable was at your disposal, yet it was boring. Maybe, Trinos thought to herself, she simply enjoyed complaining. At least it kept her entertained.

Trinos was a being from a created race that had achieved its greatest potential. Her race had been created by some other infinite being, whose race had in turn been created untold years ago by another infinite being. How long ago didn't really matter, because time was infinite. What mattered was that Trinos belonged to a race of overachievers. As wonderful as that sounded, Trinos found her life becoming grindingly mundane, to a point where she even caught herself questioning her sanity.

There had once been a time, so very long ago, when her life was filled with joy, sorrow, adventure, and love. But all her dreams had come true once her race learned the greatest secret of the universe itself. And this discovery had allowed her race to become immortal.

It was thrilling at first, having the time and the power to do whatever she wished. But now she sometimes thought it might have been better to have died. Those Trinos loved had drifted away to explore their own newfound capabilities and responsibilities. Like them, Trinos could do or create anything at all, anywhere in the vast universe. So could everyone else. Everything was easy. All too easy.

To keep beings like Trinos from going stark crazy, there were rules and tasks to keep them occupied. Some had to make new worlds and galaxies. Others had to destroy them. The majority tried to discover what had created their own universe. Despite their ability to do and create anything at all in the universe, they still could not find the end of it. It just kept going.

To occupy her time, Trinos had the task of evaluating the worlds created by the many other infinite beings. She would watch these galaxies begin and finally end. Different races would be born to these new worlds, all created by the hand of various supreme beings. But try as they may, the infinite beings just kept making the same types of worlds over and over and over again.

It was always the same scenario. A new world was made, new races gained knowledge, made fire, made weapons, went to war, struggled for survival, fought off alien invaders, and then destroyed themselves or were destroyed by others.

Rarely, maybe one race in a million would evolve to the status her own race had achieved in the universe. Trinos had seen this happen a few times. But much more often the occupants would destroy themselves through war, or natural causes such as famine and disease would finish them off. In some cases the infinite creators didn't even build worlds that could last forever. It was always much the same. Trinos had become aware that, in the grand scheme of things, her monitoring was entirely pointless.

Trinos always reported her findings to the galaxy creator, who would ignore them and simply make another galaxy. Yet it remained

Trinos' job to watch after them still. Sometimes, just to pass the time and try to get a taste of life, Trinos would show up on one of the created planets. But it made no difference what she did; she had become redundant.

One time, Trinos was busy evaluating a newly created world in small galaxy. It was blue and brand new. Trinos had visited for a few hundred years, and could feel that this race had the potential to become infinite. It was a rare treat, indeed, and Trinos felt something almost like excitement, if such a thing were ever again possible.

The beings of this planet were by far the most promising and colorful Trinos had seen. They made great strides in technology, medicine, and science in short spans of time. One of the cultures of that world had become a melting pot of all its greatest minds and races. They showed so much promise.

Trinos had begun to enjoy the lively characteristics of this race. It seemed to her that when they worked together they were unstoppable. Maybe they would make it. Maybe Trinos would not always be so bored in infinity. But her moment of hope was brief. They were not going to make it after all. The prominent young race had had too much success too early. They lost too much of their creativity as technology and convenience led them to self-indulgence and internal strife. They who had overcome so much now began fighting among themselves. Their pride and greed was to be their world's undoing.

It became clear to Trinos that it would not be long before they were all gone from this galaxy. But they still had some time. Unfortunately, much as Trinos liked this world, she could not interfere. It just wasn't allowed. What a shame, Trinos thought in her infinite restlessness. None of these worlds ever lasted long.

Of course, not every world could achieve infinite status, but why did they always have to become extinct? Couldn't some of these worlds remain in an interesting state forever? Why did all the infinite and knowledgeable beings keep creating such short-lived worlds?

Trinos pondered these questions endlessly. She had had enough. There had to be something, somehow, to look forward to. Yet every time she went back to check on a promising race, they were gone.

Finally, inspiration struck. Trinos would build her own world in her infinity. She would build a world that would remain locked in strife and survival every minute, always. She would build a world that could keep her eternally entertained, one that would always be there for her to come back to.

Trinos took great care to plan her new creation. She selected the unique characteristics of that shiny blue world she was so fond of, and then added in some of the otherworldly races she particularly liked. Survival was of the utmost importance when developing their genetic codes. There were millions of details to attend to. The basic laws of the universe would apply. The laws of alignment of good and evil were to be in place. Races would only achieve an archaic form of technology, to prevent them from ever leaving the planet. The study of science would be replaced by the study of magic. Lifespans would be normal. Humanoids would rule. And an equalizer would be in place to prevent either good or evil from fully achieving supremacy. No evolution.

It would be a brutal world, one that would run the gauntlet of emotions every second. Man would rule beast. Monsters would cause mayhem. Heroes would be born with great willpower, and villains with unparalleled greed.

These people would like it here, thought Trinos. And she would like it there.

Trinos tucked her little world away, deep in the plethora of galaxies within the universe, in the hopes that none of the other superior beings would come across it or tamper with it. Finally, after many moments in infinity, Trinos gave birth to her new world. They called it Bish.

Master Sinway had arrived. From the deep caves he came to where Lord Verbard and Lord Catten had just put the finishing touches to their finest piece of human artwork. The two furry underling commanders stood to attention, sort of, while Master Sinway quietly made his way over to inspect the hanging humans. Dark-robed and hawk-nosed, much like Lord Verbard and Lord Catten, Master Sinway's greater height and breadth easily distinguished him from others. His colorless black eyes were as deep as space and spoke of matchless wisdom and knowledge. His clothing was nothing more than a thick black robe traced in exquisite patterns of light silver dust, with a matching lining that radiated great magic. Oh, how the underling brothers craved that magic. As ancient as Master Sinway was, one would never know it. His face was broad and hairless, somewhat humanoid. His hair was black and short, just below his ears. His thin lips hid straight gray teeth and his hands were large, thick-knuckled, and hairless. He was certainly different from the rest. Underlings generally aged slowly, and didn't change much in appearance during adulthood. This was particularly true in Master Sinway's case. His robed figure glided like any other underling. But as underlings grew in age and power, they also grew in height. Master Sinway was the tallest, cruelest, and most powerful underling on Bish. Before him, the powerful five-and-a-half feet tall twins, Verbard and Catten, seemed diminished. Master Sinway stood a towering six feet tall.

But Sinway was not alone in this. His masterguard escorts were two of the most impressive sights in the underland, known as "the Vicious". The Vicious were nameless creations of the ancient underling ways, possibly as old as Sinway himself. Sinway was believed to have been an apprentice to the underling Master Sidebor when the greatest of all underlings created them from a blend of man, underling, and magic. Master Sidebor had perished in long past centuries, in a great battle believed to have been against Sinway. No underling knew for sure what had caused the demise of Sidebor, other than Sinway. The evidence casting suspicion on Sinway was the powerful magic robe he wore. Of course, as far as any the Underland knew, Sidebor could still be alive, for his body had never been found.

The imposing Vicious had naked skin that was almost black, and they appeared to be genderless. They stood just over six feet but were heavily muscled like the dog-faced gnolls of Bish. They were hairless, and their skin was smooth and thick like tanned leather. Unlike underlings, they had round, cat-like faces with long, pointed ears, and small noses with flared nostrils to pick up scents for their hunts. Thick, claw-like black fingernails came to points like five small daggers on each hand. Wide platinum eyes without lashes shone brightly under protruding foreheads. Their countenances revealed the cool intelligence of predators, and their constant smiles suggested the deliverance of a cruel and painful destruction. They did not float in the manner of Master Sinway, but moved silently and fluidly on bare feet through the cave waters, and they were difficult to see against the shadowy cavernous background. These great assassins were heralded throughout the Underland as legends of death.

Lords Catten and Verbard might have seemed uncomfortable in their presence had Master Sinway not been with them, but he almost always was. They were his bodyguards and though Sinway wasn't in need, he took no chances in the Underland, especially around the likes of Catten and Verbard. They were too much like himself, so he always stayed on guard, though one would never notice.

"A nice piece of humanity you have here." He approached the bleeding sculpture and pointed with a glowing fingernail. "Perhaps, a few finishing touches." With his left-hand fingers suddenly glowing red, he burned and slashed the three hanging humans. They screamed with what strength they had. Deep gashes opened all over their bodies, singeing blood and entrails, and a thin stream of blood mixed with sweat trickled beneath Sinway's floating feet.

"Much better," he chuckled. Catten and Verbard smiled and clapped in unison, thanking Sinway ingratiatingly for his finishing touch.

"So, what have you to report about the world above?" Sinway asked coolly. "I gather our troops have been, how should I put it, diminished over the past several months."

Caught off guard, Verbard's and Catten's eyes widened, but Catten quickly recovered.

"All is fine, Master Sinway. The troublemakers have been vanquished and our troops are in good order."

"Really, Catten? The last I heard," Sinway's voice rose in a dark crescendo, "a few score raiding parties perished a few weeks ago, and two score just before that. That's about fifteen score over the past year! So, how do you consider the problem to be resolved?"

In all their centuries of contact with him, the two elite underling lords had never experienced Sinway more angered. They quickly became as submissive as children to an angry father.

"My lord, we did not know," lied Verbard, "we have been so busy with other projects. We were assured that the problem was taken care of." He stammered and cooed like an innocent, spoiled child.

"Shut up, Verbard! I am no fool. You two have never failed me. This situation is unusual but it is not the first time this has happened," He hesitated, apparently deep in thought, then continued. "It seems our troops and run-of-the-mill soldiers are no match for this Darkslayer. He kills with less mercy than we, and he hunts us down. No one dares to hunt the underlings. Anyway, I am dispatching the Vicious to finish the task you have clearly mismanaged. Assuming the Darkslayer works alone, he will be unable to handle the Vicious. They are not typical underlings, so he will be unprepared to deal with them. And none has ever lived to see the Vicious another day."

Sinway and the Vicious left without another word. But Sinway's words lingered. Catten and Verbard seemed shocked, but relieved at the dreaded Sinway's quick departure with the Vicious. Then the two faced one another with evil grins. Each knew what the other was thinking. With the Vicious gone, Sinway would be at his most vulnerable. But it was only a whim; both well knew that even together they were still no match for him. Yet the thought was pleasurable.

"Do you think this solves our problem?" Catten asked.

"I don't know, but it's one less burden. That Darkslayer is a pain in the groin, and we are lucky the Vicious are going. Now we will learn what we are really dealing with," Verbard responded.

"I imagine so. It should be a great battle. What do you think Master Sinway meant by 'It is not the first time this has happened?'"

"I don't know, but I'm not sure he intended to let that out. We need to make a better effort this time, though. I do hate to miss an opportunity, Catten."

The two mighty magi lords departed, abandoning their human masterpiece to the cave rats and other vermin seeking succulent human nutrition rather than the crisp caves bugs that always fought back.

Venir and his small party awoke just as the suns began to appear over the horizon. At the grassy edge of the Red Clay Forest the air was filled with the chittering of small creatures bouncing among the tree tops and tree roots. Unlike the dry plains they had crossed the previous day, the forest was alive, eerie, and magnificent. Though it wasn't heavily traveled due to the rough and more uncertain terrain, faint pathways could be discerned by the experienced eye. The Red Clay Forest was known for it's inviting beauty, lush vegetation, and delicious wildlife, but even common travelers felt uncomfortable amid the eerie serenity. Venir was considering their options, and pressing for the quicker but less traveled path to Georgio's village south of the forest.

"I don't wanna go into that filthy forest!" Melegal complained. "This grassy place was dead quiet last night. Now bugs and vermin are gonna crawl all over me." He swatted at a really big mosquito. "Bone!" he cursed. "How'd I get into this?"

"Yer so scrawny, Me, the bugs'll leave you alone when they realize you're made of stone," teased Georgio, fleeing as Melegal flung a stone at him, which hit the back of his head with a thunk.

"Ow!" he whined, rubbing his head. "You didn't need to do that."

The thief and the farm boy had been at each other incessantly, and Venir had about reached his limit. "Get your gear ready and let's roll. This forest isn't gonna make the trip any less miserable, so shut it, both of you," he warned.

And so the small party moved into the Red Clay Forest, the most enchanting part of the Outlands. Its trees rose out of sight in many places, with a variety of leaves in reds, greens, and blues. The leaves never fell from these trees, unlike in other parts of Bish. It could not be explained, because on the world of Bish, neither people nor creatures bothered to understand why there were differences between one forest and another. The red clay of the forest floor was covered in various mosses, shrubbery and flowers of great beauty, some of a deadly sort, and both people and the many forest creatures could travel quietly without the rustle of leaves beneath their feet. It was as if the forest had been freshly swept.

Much of Venir's time in the Outlands was spent here in the Red Clay Forest, which he used both as a safe haven and for shortcuts during his travels. Most people knew better than to be too curious about the forest, because too often the curious never came back out. The forest was risky, filled with violent natures of all sorts. At times the forest left Venir alone, and at other times it would not. By now Venir had grown used to the unexpected here, and knew that his shortcuts through the forest often threw pursuers off his trail. The Red Clay Forest was one of the few uncontrolled areas of permanent habitation on the world of Bish. Not many people lived here. The Red Clay Forest seemed not to like too much company.

The small party traveled unmolested for a couple of hours. Despite the wonderful shade, it was hot and humid and there was no breeze. Chongo panted heavily from his two big tongues. Quickster panted too, and Georgio's head was soaked with sweat. It was even more miserable than directly under the blazing suns. There was no cool comfort anywhere in the Outlands, except in caves.

"This forest makes me itch all over with the creeps," Melegal stammered.

Venir turned his head towards the city thief. "Eh, nice outfit," he chuckled, noticing that Melegal had mixed some lightly spotted forest colors with his usual grays. "That should scare the bugs away." He began to guide the giant two-headed Chongo up towards the higher ridges of the forest.

"Er, Venir," Melegal said nervously, spurring forward to keep on the heels of Chongo. "I've heard about deadly plants and animals in this forest. And strange peoples."

"Oh. Haven't I told you about this place?"

"No. When I asked you said I didn't want to know."

"Did I? Well, now that you're here," Venir's eyes darkened and he lowered his voice, "all the things you've heard are true. The worst are the forest magi. They don't sneak up, they float up and surround you. They're really all we have to worry about. The plants aren't so bad. And the animals, well, they won't mess with us if we don't mess with them. But the trees, man! They stare at every move you make, and then . . ." he paused as Melegal looked anxiously up and about, ". . . they do absolutely nothing."

Melegal hissed profanities at Venir's muscled shoulders, while Georgio giggled from his spot on the saddle behind Venir.

———

Seated in his elaborate and ornate throne room, Tonio's father, Royal Lord Almen, was clearly not pleased to hear of his son's recent demise.

"Why? Who? How?!" he ranted into his best detective's face. His bellows echoed off the high ceilings, down the corridors, and throughout the rooms of his castle-like home. Lord Almen, of the Third House of Bone, was seething at the idea that his finest son might be dead. In the eyes of their society this would be seen as a weakening of his house in the Royal community.

"I want the culprits . . . No! Why were the culprits not already brought to me?"

"It seems that the criminal has left the City of Bone," replied the smooth, swarthy detective. "There is no specific evidence, except that Tonio was mauled to death. By what we don't yet know. It's hard getting the locals to talk. And the stable master and his help are either dead or have disappeared without a trace. It seems to be the work of an assassin from another family, although the mauling is inexplicable. We don't understand it." The detective's blue eyes never met those of the Royal lord. This was not permitted; a Royal lord might be gazed upon only by family and other Royal lords. Few had survived in this service as long as McKnight. In the City of Bone, differing in opinion with a Royal easily got a commoner killed.

Lord Almen sat in thoughtful repose. "It is assassination, then?" he questioned as he dipped a jeweled goblet into his wine bowl.

"I believe so, lord, but who and why is curious."

"That much I know, fool." Anger arose in the primped brown

brow of the Royal lord. "I believe I shall deal with this without your help, Detective McKnight. I shall ask Tonio myself. Make sure this recent debacle of my son's death does not get out. You are dismissed."

Detective McKnight could not have been more relieved. Let him bring his deviant son back to life, he thought. That way my back will be covered, not buried.

Detective McKnight was the best in the business, having done the dirty work for many a Royal family over twenty-five years. He had seen the worst. This mess, however, was unique. Whatever had killed the foolish Tonio was no assassin of a Royal house. It was perhaps a clever setup, though. It seemed more likely that Tonio had gotten caught up with the wrong locals. McKnight knew all too well from experience that the City of Bone contained people and creatures that even the mighty Royal houses should not mess with. But they would never believe that. They only realized this when it was way too late and they were in the grave, he thought.

Dozens of scenarios were running through Detective McKnight's mind. His thoughts raced as he walked through the castle like a ghost in black garb, stroking his thin sideburns and pointed chin, while a thin film of sweat built up on his pallid face. Lord Almen was one of the few Royals who could make him nervous. McKnight, however, unlike most in his profession, did not feel the need to maintain a low profile. He enjoyed the limelight. He suspected that this was why Almen had hired him long ago. In the meantime, he had to find out more. He put on his wide black hat and departed, disappearing quickly into the city night.

The Red Clay Forest, as usual, was an odd mixture of loud noises and eerie quiet, when Chongo came to an abrupt halt. His four ears pricked up like horns and his tails moved rigidly in unison. Melegal quietly reigned in Quickster just before his nose smacked into Chongo's rear. The three adventurers peered about as the air began whistling through the colored leaves. This was no normal breeze. The wind picked up around the group and Chongo began to howl at the whine of the whipping wind. The party stood firm in the vortex for what seemed an awfully long time to young Georgio, who clutched Venir's broad back with all his might. Venir neither flinched nor blinked; he thought he knew what was afoot. Suddenly the wind died and the party looked about. Melegal was adjusting his floppy hat when he saw them come.

The forest magi appeared with a whoosh, like broken branches flying in the wind. They began to hover above the ground, encircling the party, their hooded brown robes shadowing their faces. Silently they circled the group. Chongo pressed his ears down and rumbled growls while Quickster chewed comfortably on a piece of grass.

"Where are their feet?" Georgio asked.

Venir elbowed him. "Be still."

The magi finally came to a stop. Two magi came toward Venir, Chongo, and Georgio, and another two approached Melegal and Quickster.

"Don't move, it's okay," Venir barked.

Like greedy thieves, the four forest magi pawed and searched the men, their mounts, and their supplies.

"Big Vee!" pleaded Melegal, who had never let another being touch any of his possessions.

"Hold off, I don't think they'll take anything."

"Easy for you to say, you don't have anything special."

"Trust me, we don't have what they want."

One of the forest magi was shaking Venir's axe, helm, and shield from his large sack. The weight of the shield threw the small mage off balance until another came to his aid. He dropped the shield and made an odd sound of complaint, then returned to the hovering circle, as did the others. They conversed in a language of gestures, motioning towards Venir's weapons. The party watched them, listening for sounds. But the magi merely circled the party in silence once more, then broke off into a uniform column and disappeared into the Red Clay Forest.

The normal forest sounds resumed, and Chongo became calm, his tails wagging happily again. Quickster was still chewing as if nothing had happened. But all their supplies were now strewn about the forest floor.

"What were they looking for, Big Vee?" Georgio asked, starting to retrieve and repack the items.

"Magic, no doubt. They're whores for magic, those smelly fiends. That's why they live here. It's isolated and the forest is supposedly magical. I don't know if it is, but then again, it doesn't change with the seasons." Venir also began to pick up their provisions, but Melegal made no effort to dismount.

"What's the matter, Me? Did they rob you of your magic hands?"

Melegal sat motionless, his face dark with emotion.

"Your hat!" Venir exclaimed.

At that, Melegal unleashed a fury of profanities never before heard in the Red Clay Forest. For minutes Melegal ranted in an unbroken stream, until at last his outburst began to subside. Finally, he stopped, took a breath, and turned toward Venir.

Venir was not there. In his place Melegal saw the form of a heavily muscled man with an ugly spiked helmet, a matching shield, and a battle axe. It was a chilling sight.

"I will get it back."

Trinos was pleased with her world of Bish. Whenever she checked in, it seemed to be thoroughly stuck in a mud puddle of chaos. Yet it was not as entertaining as she had hoped, because she always knew what was going to happen. She remembered something from other worlds that they had called repeats; much like the people of that world, she still watched even when she had seen it all before. But sometimes a ripple here and there would catch her off guard, for good and evil were always somewhat unpredictable. The infinite ones had escaped from good and evil over time, as their eternal life transcended it.

Whenever Trinos saw that things had become too mundane, she would place a ripple in the world—a new creature, race, or ecosystem—and come back later to see what effect it had had. This proved the most effective way to keep things interesting, or to create the feeling she had once referred to as fun. It was unique how the life on the world of Bish always reacted to her interventions. The balance would tip in favor of good or of evil. Currently things were much in favor of evil. So Trinos had her tool in place to protect the good for the time being. And it was a bloody creative tool at that.

Venir took off in a flat run, angling to cut off the forest magi somewhere down the winding old path. He achieved amazing speed on his rather spindly legs; scrawny, or so Georgio thought. But the warrior's unusual breadth was deceptive; he could shoot off in a blink.

Melegal forgot his anger in the shock of seeing Venir, as the Darkslayer, disappear like a shot-put, his stringy blond hair waving banner-like beneath the spiked battle helm.

"I gotta see this," said Georgio, dashing after Venir as fast as his chubby legs would carry him.

"*Bone*," muttered Melegal, placing Quickster's reins in one of Chongo's mouths and hurrying after Georgio, catching up with him almost immediately. But they soon slowed down, as they were unused to the forest, and had to pay close attention to track Venir's path. Melegal's ears were keen, though, and what he might not see, the seasoned thief could hear.

Venir stopped. He had almost overrun the barely visible path where he intended to cut off the forest magi. He stood stoutly, legs spread shoulder width and slightly bent at the knees. His banded shield lay behind him while Brool twirled in his left arm and cut the air in short strokes. His head rolled, making his neck crackle as he grumbled angrily beneath his black-spiked helm. The forest grew suddenly quiet as the forest magi rounded the bend in the path.

The tallest of the forest magi floated forward, not startled, within thirty paces of Venir. Venir flexed his grip on his axe, his arm muscles pulsating, thick blue veins rising like small roots. The rest of the magi formed two columns on opposite sides of the path, centered on their taller leader.

"One of you took something that was not yours," Venir growled. "I will be taking it back." The forest magi rarely took normal things, such as a silly-looking hat. This was considered dishonorable among them. However, though they loved magic solely, they were greedy little pests, and were rarely challenged about what they took. Most people were just too happy to have been spared their lives, and would leave the forest magi alone, though they had likely never posed any danger. Although the forest magi were considered the bullies of the forest, like most bullies they were cowards. But like anywhere else on Bish, most people feared bullies. Then again, most people weren't the Darkslayer, who knew the byways of the Red Clay Forest and had faced far bigger terrors here.

Shortly after Venir uttered those words, one of the forest magi floated forward from the back of one of the columns. Much shorter than the others, he came to his leader and removed his hood. His human face was covered in bright red blemishes, his nasty grin revealing many missing teeth as he licked dirty lips. Atop his mangy tufts of red hair sat Melegal's floppy hat.

The little creature spread his arms wide, pointing outward, then brought his fingertips to the hat and started tapping it in mockery. He then began to tap his chest, tauntingly, daring the Darkslayer to take the hat back.

Venir strode menacingly towards him. But each time he attempted to swing his axe, the forest magi floated out of reach, taunting, gloating, and weaving in and out, even taking off the hat and waving it. Despite the big man's experience, he could not square up on the floating man for a single swipe. The Darkslayer knew he was being set up for something. That was how cowards worked, and these were magi after all.

Melegal and Georgio had crept up on the scene undetected by the forest magi. To Melegal's surprise, Georgio had hardly made a sound. A mage was doing a strange dance of sorts, while the remaining forest magi seemed captivated by the spectacle. But the observant thief quickly realized that they were not just watching. They were muttering. And the sight of a small ugly forest mage wearing his precious hat goaded him to action. Nudging the boy, Melegal readied his sling and Georgio followed suit.

"I'll take the one with the hat. You take the tall one," Melegal whispered. Georgio gave a nod of excitement. Keeping still, they felt like they might explode from anticipation. Sweat beaded their brows and their breathing became shallow and rapid. They awaited their moment.

The song and dance continued as the young forest mage drew out his fun at the Darkslayer's expense. The axe-wielding warrior kept his cool under his spiked helm and kept his bright blue eyes on his antagonist. Then the Darkslayer tripped lightly on a large raised root that had been called up from the ground by one of the forest magi. As the big warrior faltered and briefly lost eye contact, he heard his tormentor take advantage of the moment by muttering a spell.

But the mage had released only a single syllable when Melegal's stone stifled the next, replacing it with blood. The forest mage spluttered and tried to spit out the stone, but the great Brool cut the air with a whistle as if shot from a heavy crossbow, and its serrated tip penetrated the magi's sternum, flinging the weightless man backward to pin him to a mighty Red Forest tree.

Georgio's sling stone struck the temple of the leading mage, who collapsed onto the hard forest ground with a thud. It all happened so fast that the other magi merely watched in disbelief.

The Darkslayer leapt over to the tree and plucked Melegal's hat from the dangling mage's head. Leaving the stone still in the man's mouth, the Darkslayer took the handle of his weapon and jerked Brool free of the tree and the mage's body, whipped the blade in a full circle and severed the ugly mage's head from his body. Oddly, the lifeless head floated away from the still floating body, leaving a trail of red blood bubbles in the air. The forest magi had fled, and the Darkslayer took the flat of his great axe and batted the floating head after them. It smacked into a tree and dropped to the ground, its body dropping in unison.

Today, the forest bullies had lost.

"Whew," muttered Georgio.

"Here." Venir tossed the thief his hat. "You should wash it."

Melegal scowled and jammed it onto his head.

"Nice job, you two," Venir added. I don't think the forest magi will mess with you two again."

"Yeah, because next time they won't just get a few sling bullets," Melegal grinned, "but the whole bloody Melegal battle package!"

Georgio and Venir laughed. It was the jolliest statement Melegal had ever made while sober.

"Well, it turned out to be a fine day in the forest, didn't it? They might regroup, but I doubt it."

"Now let's get our butt's out of this forest, Vee," Melegal laughed.

CHAPTER 5

THE DETECTIVE AND THE CLERIC

A Badoon brigade was traveling at a rapid pace towards the great caves in the Underland. It was made up of five squadrons, each with twelve elite hunter-warriors. The Badoon underlings were known for their stealth, skill, and surprise tactics. They were the most sinister warriors in the underling world. This Badoon brigade, in particular, had been battle tested time after time, and many of its group had somehow escaped the wrath of the Darkslayer. Their stories inspired the other seasoned soldiers in their cold, silent marching column that crossed the land like a silent black caterpillar. It was night and the barren fields of cacti that lay between the dark hairy little race and the great mountains of Bish did little to slow their pace. Motivated by the two leading Vicious, the Badoons seemed to take on the mission with great vigor. Of course, slowing the Badoon brigade for any reason would only incur the instant wrath of the Vicious, and as a reminder to keep up the pace, the heads of comrades who had fallen to an angry Vicious were mounted on spears at the fore and aft of the ranks. It was a sad sight, unless you were an underling. For an underling it was a great honor to die at the hands of a Vicious who ripped your head clean from your shoulders. Witnessing this taking place had made the Badoon brigade feel as invincible as ever. They had lost more than enough men to the Darkslayer over time, and they felt a shared hatred for this enemy of their kind. No matter their numbers, they had never seemed to be enough, for the Darkslayer had foiled them time and again. But this time the odds would be in favor of the Badoon brigade. This time they were united in their revenge.

The celebratory mood of the small party in the Red Clay Forest ended abruptly when Venir discovered that Melegal and Georgio had abandoned their mounts in the forest.

"You'd better hope Chongo hasn't eaten yer little pony," Venir snapped.

"You'd better hope he hasn't, either," muttered Melegal under his breath, agitated now about having left Quickster with the giant drooling double-dog as babysitter, but not wanting to antagonize one who had just beheaded a foe.

On the trip back, Georgio bounced in and out of the trees mimicking the now perished forest mage. "Nya, nya . . . you can't catch me," he chimed. "I'm the goofy magic moron and I'm too fast for you." His attempts to float repeatedly failed, causing him to giggle incessantly, and he occasionally pretended to impale himself to a tree with a stick. Melegal grew edgy from the boy's distractions but Venir paid him no mind.

As they approached where the mounts should have been, Venir suddenly stopped, peering ahead and listening. Melegal did the same, swatting Georgio on the back of the head.

Venir motioned them to follow quietly. Melegal nodded, towing Georgio carefully behind him. Cautiously they approached the clearing. Venir's muscles rippled with the motion of his quiet steps. He came to a stop and coiled like a big ape ready to spring. Patiently he peered about. Quickster and Chongo seemed undisturbed. Chongo's ears and snouts perked up, his fat paws began stamping, and he howled softly in recognition of his master's scent. Venir emerged into the clearing and his pup began frantically licking his face.

"Why all the excitement, Chongo?" Venir looked puzzled. "I haven't been gone long." He scratched Chongo's ears while trying to avoid the soaking saliva. "The last time you acted like this . . ."

Venir whirled suddenly, his axe ready.

"Ahh!" came a booming voice. "Humans! More scrawny little humans in Mood's forest?" A figure broader than Venir and almost as tall had hoisted Georgio and Melegal off the ground like rodents. They kicked and flailed helplessly as the red-bearded fellow pinched the life out of them in the nooks of his elbows.

"Put them down, Mood, you're gonna kill them," Venir laughed, dropping his helm and Brool, spike first, to the ground. Chongo howled and hopped excitedly at the sight of the giant red dwarf of Bish.

"Oh, why not let me kill them?" Mood huffed, dropping them unceremoniously to the ground. "Humans are about as useful as underlings nowadays." He came and stood toe to toe with Venir, his mighty hands grasping and almost engulfing Venir's forearms. It was a rare sight for Georgio and Melegal to see anyone or anything the size of Venir. Mood's head was almost as wide as one of Chongo's, his features indistinguishable behind his bushy red hair, eyebrows, and beard. Only a pair of glinting, green eyes gave evidence of the dwarf within. Beneath a heavy chainmail shirt Mood wore a long-sleeved leather jerkin with matching pants and high, floppy-cuffed green boots. Two giant hand axes were strapped crisscross over his broad back, and a large belt pouch was wrapped around his waist. Melegal took in the sight of the giant red dwarf, wondering who he was and where he came from. How did Venir know him, and why hadn't they heard him sneak up on them?

"It's great seeing you, Mood! I think Chongo's even more pleased," said Venir.

"Oh Chongo, it's been too long!" Mood didn't seem to mind Chongo's two big tongues licking his broad face. "You just keep getting bigger and bigger." Mood reached into his pouch and produced two round, purple fruits, which he tossed towards Georgio. Chongo leapt after them, almost crushing Georgio and nearly giving the young teen a heart attack.

After a few moments the commotion wound down and Venir began making proper introductions.

"Melegal, Georgio, this is my friend, Mood. He's the red dwarf who used to look after Chongo."

Mood patted Melegal on the shoulder. "Hello to you. And to you, too, little fella," he added in Georgio's direction. Georgio stared back at the wide, fuzzy face, trying to see more of the bright green eyes beneath the bushy brows. The dwarf seemed to be squinting all the time.

"Yer bigger than Venir!" Georgio blurted. He stared in awe until Mood felt uncomfortable enough to turn his back.

"So, I saw you and those little forest magi having a tussle, eh?" Mood chuckled. "You sure scared the bones out of them, I'll tell you! Never seen 'em scatter like that."

"That's the first time they've done something so blatantly ignorant," Venir replied.

"Times are tough. The underlings have been making raids on them. They aren't used to anyone messing with their magic, never mind stealing it. But you'd think by now they'd know you're on their side."

"Whose side?" Melegal interjected. "Sorry, I'm a city boy. What's all this business with forest magi, underlings, and giant dwarfs for that matter?" the thief demanded. "What in Bone have you gotten me into, Venir!"

It wasn't as entirely new to Melegal as he was trying to make out, but venting seemed to make him feel better. Mostly, he just didn't like surprises.

Venir and Mood looked at one another and laughed. Mood had such a belly laugh that he had to kneel, leaving Melegal feeling foolish. Venir struggled to hold back his own laughter, but finally settled down and began to explain.

"Sorry, Me." He almost lost it again, took a deep breath, and smiled. "You don't need to worry about the forest magi, they're lightweights. You and Georgio could have handled them, you just didn't know it. As for Mood, he's a good guy and so are his people. He keeps me posted on the goings on out here. As long as you're a good guy, or a pretty good guy, you don't have to worry; I'm sure of it. I try to tell you about these things, but you don't like to listen."

"As for the underlings," Mood piped up, lounging against Chongo who was lying down, "I don't think you need to worry about them, either. Your buddy with the big axe over there goes through them like crap through ah . . . Well, I forget how it's goes, but you get the idea. It's like nothing I ever saw. Almost fun to watch."

"Anyway, we're perfectly safe," Venir finished, relaxing.

Melegal strolled forward, arms crossed. "And what about the Royals that we assume to be chasing us? Is that no longer a concern?"

"Nope. They won't find us."

"Royals?" Mood sat up. "Uh, that would be something I'd definitely worry about. They kinda run the show on Bish. Why are you running from the Royals, Venir?"

"You're leaning up against the reason."

"Oh." The answer sobered the big dwarf and he leaned back, deep in thought. A silence fell over them, and the forest quietened. A breeze wheezed through the blue, green, and red leaves of the Red Clay Forest, calming their spirits, even for the agitated Melegal. Feeling safe for now, they all took a nap.

Two days had passed since Tonio's demise in the stables at the south gate of the city. And in those two days Almen's house detective, McKnight, had figured out that Tonio had not been assassinated.

"So, you don't know what on Bish it was, do you?" McKnight was questioning an older stable hand whose leathery face was as wrinkled as his hair was salted with gray. The old man trembled through the interview with McKnight, knowing full well the penalty of upsetting a Royal.

"Yes, a two-headed monster dog it could have been, sir," he quavered. "I don't know who owns the ugly thing but it is indeed unique. I've worked all my life in this stable and only saw this creature once, a few months ago. Me thinks it did it, judging by what you say."

McKnight pondered, twirling his razor-thin knife blade coolly between his fingers. The older man watched, anticipating instant mutilation if he said a word wrong. He had never encountered anyone like this in his life, but he hadn't seen many people anyway, being born and bred in a stable.

"Well, old man," McKnight replied, "I don't like your story, but I've gathered pretty much the same from others. You say this is the stable the dog beast was in? So how did it leave without being seen?"

The old man looked at the ground, shaking his head. McKnight pulled out another knife and began poking all over the stable, alert for anything out of the ordinary. Frustrated, he left the stable and looked up and down the rows, stepping back and forth, trying to get a new angle on the situation.

"Close that stable gate, if you will."

The old hand did as he was told. It latched with a clank. McKnight then tested some other gates. They latched without a clank. He looked back at the first gate. It was set a little lower than the others, McKnight noticed. He had it! Brushing the old man aside, he opened the stable gate and closed himself in. From there he tried to find a handhold to lift himself up on the gate. Two big grooves lay under the main support beam of the stable gate. McKnight lifted it, felt some give, and stopped. He tried again. After moments of great strain he managed to lift the bar, and the floor at the back of the stable dropped open into the corridor through which the giant two-headed dog had left days earlier.

"Well, there we have it. Fascinating." He beckoned to the old man to enter, but instead saw him running away down the main corridor. He was horribly slow, McKnight thought, pondering whether to kill him or let him go. But McKnight was not a killer, for he wasn't a Royal, although he was in need of some practice. Instead, he decided to see where the secret corridor led. But first he spent some time studying how the mechanism worked. He was a thorough man, after all. He then gathered a small bull's-eye lantern so that he could let himself down the corridor and into the darkness. But he did not leave until he had found the lever that allowed him to close the passage again. McKnight was beginning to enjoy this task.

Earlier in the day, Lord Almen had been summoned from his chamber. The handsome man strolled through his grand home, which was decorated with the finest materials available in Bish. Marble pillars sparkling with intricate inlaid copper designs reflected candlelight from wrought gold chandeliers. Every chamber oozed wealth. None on Bish ever needed so much, but the Royals were the most selfish beings on the planet, and competed with one another to obtain more, more, more. It was their passion, the acquisition of beautiful things, but how they acquired them was dark, dark indeed. Fear and killing was the formula for success in this cruel world, and the Royal Almen family had perfected this.

Lord Almen had taken himself to Tonio's plush chambers to meet the house cleric, Sefron, and a scrawny black-robed rat of a man with a sharp fuzzy face and sparkling black eyes—an underling. Sefron was large and out of shape, entirely naked, and shaven from head to toe. His crystal blue eyes bulged with a look of questionable sanity. Most clerics in the city of Bone had disturbingly odd ways, and Lord Almen certainly found Sefron disturbing. The cleric went down on his knees before the Royal lord, while the underling guest did nothing.

Lord Almen then inspected the still body of Tonio that lay in the king sized bed, decorated in exquisite blue silk sheets and spreads. Tonio's face was heavily bandaged with wet salves of thick damp cotton. Only his nostrils and eyes remained uncovered. The freshly chewed body was similarly covered, but more heavily, so that he appeared almost mummified.

"He lives?"

"Oh yes he lives, dear Lord Almen. He lives indeed. I did not think it could be done after we found him so many hours in the dead," Sefron answered excitedly in a soft lisp, looking very pleased with himself. "Of course, I merely applied the bandages. Your lordship's underling acquaintance brought him back to life, it seems." Seeing Almen's flicker of irritation he added, "Of course, you know that." He edged back and began checking Tonio's bandages.

"I appreciate your service to my son, Oran." Almen gave the small underling a slight smile. "My most promising son would have been a great loss to the family."

"I care not, Royal Almen." Oran's hiss was almost insulting, but that was how underlings spoke, for the most part. "My race will never understand this human attachment to family. We underlings do not mourn the dead. It is pathetic. There are always more to take a dead one's place," he finished. Oran, black to the bone, was also a cleric for his kind. The underlings were Bish's most prominent race in the mastery of magic and healing. However, they focused more on the aggressive forms of magic than healing forms. Still, in order to dominate, even underlings sometimes needed their lives saved, though none would normally admit it. Oran was unique among underling clerics, for rather than merely healing, he had also mastered ways of causing great harm—especially to other races. But, much as he hated humans and other races, he could not help but be fascinated by them. Oran's meddling with other races had made him a renegade among his kind. He was a studious underling whose dark violet eyes revealed a deep knowledge of the black arts. His coal black hair was thick, long, and matted, just a shade less black than his simple robes and soft-soled shoes. His furry face was narrow, with high cheeks, a strong chin, and gray teeth that looked filed, as teeth often did among his kind. His eyes, round and engaging, were hypnotic. Almen was hardly able to look into them himself, though he feared no underling, or he would not have been where he was today.

"Do you have my payment?" Oran began. "I have no time to waste like a human. I have studies to complete and travels to make. "I would like to inspect the specimens now if I could."

"I was wondering if you have discovered the cause of my son's death, Underling Oran." Lord Almen sounded agitated. "Your work is not complete until I know this. Surely you know what brought my son to such a brutal end, Oran?"

Oran huffed, gritted his teeth, and answered, "I don't know what stabled beast could have done this. It's not the bite of a horse, a mule, or a giant bug, for that matter. It seems to be an Outlands creature but I cannot say what. It had four legs with paws and canine teeth, possibly a Fenris wolf. Which is odd, as they are mostly in the far north. Big though, big enough to ride, I would say." He rolled his eyes in indifference. "He has spoken a bit. He has said 'two headed' over and over. Odd. He may mean a symbol, or multiple monsters or people attacking him, but I found no evidence on his . . ."

"How about a giant two-headed dog?"

Sefron and Lord Almen looked up to find McKnight standing in the entrance of Tonio's chamber.

"A what?" Lord Almen looked surprised but not agitated.

"I am sorry to interrupt, Royal Lord Almen, but I could not pass up the moment. A giant, two-headed dog."

"Are there such things in Bish? I have never heard of such a creature. Did you see it?" snapped Oran. His eyes were wide now, almost fearful.

"No, but I've questioned enough people to know there is such a creature. And I've tracked it outside the city toward the Red Clay Forest after the attack on Tonio."

Shock showed on Oran's furry face, but he quickly composed himself. "How many were there?" he asked coolly.

"The dog thing, a pony, and three people; two men and a boy, based on the tracks I found."

"It seems you have earned your keep this day, McKnight," said Almen. "Your interruption is forgiven. Ready a score of my finest . . ."

"Wait, Lord Almen," interjected Oran. "I can help you here. I think I know who and what attacked your son."

"Do tell?"

"We call him the Darkslayer."

"And why is that?" questioned McKnight.

"Well, he has been a scourge of my people for quite some time now," Oran added somewhat ashamedly.

"A scourge of the underlings?" Lord Almen was incredulous. "Can this be? Hah!" he chuckled, smiling at the thought of a man that slayed underlings.

"Is it the beast or his rider that you call the Darkslayer?" McKnight asked.

"Oh," Oran grew flustered, "he is a man. A thick man with a black helm, a black shield, and a spiked battle axe that he wields like a stick. He is the only one known to ride a two-headed beast. But maybe I can help track him down and kill him."

Almen, McKnight, and Sefron were silent. Underlings feared neither humans nor any other race. The fear and respect with which Oran had spoken of the Darkslayer was unheard of; not that any man ever dared—or survived long enough—to repeat what an underling had said. It was an amazing turn of events.

"What now, Oran?" Almen asked.

"Let us finish today's business with my payment. I shall contact you tomorrow. Your servant has provided helpful information to me and my superiors," he said.

McKnight cocked a brow at Oran's words.

"Tomorrow then, Oran," Almen said. "I think you know the way to your payments. I bid you farewell."

Oran turned and walked out without any further courtesy.

"My lord," McKnight said, "may I ask what his payment is for the resurrection of your son?"

Sefron looked up from checking a bandage to listen.

"More humans. He wanted twenty of them; men, women, boys and girls. Some elderly, too."

"What does he do with them?" McKnight asked, not sure that he wanted the answer.

"Various experiments," Lord Almen answered. "While they are alive he studies their reactions to torture, mutilation, rape, and breeding with various sorts of creatures. Once they have breathed their last he tries to find other practical uses for their bodies. Yes, McKnight, we are cruel. But the underlings are crueler."

With that, he walked out, leaving Sefron and McKnight to their thoughts.

CHAPTER 6

HERE COMES THE DARKSLAYER

Venir, Melegal, and Mood made their way through the Red Clay Forest along deep paths that Mood and Venir referred to as their shortcuts. The terrain was rough, slick, steep, and narrow. Mood led, chopping brush like wheat with his hand axes, and Venir followed towing Chongo behind him. Georgio rode on Chongo, sweaty but perfectly happy, while Melegal brought up the rear on Quickster, scowling in discomfort.

"When will we see the suns again?" Melegal whined. "We've been half a day in this tangled mess, and then some. My butt hurts, the bugs are eating me, and the humidity's sweating me dry."

"Shut up, Me, it won't be much longer," Venir barked. Too much time the city, thought Venir. The climate could be perfect and Melegal would still complain. Venir had come to expect this from the thief, but it was still annoying.

"Almost out," added Mood. "A few more miles and we'll be back in the blazing desert." Mood was unfazed despite his preference for cooler, darker, and damper places. Dwarfs were tough and not ones to complain, especially giant dwarfs. Venir had seen dwarfs lose ears, even limbs, and never shed a tear. They were tougher than chewed leather, Venir always said, and Mood was no exception.

They had not crossed paths with any other forest creatures since the incident with the forest magi, other than a hungry grizzly bear earlier in the day. Mood made quick work of the animal, slitting its neck in a blink. Mood and Venir quickly skinned it and Mood devoured lumps of the flesh raw, its blood deepening the color of his beard. Chongo devoured his portion of the treat with vigor. Venir, however, had no taste for raw meat, and Melegal went pale and had to turn away. As they were not far from Georgio's village, Venir bundled up the remainder of the meat and gathered the hide and the head for Georgio's impoverished family. They would be thankful for such a fine gift.

Tonio's near-death experience still didn't completely add up for Detective McKnight. Why was the young lord seemingly alone at the stables on the day of his murder? Did he encounter the Dark-slayer? And why was he armed with a heavy crossbow—a weapon rarely carried around unless to ensure that your prey died instantly. Hopefully, Tonio would be able to recall why he was there, if the brat wasn't too ashamed to tell. Even with his pride on the line, Tonio would not normally venture into danger alone. A friend or an ally had probably accompanied him. Had someone set him up? The younger Royals formed tight packs and loved an opening to grab more power from another Royal house. After all, his father's house had been moving up, and so too would his son. Had Tonio been set up by another pack, or had he messed with the wrong man this time? McKnight was out to get the whole story, even if Tonio was not willing to talk.

Having gathered a bit more information about Tonio, McKnight headed for a noble tavern called the Chimera. The place was known to be a favorite hangout of his and many others among Bone's finest Royals—or possibly Bone's most pompous snobs and overbearing jerks, McKnight suspected. He would find out what he needed to know, with or without their cooperation. And their evil little minds need never know.

Oran did not waste time relaying his new information about the Darkslayer to the lords and masters of the Underland. Hopefully, he might regain some favor, for they were not very approving of his dealings with other races, fearing that he might reveal too much about his own kind. So far he had not betrayed his kind, but still he was mistrusted and shunned. He was an odd underling, for he was more concerned with the pursuit of knowledge than the pursuit of world domination for underlings.

Oran was one of the few underlings to have stepped inside a human city. An underling in the City of Bone was unheard of, even by the majority of Royal families. But Almen was a dangerous man who liked to take risks, one of the main reasons his house had moved up so fast over recent years. So far, his dealings with Oran had paid off, for Oran also liked risk—and its rewards. One day, Oran would make Almen pay much more for his services, but so far Almen had served his purposes well.

Oran had left Almen's mansion via the dungeons, and through a secret tunnel that led into massive caves far below the castle. He traveled quickly with his twenty new captives until they reached an underground river. There an ample barge was waiting, and he loaded the drugged humans aboard, where he shackled them with thick chains and gagged them. The only illumination was a burning torch that Oran had carried from the Almen mansion. But there was no further need for light, so Oran tossed it into the murky black river. It was extinguished with a hiss, and then sank.

The cavern that held the river was blacker than the night, and the sound of rippling water echoed along the river tunnel. Oran sat soaking up the darkness and then muttered an incantation. The barge moved quickly thereafter, deeper and faster into the darkness, and a mild breeze ruffled Oran's dark robe as well as the hairs on the naked prisoners. They had no concept of where they were; not did they care once Sefron had subdued them with his special toxins. They sat, silent and helpless in the darkness, in the last moments of peace they would ever know. Oran's sanctuary was only a few score miles south of the City of Bone, where they would come to learn that true horror lay not in the hearts of men, but in the world deep below.

The adventurers arrived in Georgio's village just as Bish's two ruddy red suns were setting on opposite ends of the skyline, casting long shadows over the burnt plains. Why the suns rose and set in opposite directions the inhabitants did not know. What they did know was that the suns would rise, pass one another, and set again at precisely the same time every day. This made for tough people on Bish, but they knew no different. They lived for the day, whether in pleasure or pain, and whatever brought them greatest enjoyment took priority. Who cared why or how the suns set? Oddly, someone did. For some inexplicable reason, Georgio cared.

"Stop staring at the suns, Georgio," Venir snapped endlessly. "It'll burn your eyes into the back of your head." It was a fair warning, for many on Bish had lost their eyesight trying to stare down the suns.

Georgio, however, loved the suns and seemed unfazed by his staring. Even Mood seemed perplexed by the tubby teen's obsession. But they gave it no serious thought. Venir and Melegal were keen to dispatch the boy and get down to the comforts of Two-Ten City.

Their stop at the village of Throhm was very brief, but Georgio strongly resisted being left behind.

"I'm going with you guys!" he pouted. Though they turned deaf ears to his pleas, Venir finally had to bargain with the boy.

"Now Georgio, you keep your mouth shut. No talk about Mood or Chongo. Your people here won't understand," he lectured. "Your folks don't trust outsiders, so you're lucky they finally came to trust me, what with savin' your whole bloomin' village from bloodthirsty brigands. So, keep your silence and we'll come get you in a few weeks. If you don't, you won't see me or Chongo again for a very long time."

"But Vee . . ." the boy's large brown eyes filled with tears.

"I said not a word."

"How am I s'posed to last that long? You know I can't shut up forever."

"You don't have to," Venir growled. "Just a few weeks!" He shook the boy tightly in his mighty hands.

Georgio seemed to get the message. "Okay," he said dejectedly.

Venir and Melegal spoke a few moments with Georgio's parents, who were thrilled to see their boy and very happy with the grizzly meat and pelt. "What a good influence you've been on Georgio," they said. It was true, Venir knew, although not quite the way they thought; yet he took pride in the matter, and their comments warmed his battled-hardened heart.

They said their goodbyes and headed south out of the village to where Mood would be waiting with Chongo a few miles out of sight.

"So what's this about bloodthirsty brigands you saved the village from?" Melegal inquired once they were out of Throhm.

"Oh, Me, I wouldn't want to take any time away from your complaining." teased Venir.

"Don't worry, Vee, I'll get my complaining all in, in due course," the thief smiled.

"I think you already know that story, Me," Venir sounded heavy now, and Melegal let it go. He knew that Georgio and Venir's relationship's was born not from sunshine and rainbows but from tragedy and loss. That was why the big man cared for the boy and protected him from things he wasn't yet ready to know. Venir carried his burden so that Georgio could remain happy and carefree.

Venir was thinking back now to the time he'd been hired to track some bandits and had caught them pillaging Georgio's village. Venir and his small force of mercenaries managed to run off those they had not slain. Venir did not yet possess Brool, yet he was one of the most renowned young warriors in the Outlands. The battle was a big one against superior numbers, and Venir's leadership, battle tactics, and instincts had blossomed that day, and were never forgotten by the folks in the small village of Throhm. Yet, the victory was not without its tragedies. Many of the brigands had escaped with captives, and Georgio's teenage sister Silvia was among them. Georgio was just a toddler then and had barely known her. For his own good, his heartbroken parents never mentioned her to the boy, and, as far a Venir knew, Georgio no longer remembered her. But his parents had described her to Venir, and several years later he found her by chance, working in a tavern in the City of Bone. She had grown to be a beautiful woman with long thick locks of curly brown hair, and round chestnut eyes like her mother and brothers. Venir spoke with her, but it did not go well. Shame and humiliation had apparently hardened her, and she would not acknowledge any pleasant memories of family and home, so Venir wound up walking away. He kept tabs on her for a while, but soon lost track of her.

It was nightfall when Venir, Melegal, and Quickster caught up with Mood. The giant dwarf had made a fire in a steep, rocky gorge. From the dry plains the illumination was barely visible at the upper rim of the gorge, as the smoke absorbed most of the light and the hazy night seemed to consume the smoke. But Venir and Melegal saw well at night. They navigated deep into the rocky gorge and found Mood and Chongo on a large jutting crag. Venir knew this spot, as he and Mood had spent many nights here before. A few snakes and vermin ventured here from time to time, but most dangerous humanoids or predators were unlikely to find this terrain. It had been this way always, as far as Mood knew. Something in this crevice seemed to preserve this spot as a safe haven for select travelers.

"Ah, in time for some chow," said Mood as Chongo slobbered over Venir with big, wet tongues.

"Watcha got for us, Mood?"

"We're lucky. Snake, big green snake. The best. Chongo and I have had our share. You and your little buddy help yourselves to the rest."

"Ooh, Melegal, you are in for a treat!" Venir enthused.

"Not if it isn't cooked."

"It's cooked. And better than anything you've ever had in Bone," Venir took a big bite of snake meat that Mood had skewered on a stick. "Mmm . . . now that's good. Haven't had this in years."

Melegal picked off a piece and nibbled it, his skinny face drawn tight, expecting a nasty surprise. Then a look of curiosity crossed his brow, and he took a bigger bite. The meat was tender, juicy, and delicious.

"Incredible!"

"I told you it was good," Venir answered.

"Good? It's great! Is it really snake?"

"Yep."

"Bone!" Melegal exclaimed in a whisper, sinking into his soul-satisfying dinner from the wild.

"So," Mood said, "you never told me about this mess you're in back at Bone, Venir. What exactly did Chongo do?"

"Well, Melegal and I skimmed a Royal brat. He somehow tracked me and got me thrown in the dungeons."

Mood chuckled.

"In the dungeon the fool boy decided to take a whip to me. I didn't really care for that, so I gave him the beating of his life."

Mood's brow rose. "Shouldn't mess with Royals. Most are pretty bad company. Looks like you got a beating yourself—if that's what happened to your nose?"

Venir ignored the dwarf's chuckles. "I didn't really think, I was too ticked off. Guess I shouldn't have skimmed the fool, but we can never pass up a sucker, can we, Me?"

Melegal grinned as he ate.

"So, I left the dungeon and decided it was time to get out of the city for a while. But this Royal shows up at the stable with a loaded crossbow and tries to kill me. That's when ol' Chongo got hold of him." He scratched Chongo's heads affectionately. "Chewed him up good, but the stubborn boy was still breathing when we bolted. Bleedin' pretty bad though."

The big dwarf pondered this. He had fought Royals before. Crafty, selfish, and sly they were. They ran Bish despite the attempts of the underlings to subdue the surface. Good Royals were rare, and somehow the bad Royals ruled in unison with them. Whenever there was a threat to the humans on Bish, all Royals, good and bad, stuck together. They had the numbers and the resources, and they had always ruled, as far back as anyone could remember. It was okay during the wars, when the Royals left everyone else alone. But when Bish wasn't at war, the Royals didn't have much to do. Then they were a pain in the neck. If you weren't a Royal, the last thing you wanted was be a part of their daily affairs. If you crossed one you crossed the whole family, and sometimes other families, too. Then they wouldn't let up until you were in your grave. Royals considered affairs of this kind good practice for future wars. So this was what Venir and Melegal had gotten themselves into. Mood grunted, concern buckling his bushy eyebrows. Meanwhile Venir unrolled his blanket between Chongo and the warm fire.

The night in the ravine was quiet. No crickets, no howls, just a whistling between the small crags and other outcroppings at the ravine's rim. It was neither a soothing nor a threatening sound, just eerie. The blackness crept in as the party slept and the coals began winking out. Mood and Chongo snored in thunderous unison. Melegal's belly, filled now with the wonderful green snake meat, kept the edgy thief at peace. Quickster slept soundly at Melegal's side, seemingly dead but for the bursts of green snake gas that stirred from him from time to time. All were at peace but Venir. The mammoth man lay quiet and still. Above him, the two full moons, one white and one red, cast shadows that etched Venir's warrior form like a statue, deepening the stress lines in his face and searing his soul with dark dreams of death.

Venir's eyes snapped open. The light of the moons lit up the bluish hue in his burning gaze. Moving like a gray ghost in the breeze, he soundlessly gathered his helm, shield, and Brool, and moved quickly out of the ravine without disturbing his normally alert comrades.

At the top of the ravine he stood, a dark statue of man, a mighty two-bladed spiked hand-and-a-half axe in one hand and a fattened black shield in the other. The black spike atop his helm sparkled like the serrated spikes of his axe, and he murmured in fury. The burning of his eyes under the helm's iron eyelets could make all foes run or cower, even an underling. The Darkslayer and his armaments sensed the whereabouts of underlings miles away to the south. He sprang into a quick stride, running along the plains of dirt and sand like an armored panther. This big cat would have his prey tonight. The underlings were the Darkslayer's favorite gifts to death, and he was coming for them. A new hunt had begun.

Mood's fantastical moonlit dream of a bosomy dwarf woman came to an abrupt halt as Chongo let loose the barking of a dozen bloodhounds into his blissful face.

"What in all of Bish?" the dozing giant jumped up in a whirl, keen eyes and hardened senses rapidly alert to his surroundings. Melegal stirred and muttered, while Quickster remained soundly asleep on his back, bent legs up in the air.

"Get up human. Venir's gone."

"What!?" Melegal moved warily and started gathering whatever he thought would help.

"Just grab yer gear and get on that shaggy thing. Your friend has his weapons which means he's huntin' underlings. If we can catch up, things'll be . . . well . . . you can just hope to see for yourself."

Melegal got ready quickly, and within a minute Mood was on Chongo, leading them out of the ravine. The great two-headed dog took off southwards following the scent of Venir, the Darkslayer.

Melegal wondered if he was still dreaming as he followed behind the two tails of the ridiculous dog and the even sillier-looking giant red dwarf. His past adventures with his friend had been confined to smaller cities and a couple of the more common races. Only the warm night air confirmed to Melegal that he was indeed awake.

"Woohoo! Ride, Chongo, ride!" bellowed Mood from up ahead. And ride they did, through the night, over the open barren plain, beneath the bright white and red glow of the moons.

⌒

The strange moonlight on Bish hindered the movement of most

inhabitants at night. Only a few races could see at night, and humans were not among them. But at this particular moment one human inhabitant on Bish was not hindered at all. No, the Darkslayer could see every bit as well as an underling at night. Normally the underlings used their night sight to take advantage of unsuspecting people; they could see the warmth of living bodies, which allowed them to surprise the less advantaged races and instill terror in their prey. The Darkslayer loved to turn their own guerilla tactics back onto them, and although underlings never showed fear, they often showed surprise during the Darkslayer's raids.

The Darkslayer had tracked a full score underling hunting party three miles south of the ravine where he had left Melegal and Mood. His dreams had alerted him to their presence, a sixth sense he believed to be gift of his helm, along with the night vision it bestowed, allowing him to hunt in the eve like the best underling hunters. He stood quietly in a lightly forested grove around a stagnant, foul-smelling marsh. Many dark groves such as this were scattered about, providing water on Bish's open plains which, by a cruel twist of nature, was undrinkable for humans. It was refreshing for underlings, however, and they often sought refuge in such places. A few other races ventured into these groves, but humans did so only when compelled.

Tonight, the Darkslayer was compelled to venture into this nasty, dark grove to kill the filthy inhabitants that sought its sanctuary. From his vantage point in the deep shadows, he picked out the warm shapes huddled together, muttering their ratty chitchat. Silent as a cat, he crept in unnoticed, and counted twenty hunters who, foolishly, had posted no guards—or had they? He knew this race that he hunted so well; he knew they would have other guards in place who most surely would give the alarm if he ventured close enough. Magic—all underlings had magic. And underling hunters, though not powerful in magic, still had spells that would aid them. But, the Darkslayer thought, he had seen them all.

After about ten minutes of hard riding, Mood and Melegal stopped. Ahead lay several groves scattered throughout the region. Chongo had the scent still, but Mood needed to do some tracking himself. Mood's sniffers often got mixed smells in these areas, as the acidic trees and marshes gave off strong odors that could kill a scent. While Chong's two heads and two noses often made him the ultimate tracker, sometimes the personalities of the two heads clashed. Now was one such time, and Mood wanted to make sure they didn't waste more time.

"Why didn't Venir take Chongo?" Melegal asked.

"Have you ever gone with him at night?"

"No."

"Underlings can see at night, and Chongo's so big he'd be spotted. It's harder for them to see Venir. The underlings, like me, see the warmth we give off, but I don't think they see Venir when he has that get-up on."

" I've never seen Vee fight at night," mused Melegal. "I've been out here and there with him, but never encountered much. But I have seen him in his scary costume!"

They chuckled at the thought, and Mood, finally comfortable with the direction Chongo was heading, hopped back on.

"I think he's in that grove about a mile ahead, if you can make it out. Go, Chongo!"

They rode hard again, hoping to arrive in time. Melegal could make out the grove's outline in the distance. Tall, ugly trees seemed to spike the sky, and the ever-changing glow of the moons cast an eerie haze over the strange marsh. Melegal hoped they wouldn't have to enter it; the Red Clay Forest seemed far preferable to a swamp. But, for some silly reason, Melegal knew Quickster would enjoy it. What a strange pony, he thought.

A stench suddenly assaulted Melegal nose. "Oh crap, don't tell me that's the grove!" the thief muttered. But Mood wasn't listening as he moved rapidly forward.

MAYHEM IN
THE MARSH

The Darkslayer had waited a few minutes in the marsh before an unsuspecting underling hunter left his group and ventured in the Darkslayer's direction. The giant man could barely hold back the bloodlust, and his head ached from containing his fury. The underling peered cautiously about, then began to pee into the murk, standing just twenty paces from death in the quiet marsh. Finished, the underling headed back to his group, followed this time by a silent, axe-wielding shadow that closed to within five paces and mimicked the smaller underling's movements. The duo stepped closer and closer to the unsuspecting hunting party, where some acknowledged their member's approach without noticing his looming shadow. They would not see it until too late. The returning underling stood before the group and rambled something amusing, it seemed, as the group laughed and chattered in the odd way of underlings. As the humorous underling giggled, others abruptly stopped their laughter as they watched their comrade being engulfed from behind by a great shadow which, in a blink, thrust down a mighty double-bladed axe to split him from head to belly. Before the first drop of blood hit the ground, the Darkslayer was upon the surprised pack of little dark creatures.

The nearest underling stood stupefied as the Darkslayer's axe exploded into his chest, spraying blood like a rainbow across the grove. Another quickly fell victim to the spike from the Darkslayer's backswing, which punctured his throat. As the Darkslayer prepared his next swing the serrated spike ripped open the dark humanoid's neck. The next underling turned to run as the Darkslayer swung Brool around his head and down onto the creature's shoulder, crunching through the clavicle and severing the arm from his body. Stepping onto the dying underling's bloodied back the Darkslayer moved forward for more kills.

The others, now over their surprise, had gathered their short swords and hand axes and were chittering orders. But they had no time to execute a plan of defense or prepare for the second assault of this human terror that had come in the night to mow them down. Five of them, however, managed to form a semicircle before the Darkslayer.

"I'm gonna kill you dirty little vermin!" The words burst from beneath his white-eyed helm. "I'm gonna tear the Bone out of you!" It was fury enough to make grown men cry, but underlings did not cry, even when about to die.

The Darkslayer kept his right arm moving, and Brool swept left to right in wide arcs to keep the five underlings at bay, swooping smoothly through the air with a whistle many underlings had come to know as the "last call". The outer two underlings suddenly charged at the Darkslayer's flanks, but he stopped Brool mid motion and leapt forward to chop through the head of the centre figure. The two beside him swiped at the Darkslayer's moving legs, but he slammed his shield edge into the mouth of one and parried with the other, howling in bloodlust as he swept Brool into the underling's side. As the bloodied heap fell, the last two of the group gashed open his bare thighs in two places, but the damage was not enough to slow him. He quickly countered with his shield and axe; Brool attacking from the right and the shield defending on the left. But the underlings were skilled and grew patient with their swings, hoping to expose a weakness in their now bleeding nemesis. They were no match, however, and the tide quickly turned. In a blink between underling attacks, the berserk man whirled a hundred and eighty degrees, catching the two underlings off guard and cutting deep into the leg of one while shattering the other's knee with his shield. They howled in pain and fury as the Darkslayer put them to death.

Nine underlings had perished in under a minute. And though fatigued from the long run to the grove, the fury of his attack, and the loss of blood, the great man in the helm could not stop himself. He was like one possessed, all reason banished by rage, and despite his heavy breath and pounding heart he pursued the attack blindly. A voice deep in the back of his helmed head reminded him that there were still eleven more, just as the roots, vines, and grasses of the marsh began winding determinedly around his feet and legs, pulling him down. The dark magic of the remaining underlings did not so much surprise the Darkslayer as anger him, for he had encountered such attacks before. He chopped and tore furiously at his tangled assailants. If he took too long they would overcome and suffocate him, but Brool cut through the twisted foliage with ease. The underlings were not relying solely on their forest spell, though, for three simultaneously encircled the Darkslayer to spit heavy darts at their big, writhing target.

"Curse you little maggots!" he roared, trying to protect himself with his shield. Two, four, six, ten poisoned darts assailed the angry man, most bouncing harmlessly off his shield or sticking to his heavy chain shirt; but a couple hitting their mark on the arm he was using to chop himself free.

"Arghh!" he yelled as the poison burned like fire in his bulging biceps. Yet it didn't stop him from freeing the remainder of his legs and hips from the roots and vines that held him, and as the underlings prepared another poisoned assault he was among them. As the little robed man attempted to spit a few darts at the angry juggernaut, his brains were bashed in by the edge of the shield. The other two, working behind the Darkslayer's back, had pierced several shots deep into his legs, but the pain that raced to his chest didn't slow him. As he whirled to attack the two remaining fiends, they showed surprise that he was not paralyzed or at least slowed, and they kept up the attack, one firing from the left and the other from the right. The Darkslayer hurled his axe at the one on the right, impaling the spitting little face; while the other drew his short sword to fight his now unarmed opponent. The Darkslayer charged and the underling thrust at the big man's foot, but the blade bounced off his iron shield, sending shockwaves into the underling's hand. The underling drew back for another attack but could draw no breath as the Darkslayer's steel-toed boot crushed his ribs into his lungs. The underling sank feebly to the ground as the edge of the Darkslayer's shield dealt a crushing blow to his skull.

Eight left, said the voice in the back of his head as he bounded after Brool. Bleeding, poisoned, and berserk, the Darkslayer lunged into the murky darkness of the marsh. Time was running short. His body burned like fire and his strength was slowly ebbing. He knew he had to rest, but rest did not kill underlings, and he drove himself on in pursuit. The remaining underlings were in hiding, planning another attack. Some may even have fled the dark grove to warn nearby hunters. No matter, one way or another he would find them all. It would not take long to track his next victims, not with the magic guidance of his helm.

Quietly and patiently, three underlings waited together a hundred feet south of the initial melee in the northernmost part of the grove. They were well armed with hand axes and short swords, for most other weapons would be pointless against their armored attacker. The other five had moved deeper south in the grove and split up, three to the east and two to the west, hoping to circle back on their slayer. The first three stood silently, spread twenty paces apart, awaiting the approaching man. None could see their prey—or each another, for that matter—for the grove was too thick with vegetation. But they did not need to see to know where the others would be; they were experienced hunters and they had fallen back on their well-used hunting tactics as if hunting any other creature. They were all set to strike, their weapons and magic at the ready.

A deafening silence had fallen after the last death cries of their underling comrades seconds earlier. The group patiently awaited their prey, but their keen eyes could find nothing in the darkness they were so accustomed too. It was unfortunate for them.

The Darkslayer knew full well what lay ahead. He moved quickly beyond their line and circled back on the middle one, who he had seen earlier, glowing a dim red from afar. For the sake of silence, he set Brool and his shield down. Coming from behind, he struck like a cobra, soundlessly clutching the underling's neck in his mighty hands and choking the life out of him, while the underling's feet dangled, twitching in the air. As the Darkslayer set the limp vermin down, the underling's leg gave a last violent twitch in his final death throe, kicking the brush noisily. Instantly the other two were upon him, enraged at the sight of the giant unarmed man dangling their companion by the neck.

The Darkslayer surprised them. Flipping the dead underling's feet into his hands, he swung him like a sack of melons into the face of the closest attacker. Bowled over by the impact, the underling collapsed in a heap. The Darkslayer dropped his unorthodox weapon in time to dodge two vicious axe attacks of the other. Without weapon or shield he was defenseless for an unwelcome second. The underling moved in, chopping at his legs, but the battle-tested titan caught the underling's wrist as if restraining a toddler swinging a stick. The underling swung with his free arm but the Darkslayer caught it in the same manner, gripping his wrists like a vice until the pressure caused him to drop his weapons. The underling released a high pitched wail that was silenced by a crotch-crunching kick, and as he dropped to his knees the Darkslayer grabbed one of the underling's hand axes and slammed it deep into his head. The other underling was back on his feet now, just in time to receive a flying hand axe between his eyes.

Grinning, the Darkslayer grabbed Brool and his shield and headed to the northeast part of the marshy grove. He ran with fluidity and focus, not wanting any of his foes to escape. His battle rage was subsiding but he rarely needed it for this breed. He was in control this time, although his body was burning and weakening with every stride. He needed to find the last few before his body collapsed.

Neither the murk, nor the marsh, nor the loss of his bloodlust could deter the Darkslayer from his mission. But the unique underling vision that his helm provided him failed to notice one thing, although his well trained brain certainly should have.

"Bone!" he roared as he came to a dead stop, stuck fast by a giant, sticky spider web. "Bone!" he roared again, fighting to free himself.

The thick, sticky webbing was the work of the underling hunters, he knew, for he had encountered this before. Once triggered, it only held its victims for seconds—or minutes at worst—but underlings needed only moments to gain advantage. The Darkslayer could see them coming. He strained harder to push through the web, for trying to pull it would rip off his skin. He tried sawing it with his axe as the slack in the web gave him room to work. The blades cut through the tiny fibers, giving him more room second by second.

It was taking too much time. Two underlings were now tossing larger poisoned darts at him. Some bounced off his shield and helm, but others struck his bloodied and burning legs. He cut into the web as fast as he could, but the poison slowed him, relentlessly, second by second, until, at last, he no longer moved at all.

The underlings waited momentarily, then approached. One launched another dart into his leg, but the Darkslayer did not react. Secure that they had at last immobilized their prey, they gave a loud signal of safety to the other hunters; a strange, inhuman sound that only underling magic could make, and most non-underlings could not hear. It was another gift of their race.

The two underlings within range of the Darkslayer remained vigilant as they readied their swords to end his life. One went around behind the Darkslayer, where his sword could not get stuck in the web as it would from the front. The other, watching his companion approach the trapped man from behind, stepped in for a closer look. He grinned a merciless grin. If this were truly the Darkslayer, the scourge of the underlings, they would be praised indeed. It must be the Darkslayer, he was sure. But as he got close enough to see the Darkslayer's closed eyes, they were open, staring at him even more mercilessly. Brool swept clean through the underling's neck, and he dropped, gurgling, to the marshy ground. The underling behind drove his blade at the Darkslayer's back, but his shield, already loosened from the weakened web, deflected the blow. As Brool finished him off, the underling let out a warning call to the remaining survivors.

Still covered in web, the Darkslayer now moved north to cut off the final three, but the loss of blood and the stickiness of the web stopped him from moving quickly or quietly. The web stuck to everything he passed, and, frustrated, he decided to wait out the spell's magic.

"I hate webs," he muttered to himself, awaiting the other underlings. But they never came. They must have fled to get more help, he began to realize, as the web finally dissipated. Somewhat disappointed, he started running towards the north end of the marsh, to get to his camp where Melegal and Mood would be. He was going to need their help.

"Crap," he muttered as he ran through the murk, not wanting to believe that the last few underlings had got away from him.

The remaining three underlings had heard the warning of their most recently perished companion. They had also realized that this was not just any common warrior hero who had happened upon them, but the legendary Darkslayer himself. This knowledge was enough to send them well away from anywhere the Darkslayer might be found. Nevertheless, it would be very valuable information indeed, and they knew exactly where to take their gruesome news. But the first order of business was to go northwards out of this dank grove, and they made great haste of it.

Fearing no more dangerous encounters, the remaining three underling hunters left the grove and ran over the flat, dry plains of Bish. They had not traveled more than a quarter mile when they met their second big surprise of the night.

"Underlings? Bone!" roared Mood, spurring Chongo to attack. "He musta missed some." Chongo barked, snarled, and charged like an angry bull, his keen eyes immediately picking up the underlings. Two underlings broke away to the right and Chongo and Mood pursued them. They had little defense against the charging mount, other than to run for their miserable lives. Chongo closed in on the fleeing pair, barking and snapping until he caught up with the one who was half a step behind, while the faster underling swerved in another direction.

"Bite that vermin, Chongo!"

The underling ducked, hoping the dog would overrun him. But Chongo, too good at playing catch, snatched up the underling in his massive jaws. The underling flailed with his short sword but Mood knocked it away with his axe. Meanwhile, barely slowed by the activity of the left head, Chongo's right head held the scent of the other underling and was riding hard after him.

It was just a matter of time and they would catch up. The open plain and its bright moons made it even easier for Mood to keep the underling in his line of sight. The quick underling was no match for the speed of the dog, and had to resort to defense. He turned to attack, but his pursuers did not slow until Mood realized that the bolt of a crossbow was pointing their way.

"Whoa!" screamed Mood, trying hard to make Chongo swerve, without success. It was a short-range shot, and Mood saw in a split second that something or someone was going get hurt. The underling grinned wickedly as he squeezed the trigger.

A sudden whoosh thunk erased the hunter's grin as something bounced off the back of his head, dropping him hard to one knee. It was a glancing blow and he hastily righted himself and took aim again. Another whoosh thunk dropped the underling hunter like a stone. Chongo was instantly on top of him, both heads chomping and devouring bloody underling treats, the vicious bone-crunching sounds turning Melegal's stomach as he approached on Quickster, dangling a sling.

"Sorry about that first shot," he said sheepishly.

"That's okay. Where's the other underling?"

"Hard to say. He ran like he had a hive of angry bees up his butt. I never saw anything like it. He just ran faster and faster, then he was gone.

"Hmm . . . those underlings have some sneaky magic," Mood said. "That musta been their leader blinking out like that. No matter. Just hunters by the looks of 'em. I don't think there'll be any more left in this party. Our buddy musta taken care of the rest, seeing how they was run out of that grove 'n all." He seemed worried, though. "Let's head over to where they came out; Venir should be coming our way anytime now."

Mood managed to get Chongo to quit playing with the under-ling remains, and they made their way quietly towards the grove's edge just as the bloodied Venir came running out to the west of them. Muscle, sweat, blood, and metal all combined into a hor-rifying sight, a great gory man that the world of Bish called the Darkslayer. He was splashed with mud and guts from head to toe. His muscled legs were bleeding freely from half a dozen wounds, a couple of darts still embedded. His chainmail shirt glimmered slightly in the red and white moonlight.

"Any left?" he rasped from parched lips, noticing them.

"Nope. One got away," Mood answered.

Venir approached with a bitter face.

"So, how many this time?" Mood asked of the warrior.

"Seventeen." His voice was barely audible as he removed his helm, revealing long sweaty locks of hair on a damp brow. Under his helmet his head had remained as clean as the rest of his face was filthy with grit. He spat some blood.

"Seventeen?" Melegal was incredulous. "You killed seventeen underlings?"

"Would'a been more if I hadn't hit a spider web. Bone! Would've had them all." He stretched and then grinned. "That was fun."

Venir began scratching Chongo, who started to lick the dirt off him.

"Your legs are purple!" Melegal looked suddenly concerned.

"Yep," Mood said. "He's been poisoned."

"Poisoned?" Melegal cried, appalled at Mood's indifference. "We have to do something!"

"We already did," Venir replied.

"We did? What?"

"Ate green snake meat."

Melegal fell silent.

"See, Melegal," Venir added, "green snake meat does more than just taste good. It's saved my hide more than once, and it's already lessening the burning in my legs. But not many people know about it, so keep it to yourself."

The exhausted warrior's eyes suddenly rolled in his head and he fell towards the ground. Melegal leapt forward just in time to break his big friend's fall.

"Never seen 'im do that before," the big dwarf said, looking puzzled.

"He'll be all right with your snake meat, I trust?" the thief asked with some sarcasm.

"Guess so. Let's get some water in 'im. If he ran all that way and then jumped all those underlings, he should'a been dead by now anyway. Them wounds are pretty bad, and I can't say for sure green snake meat cures everything. No telling what those underlings shot him with."

Melegal returned with some water. Mood began applying first aid to the passed-out warrior whose breathing was very shallow for so robust a man. They plucked the poisoned darts from his body, revealing ugly purple wounds. Blood and pus ran freely as Mood squeezed and drained them. It looked extremely painful to Melegal, but his friend never flinched. Mood did all he could, but their friend still lay, apparently paralyzed by the poison. They kept their eyes on him well into the night, but his condition remained unchanged, and finally both thief and dwarf fell asleep at the edge of the smelly grove.

Trinos was finding something rather like enjoyment, if that were possible for an infinite being, in the effects her ripples were having on her world. Actually, it was not so much the ripples themselves as the ripples upon ripples that gave her mild amusement. Was this how some worlds were able to reach infinite status? Worlds that were not supposed to make it made it anyway, while those that should have made it did not. Had other beings like herself tinkered too much for their own good, perhaps, sending in ripples of good that turned bad? Trinos was sure she should know the answer to this, but then again, not all the laws of the universe had been explained to her; after all, the end of the universe was yet to be found. And without an objective, outside view of the universe, how could the universe ever be fully explained? This, of course, was not the problem Trinos had been assigned by her kind. But it did spark a thought now and again, as she would see parallels between her life within the universe and the life on her tiny planet called Bish.

Trinos had also found certain points of interest in her created world of Bish that required further study. In particular, there was the matter of conflict. She had created a world that contained both boundaries and conflict. The main boundary was a lack of interest in understanding any complicated forms of science. The creatures of Bish lacked either the intelligence or the drive to study why they existed or why the two suns rose at the same time each day. Nor did they care about the stars or why they were there. The only driving force was for power and control over other beings in their world. Some races wanted peace while others wanted war, and there was no way for one race to ignore another. In general, the races of Bish exhibited very little compassion, love, friendship, or joy. The people were hard and their need to survive and conquer always outweighed their need to love. Greed and betrayal kept breaking down alliances and friendships, leaving all in Bish forever watching their own backs.

The creation of Bish had also led Trinos to contemplate the nature of good and evil. She had instilled both good and evil—although she herself was unable to engage in either—in order to confer conflict. There had to be acts that resembled one or the other. Or had she merely created persons with good and evil traits for the sake of her own entertainment? Trinos began to wonder if her created world was perhaps not such a good idea after all. She pondered destroying it, though she did not carry this out. She considered more study. Most worlds were created on a basis of neutrality and shaped by the forces of nature. How these worlds turned out depended mostly on the laws of the universe, and the specific needs of the world would then either enlighten it or extinguish it. Trinos, however, had created a world without natural universal laws. And she had instilled characteristics of other worlds but not allowed room for change. She had, in a sense, created good and evil from her own free will. Did that mean she was not the neutral being she had always thought she was? Had she bent the natural laws of the universe merely for her own entertainment?

All this contemplation took place in mere seconds, and she concluded that, whatever she may have done, the world she had created could not possibly affect anything else in the universe other than itself. With that last thought, Trinos abandoned her observations of Bish, and returned to her study of the comings and goings of the worlds of other beings. Perhaps she would discover some similarities to her world elsewhere, while the world of Bish kept on going.

CHAPTER 8

MEET EEP

"Aagh!" a male voice roared through the luxurious chambers of the Royal Almen home. "My head's exploding!" Tonio, on his feet now, was screaming while rapidly crushing Sefron's fat, bald head so that the weird eyes bulged from their sockets. There were large, deep gashes in his face from Chongo's teeth and paws that would never fully heal; he would bear them always.

Sefron's eyes, locked onto Tonio's torn and twisted face, pleaded for mercy and tried to communicate his ordeal. Despite his weakness in the clutches of his assailant, Sefron was still able to hold Tonio's gaze. But Tonio had been driven beyond reason by his resurrection. Tonio's mind was maddened, but his will was weak, and Sefron was hypnotizing the tortured young man. At least he hoped he was. Frothing through his bandages—the only garments he wore—Tonio was just moments from snapping the neck of the fat, naked, and twisted cleric. But Sefron held his gaze, and Tonio's screams began to soften and his grip weakened as Sefron's hypnotic control gained strength. Slowly, very slowly, Sefron managed to rise from his knees and stand before the brown-haired figure. The mind spell had worked without a second to spare, and the cleric sank to the floor, gasping for air, while his head recovered from purple to red to pink and finally white again.

The door burst open and Lord Almen's powerful presence swooped into the room.

"What has happened, Sefron?" he demanded. "I heard screams from my quarters above," Almen's voice betrayed a hint of worry.

The naked cleric did not answer immediately. He backed away from the now mute Tonio and turned slowly toward Lord Almen. "Good news, my Royal Lord Almen," he answered cheerfully, yet respectfully. "He woke up! When they do, it is usually with a great deal of delirium and pain. But I was lucky. He is surprisingly powerful, and had I not kept my composure, I would surely be dead now, with Tonio on a rampage."

"Mmm . . . I know how this goes. But I thought you would have it under better control, Sefron."

"I though so too, my lord, but he came out of his healing slumber sooner than expected. He is a fine specimen and a true warrior. I've not seen one recover so fast." Despite Sefron's ingratiating manner, his words were true. "I have something else, my lord." Sefron bowed, awaiting notice from his master.

"Well, what?"

"He was drugged," came a new voice from behind.

Almen twisted around. It was McKnight. Sefron, shocked, glared at McKnight with hatred.

"How do you know this, McKnight?" asked Almen.

"Well . . ."

Sefron stepped between them. "I found traces of various inducers in his body, my lord. This detective is only guessing. I have proof. He couldn't possibly know this. I'll show you."

Sefron hurried to the tall body of Tonio that stood like a statue, staring blankly. Luckily, Almen was in a receptive mood and nodded for Sefron to continue. McKnight stood by grinning, happy to have ruined the cleric's surprise.

"My lord, when a person is drugged—in this case it was consumed—the inducers that are used do not dissolve properly in the system. They are thick juices of specific types; in this case it is purpleleaf from the Red Clay Forest, one of the rarest plants on Bish. The juice does in fact dissolve out of the body, but slowly, sometimes over weeks. However, the effects of purpleleaf only last a few hours, but this is quite long enough for a person to implant one, or maybe two, solid suggestions."

"I know what purpleleaf is, Sefron! You know we use it as well! Do you think I need a refresher course in manipulation?"

Sefron dropped to his knees and bowed silently to the floor.

"Get up!"

Almen's outburst caused even McKnight to take a step back.

"Okay then, Sefron," Almen said more coolly, shifting gears while walking around to inspect his son. "How did you know?"

"I cast a minor spell designed to detect such poison, and even managed to bleed it out through his bowels. And it showed up purple in his urine, my lord. I would guess that the poison was five to seven days old," he answered.

"I'm glad that you checked him out thoroughly this time, Sefron. Last time you were not so thorough."

McKnight did not know what Almen was referring to, but Sefron's eyes showed surprise and fear.

"Now, when can I expect Tonio to be back to normal?"

Sefron returned to his feet. "My lord, I am sure Oran's resurrection will have the same consequences as the others. Tonio will operate as a better warrior with greater strength and pain tolerance, but his constitution will not be quite what it was. Resurrection takes a lot out of a person—as you know," he wisely added. "But as he wasn't dead long, I think his mind will be almost eighty percent.

Such resurrections don't restore a person's full humanity. And the scars he shall wear may make him rather irritable." Sefron finished and awaited Almen's answer.

"Indeed. My son was a fine looking warrior. He will be, how shall I put it, maniacal and sick from time to time."

Almen walked around his son, continuing his inspection, running his fingers over the wounds of the hypnotized young man. "Dear Tonio," he muttered in a low, evil voice, "what a life you have set up for yourself from now on."

Then he turned to Sefron. "Make sure he is calm when I next come to see him. When you get him under control, I need him dressed—and induced if need be—so I can make sure he is prepared for his new role."

"Yes my lord." Sefron bowed.

"McKnight, come with me. I'd like you to explain what you've discovered."

With that the two men left Tonio and Sefron alone in the healing chambers. As he left, McKnight gave the cleric a little wink. Sefron responded with a rather more obscene gesture.

Oran, the underling cleric, arrived with his new company at a wide-mouthed underground cave, accessed by a hidden tunnel off the banks of the underground river known as the Current. Several tunnels led into various caves, in a labyrinth filled with stalagmites, stalactites, streams, ponds, and bats. It was a dark setting into which all underlings were born and raised. Few other humanoids or other creatures ever ventured beneath the word of Bish, and very, very few ever returned.

Oran's lab and personal lair was a large cave. Jagged stalactites jutted from the ceiling, casting shadows in the eerie light. Candles burned, large and small, not with yellow and orange flames as on the surface of Bish, but in flickering hues of blue. But Oran's prisoners were still too dazed to notice the light or the myriad glass jars containing heads, arms, legs, hearts, and every other organ and appendage imaginable. What most beings would regard as a show of timeless horror was to an underling merely stylish decor. Oran simply called it home.

The thick glass cases and jars on all the shelves and tabletops held primarily human contents. Parts of men, women, and children, sometimes even a whole small child, could be seen in their liquid graves, everlasting witnesses to pain and horror. But Oran remained unmoved. It was purely research for the greater advancement of his race, and for his own personal knowledge. The acquisition of humanoids had its price, of course, for Oran was not a hunter nor a slayer, and he had to provide payment or service for the creatures he sought. Not all races on Bish were as plentiful and as easy to come by as humans. But other races also appeared in his jars. There were dwarfs, dog-faced gnolls, orcs, and even some long-legged striders to be discovered, among others. But most of the less-common races were hardly a threat compared to the insurmountable numbers of humans. Only the underlings came close to matching them in number.

Oran welcomed the sight of his ghastly home deep in the Underland. He was smiling as he led his herd of humans into a separate cave and locked them behind an iron gate. Their imprisonment meant nothing as yet to the expressionless and unfortunate people from the City of Bone. It would matter, however, when the spell and the drugs finally wore off, but that would not be for a while. Oran returned to the more homely part of his lair and sat on a strange couch beside the pickled head of a fat dwarf. He closed his eyes and began murmuring a spell.

For many minutes, Oran muttered steadily in various high and low crescendos. Sometimes fast-paced and sometimes slow, he kept the rhythm steady. He had to, or the spell would not work. Oran had used this spell enough, and there was little chance of his making a mistake. The casting took its toll, though, and as he finished at last he collapsed back on his couch with a gasp.

Oran lay for several hours before he awoke, blurry and drooling. Staring at him was a big, unblinking eye. It was Eep, his summoned familiar, an imp creature of magic. Eep was two feet tall, with two legs, two arms, two small, leathery wings, and a head with just one large eye. His muscular arms ended in three-clawed fingers, and his thick, bumpy skin was a mixture of grey, brown, and black. His long, jagged nose with its wide nostrils seemed to point to his permanently wicked grin, full of white, razor-sharp teeth. Eep was a small horror with a very big smile.

"It's been long, Eep," Oran muttered as he stretched.

"You could say so!" squeaked Eep. "A year or two. We used to spend so much time together, hunting and doing evil to humans. Those were the days. So," he asked with great excitement, "what wicked bidding awaits me, master Oran?"

Oran had got off the couch and regained full alertness while Eep spoke. "I need you to run a message to lords Verbard and Catten for me."

"Deliver a message? To them? Can't we go and kill people like we used to? Please?"

"No, Eep. That can wait. I need haste and you are the only one who can give me that." Eep seemed pleased with the compliment. Imps fed well on those.

"Please, I haven't been summoned in a very long time. You gotta let me kill someone." He gnashed his teeth and clawed the air. "I gotta kill something, master Oran, I just gotta! It's been too long."

"Oh, quit begging, Eep, it's beneath even you. But when you get back, I have some fresh meat for you to play with. My word, if you properly deliver the message, and lords Verbard and Catten don't kill you, like last time."

"Ooh, I hate those two. They had no business doing that. It was just for their pleasure, and it hurt. Nothing can hurt me, but they did." He paced edgily. "They'd better not kill me this time, master Oran. If it happens too many times I can't come back. I think so, anyway; I can't remember because it's been so long."

"Quiet, Eep," said Oran calmly. "The news you shall deliver is positive news about the tracking of the Darkslayer. They will be pleased and we shall gain favor. I assure you, not even lords Verbard and Catten will want to tease you with their twisted musings.

"If you say so, my lord. What message am I to deliver?"

One moment Eep, the imp, was running across the open plains faster than the fleetest deer, and in the next moment the little imp had entirely vanished. The magic on Bish came from a different dimension that few could tap, but creatures who existed in those dimensions could invade Bish from time to time. Imps, however, could travel in and out of both dimensions, but only when summoned. They could view Bish from their own dimension and then re-enter it in an entirely different place from where they had left it. So imps could travel the planet faster than any other creature. There were only a few imps, however, and among them, Eep was a particularly powerful one.

When he next blinked into Bish, Eep was smashing in mid air into an unsuspecting golden eagle of his own size. Eep tore the life out of it in a lustful frenzy, its feathers and blood scattering in the sky and sprinkling the terrified farmers below. As the noble bird struggled, they plummeted together toward the ground in a gray streak. Preoccupied with biting off the eagle's leg, Eep was unknowingly plunging toward the hard ground, until his eye saw the ground rushing at him, and blinked back into his own dimension.

Below, the farmers ran in horror from the bad omen they had just witnessed. The death of the great bird signaled death for them too, they feared, and they abandoned their duties and ran home for their loved ones. They were cut off however, by the bloodied Eep whose permanent grin showed a mouthful of blood and feathers. Eep hovered momentarily, his gray wings beating like a giant hummingbird, then attacked. The murderous flying imp whizzed in and out with blazing speed, ripping out throats and pushing in the eyes of the helpless farmers deep into their battered heads. It was indeed a bad omen they had seen, and Eep disappeared again in a blink of blood.

It was not long thereafter that Eep appeared before an audience in the Underland.

"Look who we have here, Catten," said Verbard graciously. "A visitor. Underling Oran's little imp familiar." They were in their audience hall, having broken away from some entertainment upon receiving news of Eep's arrival. The darkly ornate chamber, a deep and narrow cave, held two large, heavily jeweled pewter thrones cushioned with red velvet. The two brothers sat calmly and comfortably in billowy robes that matched their gold and silver eyes, for it was common among underlings to match their clothes to their eye colors on special occasions.

"Is he not dead, Verbard?" Catten inquired with some amusement. "Did we not kill him many a time in days past?" The two lords rose from their thrones and approached the one-eyed imp.

"Ah, you know how these imps are," Verbard sighed. "Kill them and they just come on back. I wonder how we can erase this weird little one for good. After all, we don't really like Oran, nor his little pets."

"Agreed. But perhaps the imp brings good news. Or something

we can use, perhaps. What say you, imp? Have you some news to deliver?" Catten and Verbard knew the news must be important for Oran to return Eep to their lair. But they did love to torture the evil imp, although he was a creature of the magic dimension. Eep, who hated all life on Bish, did not fear death from the lords, for they could only kill him permanently in his own dimension. However, they could bring him a lot of pain and suffering while on Bish, so Eep chose his words carefully, biting his snake-like tongue. Too often his big, grinning mouth had got the better of him, for the underlings liked to trick him and then make him pay.

"Yes, Lord Catten, Lord Verbard, I do have a message of importance from the cleric, Oran." Eep grinned with feigned humility, keeping his head down. "I have been sent to tell you about a human called the Darkslayer. It seems this man was in the City of Bone and has killed, temporarily, a member of the Royal House of Almen. This Darkslayer is believed to be heading south from the Red Clay Forest at this time. Oran believes he is most likely traveling to the City of Three, or will hide in the Outlands in the southeastern area."

Impressed, Verbard and Catten hid their surprise from Eep.

"Impling, this news from Oran is of some help. But it would be better if we knew exactly where he is. Tell your master that his message shall be remembered by us. In the meantime, give him this message." Catten paused. "If he can deliver the precise location of the Darkslayer in the next two days, the chances are that our underling community could make a better place for him. If he cannot, I would suggest he never bother trying to be a part of this community again. Am I clear, wretched imp?"

"Yes, Lord Catten, very clear," Eep answered as humbly as he could bear, fully wanting to kill them both. Though it was a task he knew he could never accomplish, he thought about it often.

The imp stood silently before the two underlings for many minutes after that, his head bowed and his eye on the ground while the underling lords looming over him, recounting a previous time when they had severed his arms, wings, and legs from his body, and his head that would not die. They had then fed these parts to their starving cave dogs and made Eep's eye watch. Their talk was torture for Eep, and he knew they knew this. He could only wonder if they were going to torture him again, as they had so often over the centuries. But Eep did not move, show impatience, or even glance at either of them, for he knew full well that this would provoke them. He was unable to leave without their permission, a requirement of Oran, who would immediately banish him for a long time to a dimension where nothing existed, or until summoned again. Eep would rather be tortured than bored.

Finally, after several long and horrible minutes, Verbard broke off. "You may go, Eep."

Eep's wings buzzed, he floated up, turned his back quickly to the underling lords and flew as fast as he could, blinking almost instantly into his own dimension, with a brief rush of joy and relief.

Verbard and Catten sat back on their thrones and started making plans.

"This is good timing, Verbard. We haven't heard from Oran in a decade or more, and now this. Right when we have sent a Badoon Brigade after this human. Now we just need to get word to them and some hunters, and send them that way. We may finally catch the element we have always lacked—surprise!"

"Yes, brother, but I don't wish to take chances. We should send the Vicious and the Badoon south. And," he stressed, "I honestly think we should go as well, and head him off before he can get back to the Red Clay Forest or the Great Forest of Bish."

Lord Catten had not expected such a thought from Verbard. Normally they operated from behind the scenes, pulling the strings. Lord Catten thought, and then he smiled an evil smile.

"Brother, dear brother, if you think that is best, I have to agree.

But if we are to go out, let us make the most of this trip. Let us make it a bloody one, filled with screams of human terror."

"Well, let us not limit it to humans," Verbard added.

At that, the two rose and floated silently into the surrounding caves, leaving their red cushioned thrones in the candlelit silence.

T WO–TEN CITY

Melegal woke at dawn to a stench fouler than anything he had known in the City of Bone. Astonished to have slept through it, he held his nose and peered toward a mysterious rustling. Astonishingly, it was Venir, preparing Chongo for the next step of the journey.

"Venir?" Melegal could not tell if this was a dream or a ghost in the strange morning mist rising from the marsh. "How are you?"

"Doing good, Me," he smiled as he checked the straps on Chongo's saddle. "How 'bout you?"

"You are? Well, you were pretty nearly dead last night."

"Really? I don't recall seeing you last night."

"You don't?" Melegal stared at him, dumbfounded. "You're telling me you don't remember coming out of that grimy, stinking marsh and telling me about green snake meat and all?"

"Nope."

"Well if that don't beat all. And there I was worried about you. Bone! You are invincible, aren't you! Well, fine, I guess if you can't be killed then I don't have bother myself worrying about you," he retorted. "So hey, why don't we just go kill all the underlings right now?" He strutted angrily to Quickster and started rousing his groggy quick-pony from slumber.

"Hah! Would you rather I was dead, then, Melegal? Then you'd have a really good reason to be miserable on this trip. Would that make you feel better?"

"Maybe it would. I mean, look at you! Your legs were purple last night. Now they're just plain scrawny and white."

"It's the snake meat, Me. And besides, it's not like you haven't seen me pass out dozens of times from booze or some of the other encounters I've had. Why're you so bothered this time?"

"This is just too new to me, last night's events and all." Melegal stared uncomfortably at Venir's helmet that lay beside the long-extinguished camp fire. "It's disturbing."

"You'll get over it."

"Sure."

"Have you ladies finished squabbling over not being dead yet?" Mood's grizzly voice interrupted. "I'm ready to go."

The party was soon making good headway southwards, without further mention of the topic. They were all veterans of tough times, and last night would soon be just one more memory among many they would not care to recall. They had survived to endure another day, and that was all that really mattered, though each took pride in the thought that they had eradicated a few more underlings from Bish. Even Melegal now saw himself in new light, having helping to chase and slay underlings himself for the first time. It had been a good night for hunting, after all.

It took a full day's travel after the night of battle in the marsh before the company arrived a few miles north of Two-Ten City. Dusk was setting in, and the two blazing suns were sinking slowly onto the burnt plains of Bish. Unlike the City of Bone, Two-Ten City could not be seen clearly from a distance. It had no giant wall enclosing it, although such a wall had once existed. Now the city lay open to the plains. It had a few scattered lookout towers that were rarely posted with guards or militia, for Two-Ten City was a community without civil care. The party could see some buildings in the distance and several caravan trails leading into the city from all directions. The people of Two-Ten City lived without fear of being overrun by hordes of underlings, or any other race for that matter. It had a motley army at best, made up of various humanoids of various races, just like the city itself. Nobody cared if you were human, orc, half-orc, or dwarf, just as long as you were not an underling. This odd mixture of people on Bish made for the most unique culture on the planet. It was where all misfits, adventurers, profiteers, and thieves came when their status as an outcast or criminal had all but banished them from the other cities in Bish. For the most part, the races tended to stick with their own kind, but in Two-Ten City, everyone was welcome.

"Well, this is close enough for me, Venir," Mood said flatly as they stared along a disused caravan trail that led into the city. "The smell of city, ooh, it's as bad as the marsh. I'll take care of Chongo and the pony if you like, while you two dogs go into that hole and do what you gotta do."

"I figure it'll take us a day or two to get situated," Venir said as he hopped off Chongo and started gathering his necessities. "Then we'll run back out and let you know our next move. We may have to lay low here a good while. If that's the case, you may have to run Chongo back home with you for a while. I don't know how persistent those Royals will be. I'm sure they'll look here, but they won't get much help. The Royals here aren't like the ones in Bone. But they'll get other help, I'm sure."

"They won't find us in this city, Vee," said Melegal. And as long as we're here, I plan on enjoying myself. Oh, and I'm keeping Quickster with me," he said emphatically. "I'll be darned if I'm gonna walk any more than I have too. Especially drunk." He scratched the ears of his beloved shaggy mount. "That's one thing I like about Two-Ten. Nobody messes with Quickster."

"Fine, keep your stinky pony, little human," Mood laughed. "Sure as slat nobody'll want to eat or steal that smelly beast, not even an orc. Ha!" The giant bushy-faced dwarf slapped Venir on the shoulder as he took Chongo, and Venir and Melegal strode slowly away.

With Quickster in tow they began heading into town, big grins on their faces.

"Ah, Melegal, it's good to be back into Two-Ten City. I can smell ale, grog, and cheap perfume already. And some of Bish's best-kept secrets are in Two-Ten. There's always something new every time I come."

"Well, Vee, you got that right. It must've been years, I can't believe I've been in Bone so long. I used to like it here. Wonder if our old tavern's still standing. Didn't we just about destroy it last time we were here together?"

Venir's handsome grin broadened, his blue eyes sparkling in the dusk. "Yep, I'm pretty sure we did."

It felt to them as if Two-Ten City was welcoming them with open arms as they approached along the old caravan trail to the place they had once both called home.

It wasn't long before the neglected trail had led them toward the bustling activity on the outskirts of the city. Every type of commerce could be found scattered around the borders of the city as well as within. Merchants and farmers fought for space to sell their baubles or their food. The worst of the streetwalkers tried to foist their wares aggressively onto the two adventurers amid a continuous stream of profanity. Venir and Melegal grew excited. There was something about Two-Ten City that represented the highlife they loved most in Bish. Maybe it was the oddity of it all. The prostitutes were not just human, but orc, dwarf, and even halfling, and they were all jostling to try to find seekers of their tricks, each race offering its own specialties. The open fondness for a multitude of different races would not have been acceptable in the City of Bone, where it was considered something of a crime to intermingle with other races without proper approval or consent. But the Royals of Two-Ten cared not at all, for they, too, were of different races.

All was good as the two made their way into the city, until the grimy urchins started pestering Melegal to stable Quickster.

"Lord, shall I find you a stable for your jackass?" asked an ugly orc boy with blonde hair, snaggled teeth and the typical piggy nose.

"No," Melegal answered flatly, tugging the shaggy pony along. But the orc would not give up. He grabbed Quickster's reigns.

"It will only cost a few coppers, skinny man, and I shall groom and feed him."

"What? Go away, stupid boy, and don't call me skinny man again."

"Sorry Miss. I didn't realize you were just an ugly woman."

Venir was laughing but Melegal didn't see the humor in it. He had forgotten how ignorant and smart-alecky orcs were by nature. Melegal stopped suddenly.

"Leave me and my pony be, orcling, or I shall be forced to use this." He waved his finger across the orc boy's eyes.

"Whatcha gonna do with the finger Miss?"

Melegal grinned and poked the boy in the throat quicker than the eye could see. The orc dropped to his knees clutching his neck, unable to scream for lack of breath. Melegal bent over him.

"That's what I'm gonna a do. And if I ever see you again it'll be the last thing you ever see. Got it?"

The orc boy acknowledged his words with rapid blinks, turning purple and beginning to pee himself, but staying put. A small crowd started to gather. Not wanting to cause too much fuss, Melegal poked the orc boy's throat again. The orc gasped again, looking back at Melegal with wide-eyed fear, then turned and ran clumsily away from the city as fast as he could manage.

"Tsk, tsk. Pickin' on children already, are you?" Venir mocked.

"That wasn't a child, it was an orc. And he reminded me too much of Georgio."

"Now, Me, that's just wrong," laughed Venir. "Just plain wrong."

"You know, I'm starting to remember why we left this wretched place. Those orcs are so annoying and so stupid. They drove me nuts. I can see they haven't changed, but I hope we can be more patient than we used to. I'm starting to recall why we had to leave last time."

"Me too. I wouldn't be surprised if they were still around," Venir said.

"I'd be surprised if they weren't."

"Let the good times roll, brother," the big warrior chuckled, giving the thief a big slap on the back.

It didn't take long for the adventurers to find their favorite haunt. A run down building, it was, a full five stories of old oak, covered in dirt in grime that was as ugly as it was unnatural. Deeply grayed by time and weathering, the Beaten Boar's Bum stood in defiance of its architectural odds and decayed appearance. Some said it was magic that somehow held the giant tavern together, while others said it was the dwarfs who had built it so soundly centuries ago. The stories had grown in extravagance since Venir and Melegal had last left, and it mattered not. The Beaten Boar's Bum was the lowest, dirtiest place to be found on Bish, unless you were underground.

"Shall I stable your pony sir?" enquired a small, black human lad sporting a heavy afro, blue eyes and a slender nose.

"Keep him close to the Boar's Bum, laddie," replied Melegal, handing over the reigns and a few coppers. "And be sure to feed him well, I would appreciate it." The thief flashed another few coppers. The young boy smiled wide and white as he happily led Quickster to a safe stable.

Alone together for the first time, the two men stood outside the giant but oddly shaped and decrepit building, sighing with antici-pation. The refreshing thought of ale, grog, and women began to overwhelm their manly urges.

Venir caught himself mid-fantasy. "We'd better go in the back, offload in a room, and then come down to the main floor. Let's find that boy and have him watch our stuff. I think he's good. He looked familiar."

"I'm with you, Vee, but let's make haste. My tongue's dry for food and ale, enough to pickle me purple. And I can't wait to do a bit of skimming." He gave an excited clap. "That trip down was rough."

"Go on after the boy, then," Venir urged, smiling handsomely at a bosomy blonde lady of the tavern who stood alone, wooing him from outside the main door of the Broken Boar's Bum.

Shortly after Eep's encounter with the underling lords Catten and Verbard, the imp was once again united with his master. They were back in Oran's underground lair, and Oran had allowed Eep to let off steam by chasing and killing the humans Lord Almen had given him in payment two days earlier.

The humans had emerged from their drugged calm to find them-selves in a black dungeon surrounded by the dead. In one small cell, four stout men were presently engaged in a battle for survival against the evil imp. The men were rapidly losing, while Oran took notes concerning their various reactions. They screamed for mercy under the imp's assault, he noted, and died painfully but quickly. However, the wails of the remaining prisoners who had witnessed the incident continued fearfully for hours.

"Eep, come out of there so we can get moving," the underling cleric told him, unlocking the cell door. "It's time for part two of your journey."

"Ah, thank you, Lord Oran, thank you," hissed the blood-soaked imp excitedly. "That was just what I needed . . . I just had to rip something apart. They were perfect." He wiped the blood from his large blinking eye. "I'm sorry it went so fast. Catten and Verbard made me so angry I couldn't contain myself." His wings were buzzing him rapidly up and down in the air as he shook off the blood like a rain-soaked dog, splattering droplets all over Oran as well.

"Foolish imp!" shrieked Oran. "Look what you've done!" Oran tore off his modest robes and hurled them at the distracted imp. They caught Eep full in the face and began to smother him, literally, as if they were alive. Eep struggled, but the robes constricted around his small body, restraining his wings so that he dropped to the ground with a plop. There they continued to squeeze until there was no more air for the imp to breathe and Eep began to suffocate. Within a minute Eep became motionless. Reluctantly, Oran relented and passed his hand through the air.

"Rollahkem," he muttered.

The robes slackened, and Oran quickly walked over, gathered his robe off the limp imp and kicked him in the head.

"Ooch," the imp wimpered faintly, and, having discovered that he could draw breath again, started drawing bigger breaths.

"No more fun and games, Eep. Let's track this Darkslayer and be done with it. Come."

Eep followed Oran into a type of study that resembled the rest of Oran's cave, but with fewer experiments lying about; its surfaces were scattered mainly with paperwork.

"This is the plan. I have to return to the City of Bone. You need to head southeast to this area," Oran pointed to an old map. "The Darkslayer has to be somewhere there, between the Red Clay Forest and Two-Ten City. Our human troublemaker will most likely be in the city, so look there first. We have to resolve this within a day, to give us time to help Verbard and Catten. Even if we don't actually catch the Darkslayer, at least we'll have aided them. That will go a long way with the underling lords. Then hopefully," he paused in deep thought, "I can finally go home."

Oran was thinking back to the last time he had met with Catten and Verbard, a memory he would never forget. He had dared to speak against them in the presence of like brethren on the issue of mingling more freely with humanity. The mistake had almost cost him his life, but instead he had merely been banished. Oran had had power in the Underland, but Verbard and Catten had great powers of their own. Oran lived only because he was no threat to them, and they could use him from time to time. Now was one such time, and perhaps this time . . .

Eep nodded at Oran to show that he understood his orders, and sped out of the cave as fast as his wings could take him. Oran, not bothering to watch his departure, headed to the Current, got onto his barge, muttered a spell, and set off back up the black river towards the City of Bone. Idly, he wondered how many of his humans would die of starvation while he was gone, and whether they would try to eat one another. He hoped he wouldn't miss too much of it.

It was late evening when Venir and Melegal finally sauntered down the steps from their second floor room onto the main balcony of the Beaten Boar's Bum. Inhaling the smells of sweet-leaf smoke and long-brewed ale, the adventurers felt a burst of virility. Pumped with testosterone, Venir's lustful manliness caused all in his path to clear out of his way as he made for the bar. Not even the common orcs wanted to risk rustling the brimming human. Melegal, however, regained his composure and cruised along smoothly, slightly behind and to the side of his broad companion, who cooed playfully with the bar girls and dispensed winks, kisses, and nods as he went. A curious kind of music filled the main tavern, mingling with the sounds of laughter, anger, and triumph. The pair from the City of Bone made it to the bar and somehow managed to find an opening big enough to accommodate the two returning old timers.

Unlike the Chimera in the City of Bone, the Beaten Boar's Bum had scarcely any human occupants. There were plenty of part-humans, but the full-blooded ones seemed a rarity in this tavern. Also absent were the expensive perfumes and beautiful ladies in elaborate silks and colorful make-up. Customers in this tavern didn't seem to care much about appearances. As long as you kept to yourself and stayed out of their business you were as safe here in the City of Bone. The room was weathered yet maintained, and the floors, tables, chairs, and wooden mugs seemed as well-worn and hardy as the floor itself. Torches lit the room on all sides, their orange flames casting shadows onto the faces as they laughed, drank, smiled, cursed, and even wept. Despite the plethora of torches it was not hard to find enough privacy to commit an illegal act or two. The room was lively and engaging, and it provided a respite for its occupants from the harsh realities they all faced, whether due to shame, ugliness, or crimes. It was a tavern that didn't know a stranger even though it was full of them, coming and going at all hours. And tonight, two old faces had returned to a scene they had once loved, but had to leave behind.

Venir felt memories swelling up inside him that he hadn't anticipated. The room and its ambience made him feel as if he had stepped back in time. He felt like the younger man he had been before he became the Darkslayer. He thought back to other nights like this and to what had happened before he acquired Brool and the gang. In those times he had lived so freely, as a soldier, a mercenary, a scout, and even a brigand. The best of all were the days when he had lived for the hunt, as his reputation to find, track, and kill man or beast preceded him. He had been vibrant, with a full head of thick blonde hair that drove the ladies in the taverns wild. Venir had occasionally felt a vague longing for those days, but tonight it hit him like a great slap in the face. So much had happened since he last left this place. Melegal had been with him back then, sharing some of his daring, foolish, and even childish adventures. It seemed as if they had come from nothing, only to have the whole world of Bish at their very feet.

But she had changed it all. A woman, a fully human woman, whose exploits he had heard about in Two-Ten City one night, a hot sweltering night that had changed it all. It was with more than a mere glance that Jarla had caught his eye. Friendships like his and Melegal's were put to the test, and changed forever.

"Hey, Vee, it's the same band!" Twin orc men with large noses were strumming tall basses, one with three strings and one with four; a halfling man banged a tambourine and danced; while a dwarf was playing a cone-shaped flute. It seemed as if the band had never changed, never left the stage since the day they were last here, five years ago. Venir snapped up out of his daze before his distracted friend had even noticed it.

"Yep, same gang." Venir's booming voice seemed to cut through the room like a cymbal, causing heads to turn.

Venir was starting to lose patience waiting for the barkeep to take his order. He couldn't order because the barkeep was at the far end of the oak bar that ran the full length of the tavern hall. Venir and Melegal could see the barkeep's big bald head at the opposite end of the bar, keeping his back turned on Venir and Melegal. He hadn't so much as glanced their way. It was clear that they were being ignored. Or were they?

"Hey, you big black son of a boar," Venir bellowed, grinning, "how about some ale and grog down here!" Most of the tavern fell silent, but the band played on, and the bartender didn't even seem to notice.

"Hey! Are you deaf? If you don't give me some drinks I'm gonna come back there and get them myself." With that Venir stood up and began to climb onto the bar counter. The barkeep, all muscle and six foot four, didn't turn, but slung a small but full cask of ale across the counter, which hurtled like a missile toward Venir, who was now squatting on the bar top. Off-balance and unable to dodge it, Venir caught it fully in his chest, and was sent tumbling off the end of the bar with a resounding crash.

The tavern fell silent, although the band were still playing. Melegal stood calmly by.

"If I catch it, it's free!" Venir roared as he bounced up, hoisting the keg over his head with a big smile. The crowd stared in astonishment.

"You better be glad you didn't spill any, you big jerk, or I'd a busted yer tail, Venir!" the big black man roared with a broad, white-toothed smile. "What on Bish brings you back to this filthy dump? I didn't think you could leave the pretty women of Bone behind!" The man reached Venir's end of the bar in a few strides, leapt the bar in a single bound, and snagged his keg of ale.

The two men stood eye to eye, the black man taller but less broad. They were clearly both more than ordinary men, like men among babes. The ragged and motley crowd of humanoids, momentarily awed, quickly returned to their own desires.

"You know me, Mikkel." Venir slapped and clasped the bartender's shoulder. "I can't stay in one place too long. Besides, I missed the finest ale ever brewed. By a man, that is!" The two laughed.

"Yer not saying I don't make the best ale in the world?"

"Come now, there is one better, made by a beautiful black gal in Bone. . ."

"You shut your mouth, Vee!" Mikkel was instantly in a lather. "You know that heifer stole my recipe!"

"She said it was hers."

"Bone! It's from my grandfather's grandfather and old as this tavern, you know that! Why do you torture me with her memory?"

"Ah, I just like screwing with you."

"As long as it ain't with her." Mikkel gave him the eye.

"You know me better than that. Last time I saw her she was as big as a six-legged cow, you'd be happy to know."

They laughed. "She was that big when I kicked her out. Now let's drink the best stuff ever. Nikkel! Get us some glasses and a bottle of grog. Today your daddy drinks with old friends!"

The three men took a separate table near the bar and pulled up a chair, while the young black Nikkel with blue eyes and a large afro brought over the grog and glasses. It was clear who the boy's father was, although Mikkel wasn't sporting an afro anymore.

"Hey, why did you start shaving your head?" Venir asked.

"Don't ask."

Puzzled, Venir started pouring some drinks before it hit him. "You went bald!"

"Well, you aren't so far off yourself. But I'm older than you, so show some respect. Now let's drink, all this talkin's made me thirsty!" Chuckling, the men swallowed down a large sip each and began to relax.

"So, what's up, Me? What kinda trouble has big stupid got you into this time?"

"Oh?" Melegal feigned surprise. "Are you going to start acting as if I'm here, now?" Melegal felt snubbed and didn't like it; at least he felt it was rude, anyway.

"Ah, come on, Me, you know yer my main man. I'd never intentionally snub you," Mikkel apologized.

"Okay then, Mick, I'm just messing with you. Anyway, to answer your question, let's just say some simple skimming turned ugly and we're trying to avoid any further Royal trouble." The slender thief took a solid slug of the delicious ale. Mikkel nodded in a moment of thought, blue eyes pondering what might have happened. Venir and Melegal never flirted with those types—as far as he knew, anyway—so his old friends must really be in it to have come down to Two-Ten City.

"So we thought we'd lay low awhile and assess our situation a little," Venir piped up, scoffing down a pitcher of ale. He was plenty happy in present company, and didn't seem too worried for the moment. The smells of sweet smoke, ale, perfume, and various body odors seemed to relax the men, or maybe it was just Mikkel's ale. Either way, the tavern of the Broken Boar's Bum was alive and kicking, and the thief and the slayer quickly began to unwind. They ate and drank like they were Royals themselves, and far into the morning they sat and talked about past adventures together, marveling at their somewhat exaggerated exploits that may or may not have actually happened.

Venir was quite the warrior and storyteller, and one tale after another rolled off his drunken lips. The women that gathered about swooned at his words, as well as those of Melegal and Mikkel. It was rare that such hardened men opened up like this in Two-Ten City; it was rare enough anywhere in Bish. Yet Venir's boisterous voice did not impress everyone, and his return to the Beaten Boar's Bum was quickly noticed by old enemies.

Finally, Venir ran out of words for a spell, and fell asleep at the table, along with his comrades. They remained passed out for the most of the day and into the dusk. But when night came they revived and resumed their eating, drinking, and storytelling. Melegal and Venir were having their best time in years, and the tightness in their faces had softened for a change.

However, peaceful moments never lasted on Bish, for the world of Bish had been created for chaos. So as a silence began to settle in, it was a sign that their peace was about to end.

There were many kinds of silence on Bish. There were silent nights, silent shadows, silent terrors, silent murders, and silent suffering. But this silence, the silence that fell now, was perhaps the most unnerving and unpleasant of them all. The band, the band of the Broken Boar's Bum, had fallen silent, and so had the rest of the occupants, as if a spreading doom had crept upon the room. All were quiet, all sat wide-eyed and unmoving as a bulk stepped into the room. All living creatures in the tavern were transfixed, except for one that is, one who never seemed to know better about anything once alcohol had fueled his veins after a few hours of steady drinking.

Venir, still talking of lowly adventure to the boy Nikkel, was rambling as loudly and offensively as ever. Seldom was such talk even noticed in a place such as this. But when all went quiet, including Mikkel and the band, something about this talk seemed out of line, inappropriate. It had been five years since a younger warrior had caused such a silent stir, and, apparently, that moment had not been forgotten.

"Oh no," Mikkel breathed, "not again!"

A giant humanoid shadow had fallen over the massive shoulders of the ever-rowdy Venir.

"Hey, who turned the lights off and the stink on!?" demanded Venir, as he turned about to see the source of the disturbance.

He looked up to see one of the biggest humanoids he had even seen. Broader and far taller than himself, a rare half-ogre man loomed over him, arms crossed over a hairy, muscled chest, peering down at Venir through what appeared to be only one good eye. Ogres and half-ogres were the largest speaking race on Bish. They had thick black and brown hair, brown eyes and some canine teeth. Although they had no facial hair, their arms and legs were covered with much thicker, darker hair than those of humans. This one in particular stood nearly seven feet tall, and must have weighed well over four hundred pounds. He seemed older than Venir.

"Ah, it's Farc," Venir peered back through one eye. Using both at once would only have made things look twice as bad. "I gather you haven't taken a bath since I last saw you. You smell like crap."

"Venir, close mouth, listen while Farc talk," sneered the half-ogre, bending towards the sitting man. "Farc not forget you smashing eye! Farc pay you back. Farc pay you now!"

Gasps filled the room, and those who had actually been around at the time the two had clashed scattered to spread the news.

Venir sat coolly. "And how do you plan to do that?" he slurred lightly. "I crippled your career, Farc. And even you wouldn't be stupid enough to fight me again, 'cause then your other eye will be useless, too," he mocked.

Farc leaned in. "You promise Farc another fight. Remember, human?" he whispering heavily.

Venir nodded. "But I not said you fight Farc, did I? I just said you fight. Right? Yep." Venir nodded again, slurped the last of a mug of ale and wiped his mouth on the inside of his arm. "Hey Farc, why don't you buy me another ale? I'd like that, I'm all empty."

Farc, apparently not feeling too generous, slapped Venir's mug across the room. "You say anytime, anyplace, last time." he growled. "Time now! Place where last time. Me and boy will be waiting."

The half-ogre stormed through the crowd like a behemoth dancing at a ball.

After he had left, Venir looked round and smiled. "I bet he's got one ugly boy, and I bet that boy has an ugly mother to boot. Poor lad!"

Melegal chucked, but Mikkel looked grim.

Then Mikkel cleared his throat. "Uh, Venir, I think it's his boy he wants you to fight. He's been the champ for the last two years. You might wanna stop drinking. This is gonna go down soon.

"I thought you were the champ, Mikkel."

"Not since Farc beat me. Then you beat him, and after that it was wide open for awhile. His boy's better, Vee. Much better, and younger. Farc wasn't the youngest or even in his prime when you humiliated him. But his son! Well, he's an abomination. He makes his ugly old man look like a school teacher."

The young Nikkel was just putting another ale and a grog in front of Venir, when Mikkel grabbed them away.

"Gimme my drinks, now, Mikkel!" slurred Venir, fully agitated.

"You better stop drinking and start thinking, Vee. You're on in about an hour!"

Venir brooded, but finally gave in with a sigh.

"Coffee, please," he growled.

CHAPTER 10

FARC'S RULES

The Badoon Brigade led by the Vicious had moved fast, cutting through the southwestern part of Bish and leaving a trail of blood over hill and dale. Most humanoid inhabitants that hadn't have time to flee had died screaming for mercy in their own trail of blood. The possibility of surviving a Vicious-led Badoon attachment was very, very slim. Dozens of Bish's more peaceful inhabitants had already died, and dozens more would meet the same fate before the brigade caught up with the Darkslayer.

The two hulking Vicious led the trek through high and low landscapes, unhindered by terrain, inclement weather, or natural hazards. Even the most senior and weathered elite underling hunters had trouble keeping pace with them. The best of the Badoons, nasty as they were, felt uncomfortable in the presence of the Vicious. For the Vicious, more evil even than they, did such things to torture and mutilate their victims that even a Badoon had never imagined. The word "cruel" was entirely inadequate. The worst they could imagine was merely a bad dream compared to what the Vicious would, could, and did do.

Much of Bish had heard about the unspeakable acts of the Vicious, but none had lived to witness such events actually unfolding. But just recently, from high in a tree, a halfling, a rare yellow-haired halfling boy named Lefty Lightfoot had seen the bodies of his family and friends torn, shredded, bludgeoned, and strewn from one end of his village to the other. All were massacred by the two Vicious, but for the few lucky ones who had fled into the arrows of the surrounding Badoon Brigade. The small halfling boy's mind was seared with the nightmarish screams of his brothers and sisters, bigger and smaller, being bitten, broken, and even eaten, their little heads squeezed to pulp or smashed together like pumpkins. He only wished he had not survived to see such horrors befall his people. He wept until he could weep no more and then ran as fast and far from the Badoon Brigade as his speedy little legs would carry him.

Oran had taken little more than a day to return to the City of Bone for an audience with Royal Lord Almen. The Current ran just below Castle Almen, as well as many other castles, unbeknown to Almen. The cavernous stone-cut chambers far below the castle, ancient beyond recorded history, could not possibly have been the handiwork of humans. Dwarfs possibly, but even dwarfs were not known for engineering feats as spectacular as this. In an eerie cave room, Lord Almen stood in the torchlit semi-darkness with the resurrected Tonio, Sefron, and detective McKnight.

"What information do you have for me, Oran?" Almen's voice boomed through the large chamber many times louder than normal. The underling cleric feigned a step back, for such gestures seemed to please the Royal lord's ego.

"South, most positively. He will be cut off whether he goes further south, north, east, or west. An underling Badoon is en route to dispose of him now."

"What is your point, Oran?" asked Lord Almen coolly. "I thought underlings could not handle this Darkslayer." He folded his arms across his gold-laced and diamond-studded robe; like most Royals, he loved to show off with gold and precious gems. "So what makes you think he'll be dispatched now?"

He began to pace around the little underling, enveloping him with his large, flickering shadow. Oran felt no fear of this powerful Royal, however. He respected the man, but it was beneath an underling to fear a human.

"Lord Almen, my reliable sources leave me in no doubt that these are the final days of the Darkslayer's scourge. He has never been taken seriously by our people, but over time, word got back to some of the upper underling management, so to speak, and they were not happy with their losses."

At this, Lord Almen let out a deep chuckle. "Ha, Oran! Yet you tell me that this man, this one man, has required the effort of a whole underling Badoon? My, what I wouldn't do to have a fellow such as that on my side. This has to be the most astonishing news I've heard in over a decade!" He continued to chuckle, stunning the onlookers who had never before seen Almen laugh. Oran, equally stunned, had been too busy to give the situation much thought. Struck now by the preposterousness of it, he felt somewhat embarrassed for his kind. Sefron laughed along, his naked belly jiggling, while McKnight grinned sheepishly, not knowing what to think, so surprised was he by Almen's mirth.

"Huh . . . huh," was all the revived young Tonio could muster for a laugh. Once a loudmouthed braggart, Tonio was now much quieter and focused solely on the Darkslayer. Since his resurrection he was clearly not all there, but he was still a soldier to contend with.

"Lord Almen, you need no longer trouble yourself with this matter. I could try to recover the body of the Darkslayer for you, or a piece of it at least. It is unlikely even a shred will remain, but I will do my b . . . urk!"

Tonio's strong, slightly grayed hands squeezed the neck of the underling cleric. "Lead me to this Darkslayer," he growled, spitting in Oran's stricken face, "or die now, underling!"

In that instant, Tonio's impulsive action decided the fate of the underling cleric. Almen had considered sending Tonio in search of the Darkslayer, and now it struck him as prophetic that his once finest son should undertake a personal mission of revenge.

Oran had no words to argue. He was only happy to breathe again as Sefron calmed his zombie attacker.

Few words were exchanged as Almen clasped his son's hands and gave him a final blessing.

"Kill him without mercy, son. Avenge yourself. Good hunting."

And that was how one of the most unlikely hunting parties in all the history of Bish was formed.

Oran could not believe how quickly his predicament had actually worsened. Thinking himself free from the Royal lord and the underling lords Catten and Verbard, he now found himself smack in the center of the mess he had been trying to avoid, now that the Royal pain-in-the-butt Tonio had insisted to his daddy that Oran lead him and that other human fool, McKnight, straight to the deadly Darkslayer. Oran was upset more at himself than he had ever been, and with those he had foolishly placed himself in league with.

"I am an idiot," he muttered to himself.

"What's that, underling?" enquired McKnight, brandishing two long, silver-hilted daggers of unique design.

"Oh, shut up!" was all Oran would say throughout the rest of their journey southeast, down the Current toward Two-Ten city. The underling cleric was used to travelling in total silence and darkness, but the humans had brought along lanterns so their feeble human eyes could keep watch over him and everything else. It was a sad mess, he thought, guiding his craft with the shiny weapons of two paranoid yet deadly men constantly pointed at his back. Luckily, the trip would take less than a day. For Oran, it felt like an eternity.

With the end of the universe still not found, as far as any eternal being knew, Trinos found herself stymied from time to time. A degree of frustration had even set in, which should not happen to one who had the ability to do anything; yet it did. More often than one would expect, created things would evolve into things they were not supposed to. Still, the endless universe at least held surprise for the omnipotent ones who seemed to roam and do whatever they pleased. Trinos would run across unique changes to worlds that had come and gone, and she would be fascinated and begin to study them, looking for answers. It did not happen as often as she would have liked, but by her eternal frame of reference, that was still quite often.

However, within the infinite there remain infinite possibilities. And so it was that the tiny world of Bish, hidden deep in the universe in a place impossible to find, was about to be discovered by another Trinos-like being. Scorch discovered this odd world quite accidentally, and began to study it with divine interest. He enjoyed its unique set-up.

But, he thought to himself, it could be even better.

After an entire pot of Nikkel's strongest coffee, Venir's blonde head was only slightly clearer. Things were beginning to annoy the great muscled brute as he contemplated how such a promising night was about to turn bad in just a few more minutes. And as if things couldn't have been worse, he was now being constantly harassed by things that couldn't have been better.

"Ooh, honey, now don't get beat up too bad," crooned a comely-as-they-come part-orc woman whose purple satin dress was slit to reveal one of the most curvaceous bodies he had ever seen on Bish. "I just love the rough and rowdy type, and I was counting on you the moment I saw you walk through the door." The part-orc women of Two-Ten City could curl the toes of men and dwarfs as well, so they said, and Venir and Melegal had been all too eager to find out, until this fight had come about.

"Don't worry sister, you won't be waitin' long," slurred Venir with a wink. The sight of the sexy part-orc pumped testosterone through his body, but not through his mind where it was most needed. The orc woman's muscular thighs and big round behind caught his attention so completely that he didn't even notice her pigtails, sweaty lips, crooked teeth, and piggish nose. After countless drinks compounded by days without companionship, such things just had not registered with Venir.

"See you later, big boy." She blew him a kiss and waved as Melegal, Mikkel, and Nikkel led him to where the match would take place.

"Man, Vee, if you survive this, you might not survive that!" grinned Melegal, happy for his friend.

"Me and Vee, you guys are both sick!" Mikkel shook his head in astonishment. "She is bad news, trust me. I know. Win, lose, or don't fight at all tonight, she's still gonna try and tear your legs off!"

Venir and Melegal just grinned foolishly. Poor Nikkel just gagged at the thought of something so violating to his innocence.

The door to the stairwell opened. In the torchlight, A wide, deep stairway could be seen leading steeply down into an open room. The warmth and smell of sweating bodies flared the nostrils of the manly party. All races sweated, but half-ogre sweat distinguished itself above and beyond the rest. You could not smell it from a mile away, but you always wished you had, because once you got too close, it stuck to you. Most agreed that it smelled like a mix of manure and salty urine. It was something most races could never get accustomed too.

The room opened into a large, circular arena where several hundred foolish gamblers were betting on the greatest game on Bish: pit battles. This was the only place known to host fights between all the races on Bish except underlings. Which was lucky for the underlings, because, typically, they couldn't box worth a darn. All sorts of races and questionables were about, drinking, screaming, cheering, and jeering over the fight currently in progress. Fights were ongoing, twenty-four seven. Many of the spectators hadn't left in over a week. They couldn't. They either owed the Royals of Two-Ten too much, or they were just plain addicted to the madness.

The pit itself was a simple setup. It was a six-foot deep and thirty-foot wide circle cut into a stone floor. Thick iron bars were bolted into the lip of the stone circle and ran in a crisscross pattern to about ten feet above the main floor and across the top of the pit to form a sealed cage. Two large gates on opposite ends of the ceiling allowed the contestants to drop down into the pit. Smaller races, like dwarfs and halflings, hated this drop; they often got their fingers smashed while hanging on for their lives to the upper gate, or broke their legs or arms from the fall. The Royals of Two-Ten always had a presence in place, giving their debtors a chance to fight in return for waiving their debts. It was a cruel way to go, to say the least. Most were out-matched and died brutally.

The pit rules were simple: no weapons other than a single blunt weapon that hung from a chain in the middle of the cage. The weapon varied; it could be a staff, a mace, a flail, or a big wooden club. Whoever got it first would often have the advantage, and, once again, dwarfs and halflings had a hard time jumping up to reach the weapon, especially with an already broken leg.

Currently, sitting on the far side of the cage from the opening through which the four men had entered were many of Two-Ten

City's so-called Royals. No doubt many more of the outcast Royals would be along soon enough, as word got out that Venir would be fighting Son of Farc. His battle with Farc had become a classic that had spread throughout the land, taking the shape of a legend over the years. Certainly this battle would be no different; possibly even better. But this time the older Venir, the Darkslayer, was more than likely to have met his match. As for the Royals of Two-Ten City, they were unlike any other Royals on Bish. The Royals on Bish were pure human, while the Royals in Two-Ten City were humanoid, but not all human. Long ago, Two-Ten City had been pure human, until it was invaded by a multi-racial horde who took over the city, bred with the Royal humans by force, and became Royals themselves. Of course, the other Royal families of Bish no longer recognized a Royal from Two-Ten City. They considered them a disgrace and a mockery of humankind, so Two-Ten City was left in its own tiny little world.

The ten or so Royals currently sitting at the pit were mostly part-orc men and a few part-orc women, so to speak. There was clearly some portion of human in all of them, maybe an eighth, a quarter, or hopefully half or more. Typically the small, piggish noses and rough, dark skin were features that identified their kind from humans. They were bigger and more muscular, on average, but mixed orcs some-times looked very much like their pure human counterparts. If there were uncertainty about whether one was more orc than human, the brash orcen personality would usually reveal the more prominent lineage. The more human, the more bearable in all cases, as the orcs were one of the strongest but ugliest races on Bish, as well as being known as the stupidest. They all hated humans, and of course denied being any part human, yet they certainly tried to imitate humans as best they could. But they were tolerated in Two-Ten, the city they had ruled in comfort for a long, long time. At the moment they were watching the combatants of the pit as a tall, heavy human was dispatching a family of six halflings. The ponytailed man seemed intent on breaking every bone he could, rather than killing them all quickly as he should. The badly crippled halfling family begged for mercy and were finally dragged up out of the cage. Melegal shuddered at the thought of what might happen to them next, but he hoped it would be quick. Bad memories began to swim in the drunken thief's head as he began to recall why he had preferred the safety and civility of the City of Bone all these years. But he moved on, and started taking bets.

Finally, the one-eyed half-ogre, Farc, appeared before them. With what just could have been mistaken for a smile, he leaned down and pointed into Venir's somber face.

"Tonight Farc finally pay you back." He spit as he spoke, his rotten breath gagging them all. "Tonight your eye get smashed for good and other eye. Then you know what it likes for Farc. Son of Farc bust you good."

Mikkel had turned away, holding his nose, But Venir held Farc's eyes unfalteringly as his blood pumped harder and began to clear his head.

"Whatever makes you happy, Farc," he replied coldly, and the two opponents stared hard into one another's eyes.

"Time to get in."

Farc broke off his stare and strode off to where the Royals sat.

All the while, the cage was being cleared, and the room had now filled beyond capacity. The betting now started. On top of the cage, two full-blooded orcs in armor opened the drop-down gates and beckoned for Venir to come. Venir strode to the cage and climbed the steps to the top. The crowd became silent, studying him and his approach. The two armored orcs had done this job a long time, and would normally badmouth the fighter and work the crowd. But they remembered Venir and showed him uncharacteristic respect. The crowd was puzzled momentarily, but when Venir hopped down into the pit and the orcs slammed the cage door shut they started cheering. Then the chanting began.

"Son of Farc! Son of Farc! Son of Farc!"

It began to annoy Venir that he was seen as the underdog. But he was older and smaller, and it seemed to the crowd highly unlikely that he could beat the younger, bigger, and undefeated Son of Farc. Venir gritted his teeth and stared hotly down the corridor toward the current champion.

When the large head of Son of Farc appeared from the dimly lit corridor, the crowd's roar became deafening. Things got so loud and out of control that Melegal and Nikkel could no longer even negotiate bets. Son of Farc made a grand entrance, pumping his arms up and enticing the crowd, which roared in return. Venir studied the him. Unlike his father Farc, he was much more ogre than man. By the looks of things, Son of Farc was all ogre, but for his pale blue eyes, which showed some humanity within him. He must have closed in at seven feet and over four hundred pounds. He had coarse black hair all over his half-naked body. His muscles were thick, his heavy brow protruded, and his legs were like solid oak trees. His nostrils flared wide under a fat, flattened nose and his shoulders were bigger than the biggest of bulls. All Son of Farc wore were faded blue pants, torn at the bottom, with a rope belt. A rope, that is, of a variety of hair pulled out of the heads of previous opponents. Venir wasn't surprised, for ogres always liked strange trophies.

Son of Farc seemed fairly agile as he climbed the cage like a gorilla, shoved the two armored orcs off the top, opened the drop-down gate and hopped in to face Venir. His big smile showed his rotting yellow teeth as he jutted his jaw tauntingly. The orcs slammed the gate above his head and prepared to lower the weapon. But as a morning star was about to be lowered, Farc, from the audience, made them stop, signaling "no weapon" with his fists in the air. This fight was to be strictly bare knuckles, teeth, knees, elbows, you-got-it you-use-it; just the way it was last time.

Staring at his ogre opponent, Venir removed his leather tunic and started doing short flexing and stretching movements that pumped more blood into his veins. The crowd was surprised at the powerful appearance of this human, and the big "V" tattooed on his thickly muscled back caused them to wonder what kind of man he was. A few more bets came in on behalf of Venir. Farc and his son seemed leery, for Venir was noticeably bigger and thicker than five years before. Even Mikkel had begun to look puzzled. Only Melegal showed no reaction, but took note of the crowd's response.

Things began to quieten to a manageable rumble as the crowd waited for the pit battle to commence. Down near the cage, a grey-bearded dwarf waited beside a gong that was taller than an orc. The elderly dwarf stared up at the Royals in the bleachers, awaiting the signal. A tall orc man, lean for his kind, stood and raised his arms. The crowd quieted in anticipation. In the pit, man and ogre faced each other, eyes locked, sweat beading both foreheads. All Venir could hear was his own heart pumping.

Then the tall orc with the raised arms formed fists, and suddenly flicked up his thumbs.

BONG!

Venir sprang like a panther and punched Son of Farc straight in the nose. The ogre's head rocked back with a crack as his nose broke. The first blood had been drawn by the warrior from the City of Bone. The crowd began screaming for more blood.

Furious, the ogre was managing to remain composed. He turned and smiled a bloody grin at the man, and then beckoned to Venir with his finger, playing to the crowd. The crowd went wild. Watching the ogre's response, Venir realized it was going to be one long, hard, and dirty fight.

The two circled each other, then Son of Farc made his move. He lunged in low with a powerful right upper cut. It just missed Venir's head as the warrior stepped right into it and pounded a couple of shots into the ogre's ribs. Any man would have dropped like a sack of broken glass, but ogre bones were very hard to break. Venir tried to move back before Son of Farc could grapple him, but the ogre was ready, and his left fist slammed down, glancing off Venir's head and onto his neck and shoulder. Venir dropped to one knee, unable to back away before the two huge fists slammed into his shoulders like hammers, driving him to the ground. Pain exploded in his upper body, but he didn't show it. With Venir on both knees, Son of Farc tried the double hammer move again. But this time Venir caught both wrists and rose up, staring the ogre in the face.

"You got nothin', human!" the ogre said. "You gonna die."

Venir kept pushing up and back, but the bigger ogre had the advantage in leverage. Then, using the ogre's weight against him, Venir suddenly yanked the ogre down and inward, rolled onto his back, planted his feet in the ogre's stomach and launched him over his head, slamming him surprisingly hard into the arena wall.

The ogre lay momentarily stunned. Venir pounced on the ogre's back, raining down punches as hard as he could into the ogre's ribs and kidneys. Howling in pain and anger, Son of Farc managed to break from the vicious onslaught and square up again. Despite Venir's best efforts, the ogre still wasn't too damaged, just a bit slowed. Son of Farc did spit blood however, but whether from bloodied lips or a busted rib Venir could not tell. It was difficult to work with such a size difference, and Venir thought he'd better be more cautious, but the alcohol was still in his system, and seeing double wasn't really helping. Venir knew one thing, however. Son of Farc was a lot tougher than his father, and it had been a close fight last time. If Farc had not become overconfident, Venir might not have won that battle. Farc had certainly prepared his son well for this day.

Even though Venir sensed his timing was off, he rushed in, hammering powerful haymakers and uppercuts into every vulnerable spot on the ogre's body. The ogre returned in kind, and the apparent mismatch became a clash of equal titans. In a furious assault, they struck, dodged, and countered. Venir was quicker and more precise, but the ogre was taking the pain and keeping him from getting in the critical blow he needed. Farc wasn't used to defending himself in battle, but his big arms served well to block his opponent's powerful blows. The ogre's massive arms flailed all around and Venir had to be careful not to take one to the head. His quickness and instinct saved him several times from punches that would have killed any average man. Stunned at what they were witnessing, the crowd squealed in delight.

Battered, bruised, and bloodied, the seconds began to feel like minutes before Venir backed out and broke it off. Both were breathing and sweating profusely, and determined to crack the other's defense. Then the mighty half-ogre charged. Venir tried to dodge but was barreled over. From beneath he tried to break free of the big ogre's grapple and squirm away. But he couldn't escape the mighty ogre grip, and began wrestling back instead of punching or kicking his way out.

It was a fatal mistake. There was an old saying in Bish: "Don't wrestle the ogre, wrestle the bear instead." You didn't wrestle ogres because they were smarter than bears. Once an ogre locked arms around you, the ogre had won, and you were dead meat.

Outmatched under the ogre's weight, Venir's wrestling was fruitless. Though he was a good a wrestler as any man on Bish—maybe the best—humans were not natural-born wrestlers as ogres were, and Son of Farc was possibly the greatest ogre wrestler to date. On the defensive now, Venir began countering all he could as he tried in vain to grapple back and escape. Finally, in a bad move, Venir got turned with his belly to the ground. The ogre grabbed his long sweaty hair in his hand, jerking Venir's head back with all his might. The warrior roared in agony. Sensing that the end was near, the crowd went wild. Melegal, Mikkel, and Nikkel became suddenly uneasy.

With his neck exposed for that one instant, Venir was doomed. The ogre wrapped his left arm under Venir's arm and neck, locked it over his back with his right, and began squeezing with all his ogre might. Venir tucked his chin in as far as he could to avoid completely exposing his neck, and held on for his life, hoping he could last long enough for the ogre's grip to give. It wasn't likely. The pressure in his neck kept growing, and his nerves were on fire. He struggled fiercely, trying to tear himself free from the powerful grasp. He was turning red with rage, his veins bulging like purple snakes. His air supply was almost exhausted, and, for the second time in his life, he started to suffocate and black out.

CHAPTER 11

THE PIT

O ran, McKnight, and Tonio ended their rather dreadful journey along the Current in what seemed to all parties to have taken an eon. The sound of rippling water and Tonio's raspy breath had worn down McKnight like a festering earache. Just when he was contemplating stabbing his own dagger into his ears, they arrived, and McKnight was never more thankful for the ground below his feet as they climbed out of the barge and into a cave on the surface of Bish. Even underling Oran seemed more comfortable on the surface for a change. The cave, however, was still dark, but some moonlight from a not so distant cave entrance felt like warm sunshine to the men, and they made haste toward its welcoming illumination.

The cave opened somewhere in the Outlands, but where exactly Detective McKnight could not be sure. He surmised that they were southwest of where they had originally departed in the City of Bone, based on the position of the red moon.

Tonio's thoughts, however, seemed quite different.

"Let's eat," was all the big warrior had to say. He was clearly thinking other things, however, vengeful things that only his evil imagination could conjure, as his appetite for food was surpassed by a far more insatiable hunger for revenge.

The meal the men shared was brief and tasteless. Oran did not care to eat, for he was preoccupied with other appetites. Slowly the underling cleric began moving away from the party.

"And where are you trying to head off to, Oran?" asked McKnight threateningly, his daggers glinted in the moonlight.

"At ease, human. I am not venturing out of sight. I have to call for some help to know the whereabouts of our . . . I mean, your . . . prey, the Darkslayer. It would be wise to let me be, so that we can get this over with."

"I don't trust you. What you have to do you can do right here."

"Surely even you must know that I have nothing to gain at this point. You clearly have the advantage." Oran looked toward Tonio who was now also facing Oran, brandishing his long sword.

"What kind of help are you calling on, Oran," asked the detective. "At least I need to know what to expect."

"Since you insist, it is my familiar, an imp. You do know what an imp is?"

McKnight did not know exactly. But he knew that imps were creatures mentioned in stories to scare children. It had never occurred to him that they might be real, but he was not going to let Oran know that.

"If an imp shows up here, underling, it had better not make any suspect moves, got it?" He flashed his dagger and short sword for emphasis.

Oran sighed. "I only want this over. The imp won't bother you; just don't bother it."

"Do your summoning then, and tell us how long until the imp arrives," instructed McKnight.

Oran sauntered off but remained within sight, muttered for about a minute, and then sauntered back.

"Eep should be here any minute, flying or just appearing, I cannot tell, but certainly any minute."

Tonio looked all about in the sky, clutching his sword ready to attack, while McKnight's eye stayed on the dark and frustrated underling.

Eep, bored with killing forest vermin, was relieved to receive a summons from Oran. And he would be able to fly since Oran wasn't too far away. Eep wings buzzed to a shriek as he spit out a brown squirrel head and flew like lightening towards his master. Finally, Eep thought, I can get this done and receive my due.

Eep flew low over the plains, almost grazing the cactus tops, directly toward the underling cleric. His leathery wings buzzed like a thousand blinking fireflies, cutting the air with a zipping sound that could be heard for a hundred feet. As he approached, a man, a large man holding out a sword, appeared in Eep's path. Why would a human—no, two humans—be with his master? Imps, for all their magic and power, were not known for complex thinking; they were impulsive creatures, creatures of action, who followed orders to attack and kill. Split-second thinking was not their forte; they relied on instinct, reflex, and the impulse to destroy life whenever and however they could. Eep's summons had not communicated a need for help, but as the humans appeared before him, he was certain that it must, indeed, have been a call for help.

Almen had been busy with an additional investigation into the recent demise of his son. Even before the small company led by Oran had departed to find the Darkslayer, he had set things in motion to try to apprehend the villain who had filled Tonio with inducers. He felt not so much threatened as insulted by the attempt to eliminate his son. Indeed, nothing intimidated one who had raised up his house from the lowliest of Royal rankings to almost the very top, and it was still rising. More than anything, he was angered that the attempt appeared to have been made by an inferior house. Either some Royal lords within the City of Bone had a vendetta against the Almens, or someone was trying to enhance their own opportunities at the top. The use of inducers was amateurish. Though rare and costly, they were child's play for any upper ranking Royal family. This evidence eliminated the houses ranked just ahead and behind his. But with almost unlimited resources at his disposal, Almen was confident of finding his answer. In the meantime, he kept busy within his wondrous castle, entertaining the guests from near and far who came and went at all hours of the day.

It was a happy blonde-haired, blue-eyed boy who had lived the first ten years of his life to the fullest in his village, laughing, playing, and even working happily alongside many other children just like himself. For the most part they had all had it really good in the village; mothers and daughters and fathers and sons were often paired as they did their familiar tasks. They hunted, fished, farmed, bartered, camped, and cooked. Whatever the need, whatever the day brought, all the village families did their part. Yes, even on Bish there were such places, good places filled more with joy than pain.

But it was not always easy. There was still sickness, famine, and even village conflict that was only resolved by fighting. But for men in the world of Bish, this was as good as it could get, and the carefree, blue-eyed Venir understood this.

It was another sunny day and a great day for fishing in the wonderful streams that ran all around their village of Hohm. Venir's father was both a businessman and an avid fisherman; or rather a fisherman in the business of fishing. This was his family's role in the village of Hohm; they trapped, hooked, and sold the finest fish in all of Bish, as their family had done for decades. For whatever reason, Venir's father and grandfather enjoyed fishing as much as any man could possibly enjoy anything. And it provided a great life for them all.

That morning, Venir was fishing downstream from the village as his father had asked, while his father and grandfather worked the market. It was another routine day for the boy, who, though he was only ten, stood nearly a head taller than others of his age, and many passed the young lad off as a 15-year-old. The strapping boy was also a natural hunter. He could climb trees, sling a flying bird in the sky and spook a deer. He seemed a part of nature itself, and his people loved that uniqueness about him. Just like his father and his grandfather, he was a good young man; but somehow, in another way, he was special.

Venir waded in the thick silver stream, checking the trout snares he had set at the end of the previous day. His long blonde hair was pulled back into a ponytail that hung to shoulder length. Shirtless, the boy wore long brown leather pants and high leather boots made specially for wading in the streams. He had a belt with a large pouch and a very long hunting knife that hung by his side. It had been his grandfather's, and the young boy wore it with pride. His young muscles were fluid and supple as he moved the trout out of the traps and into nets, and then into sacks for transport. It was hard work but it had its rewards, for some of the fish he brought home each day were grilled or baked into delicious meals, which he never missed.

Smiling and enjoying the sunlight on his way home, with two large half-filled sacks slung over his back, he heard his pet dog barking. From somewhere upstream, his dog was agitated but coming gradually toward him. Venir wasn't worried as he wandered up to find out what was upsetting Chongo, his small mastiff. As the dog appeared, Venir noticed him barking at something floating. The young boy set down his sacks and waded into the water to try to catch it. Peering upstream, he noticed some darkening of the water. Slowly it started flowing past him, becoming thicker, darker, and reddish. Focused on the object of Chongo's obsession as it floated towards him, Venir finally grabbed as it came within reach, and then gasped in horror. It was a leg, a human leg, or so it appeared, though darkened and grayish. In shock, the boy slung it as far away into the forest as he could. Chongo wanted to go after it, but recoiled from crossing the reddened water to reach it.

The boy tried to gather his thoughts. Something was unnaturally wrong. The very innocence of his being was shaken as the water that surrounded him became redder. The once silver stream that had fed him all his life had filled with blood, and Venir ran out of it in a panic. He tingled from head to toe in the knowledge that something was horribly amiss.

"Chongo, come. We have to get home!" And they ran back toward the village as fast as they could.

It was not long before he heard the sounds: shrieks and wails from ahead gripped him with fear, but his legs pumped faster and faster, while his mind was paralyzed in terror. Billows of gray smoke began to burn his nostrils and water his eyes as he approached his village. The paths became more distinct and his pace made the wind whistle in his ears, but he did not notice it; all he could hear were screams of agony. His stomach was turning and tears streaking his face, whether from the thickening smoke or overwhelming emotion one could not tell, but never again would fate allow tears to run down his face.

Chongo burst ahead, suddenly in full charge toward the center of the village, and was quickly lost to Venir's sight as his burning eyes lit on something entirely unexpected. Furry, black and grey, hawk-nosed humanoids were running wildly through his village. Venir knew what they were. He didn't know how he knew, but he knew these were underlings. And he had heard enough terrible stories about Bish's Underland to know what to expect at the sight of an underling. But hearing about underlings and actually seeing these underlings in action among his own people were entirely different things. Venir froze, trying to comprehend the black and bloody madness surrounding him. Women, children, men, friends, and family were either dead, almost dead, dying, bleeding, or crying. Panicking in the horrible chaos, they ran all about, trying to evade their pursuers, but to no avail. Clearly the villagers had been surprised and were outnumbered by dozens to one. Many lay in bloodied heaps on the ground. Although almost overcome by fear, deep inside the young hunter another feeling rose up and overcame him. That feeling was rage.

An underling hunter rushed directly toward the unsuspecting boy and screamed in his terrified face. In a flash, instinct overcame him and his hunting knife tore out the throat of the surprised underling, who gurgled into a pool of dark blood. Now Venir was in motion, running, screaming, and slashing wildly and accurately at the evil horde. The adrenaline that had surged through him from fear was now fueled by rage, as he punched in the bodies of his newfound adversaries. In the confusion, many underlings were completely surprised by their wild attacker. Amid the smoke, fire, and chaos, the underling hunters believed that they faced a human, though the boy was already as big or bigger than them, and a couple of them were felled by his anger.

It didn't take long, however, for the seasoned underling hunters to recover from the surprise attack and corner the brave and formidable boy. Venir squared up to three underlings in his path, stabbing and slashing with all his heart, but they parried his attacks, toying with him mockingly, awaiting their moment. The young hunter didn't care what they did, so determined was he to spill their blood. But as suddenly as it had started, it ended, as several poisoned darts shot into his neck and legs quickly paralyzed him, and he fell backward onto the ground.

Before his frozen gaze he saw faces of underlings passing, and felt himself being dragged across the bloodied ground and grass. He could hear their mocking, smell the sweat and dark blood on them, and feel the pain they inflicted on him. But he felt no fear of them, and his rage protected him from utter despair. The moments became like hours, tortuous and dragging as the young hunter could hear the sounds of shovels digging in the ground, one shovelful at a time, at a pace so steady that it ground into his brain.

Venir lay on his side, with his back to the sound of the shovel. His frozen eyes could see other paralyzed and bloodied bodies of his people, all of whom he recognized, who were now lost and futureless at the hands of the most evil beings on the planet of Bish. Mable, a girl he had been fond of all his life, lay helpless, bruised, and broken, her clothes in shreds. Her eyes, though unmoving, showed no desire to live, for only death could now bring her peace. Venir's rage flared so strongly that he flinched despite his paralysis.

His subtle movement was caught by the digging underling hunter. Shirtless, blackened, and filthy, he was one of only a few underlings left behind when the raiding party cleared out. The wiry-haired little humanoid came forward to peer curiously at Venir, waiting to see if the flinch was for real. He studied the numerous poison darts in the haggard young body, wondering how it was possible for him to have moved so soon. He crouched, shovel at his side, and looked directly into the eyes of the paralyzed boy, studying him. Venir saw the cold evil deep in his eyes, and his rage burned stronger still. The foul underling smell disgusted him, and the underling's insidious, mocking chatter repulsed him. But he could do nothing, absolutely nothing, and deep inside it enraged him further. Then, as the underling started to move away, he blinked. The underling stepped back and hissed in astonishment, then picked up the shovel and lifted it to smash Venir's skull. But then he stopped, put down the shovel, and walked out of sight.

Now Venir was grabbed by his feet and turned around, so that he was able to see many more of the bodies of his people. Then the underling walked into his line of sight, shovel in hand, and began systematically killing Venir's people with the blade of the shovel. Men, women, and children died before his eyes, one by one, senselessly and cruelly. The evil underling was deliberately trying to get a rise out of the young warrior. Venir's heart cried out, bursting in his chest, burning with fire, and as it all came to an end, a single tear ran down his filthy cheek. The underling laughed in his face, laid the bloody shovel down before Venir's eyes, then grabbed his legs and dragged him away. As he was being dragged he could see dozens of bodies, buried head first in the ground, with only their legs sticking out. Buried alive, thought Venir, and fear finally gripped his heart as he was pitched, face first, into a large, man-sized ditch.

And then, in a final, tortuous twist of fate, the dirt hole, his own personal grave, was being filled in, shovelful by shovelful. Each heap of dirt brought him closer and closer to his very last moment on Bish. Soon the light was no more as Venir was finally covered and laid to rest, not hopeless but angry. The blackness suffocated him, but his rage burned bright to the end. Yet without oxygen, all fires go out, and finally the young hunter from the village of Hohm blacked out.

It was not the choking hold of Son of Farc that was to be Venir's final memory. It was the blackness, the sinking into unconscious, that overcame his senses in his last gasping moments of desperation. Venir's colleagues, Mikkel, Nikkel, and Melegal, cried out in horror as they watched their pummeled friend's body go slack in the hands of the mightiest of ogres. An odd silence began to settle on the battle arena as the excitement in the air changed from a blasphemous hostility to a collective shiver, in anticipation of that final snapping sound they had heard so many times before at the hands of Son of Farc; the sound of the ogre snapping his opponent's neck or back.

Son of Farc roared in triumph as he prepared to apply his final spine-shattering twist to Venir's neck, and all held their breath anticipation, staring wild-eyed as they awaited the final battle sound. They waited. Had they just not heard it? Bewildered, they peered deeper into the caged arena. And then they saw it. Venir's body suddenly flexed and become taut. Then he growled in rage. The crowd went into a frenzy.

Venir had remembered. Son of Farc had triggered the memory: the most hated and despised moment in his violent life; the day that the innocent boy was supposed to die in a ditch; and the rage that had come upon him, that had drawn to him a power far greater than his own. And now that rage, that uncontainable rage toward all underlings, had been triggered as Venir began to black out. And so the boy who should have died that day but was now a grown man would not die this day, either.

Venir lurched up, his bloodshot eyes bulging in his purple face, and as the crowd looked on his face, fear and excitement surged through every one of them. The warrior had somehow managed to get into a sitting position, and although Son of Farc had his hairy forearm still tightly wrapped around his neck, soon it was not going to matter how tight his hold was. Venir began to shake in unfettered fury, his rage and bloodlust blocking all rational action, only his instinct to survive was thinking, and that kind of thinking meant destroying whatever he saw. Elbows began hammering rapidly into the half-ogre's ribs, and though they were only glancing blows, Son of Farc felt them. And now, after all this time trying to squeeze the life out of the human, the half-ogre's strength and wind were beginning to wane. And the Darkslayer sensed it.

"Get him, Venir!" roared Nikkel, his excited young voice shattering the silence of the crowd and getting them going again.

"Go Vee!" Melegal and Mikkel began yelling in unison.

"Vee. . . VEE. . . VEE!" The name rang out over and over as the crowd throughout the arena began to turn on their own champion, while others were utterly outraged that the human had survived the beast.

Now off his knees and on his feet, the mighty Venir began to rise up with the big hairy ogre on his back. Every muscle on Son of Farc was straining as Venir's own muscles seemed to knot all over his body in thick cords. Son of Farc bellowed mightily in one last effort to restrain the human, but Venir could not be restrained any more this day. Bursting forward on corded legs, Venir charged toward the circular stone wall of the arena, moving rapidly and dragging the half-ogre toward the wall. Ducking in a blink, he slammed the man-beast's head full into the wall. The thrust jarred the ogre, cracking the stone and opening a gash in his head from which blood gushed onto his hairy arms that were still gripping Venir's neck and throat—but not for much longer.

Somewhat stunned, the ogre could not regain his feet, and Venir started toward the other side of the arena, repeating the tactic with a tremendous thud. This time, Son of Farc lost his hold for good.

The crowd was split and fights began to breakout all around the arena as the shocking event unfolded. None was more shocked than the elder Farc. In disbelief he waded unnoticed through the fracas toward the arena. Inside the arena, an enraged man was about to give the Farc family just due. In a scant few moments Venir had managed to untangle himself from certain death, and now the enraged Darkslayer quickly squared up to Son of Farc. The two giant warriors charged each other. As they clashed, Son of Farc tried to pound the battered warrior down, but the berserk Darkslayer would have none of it. This time he was far too quick for the ogre to land a solid hit, and his punches were like mallets driving spikes through the ogre's body.

Venir could not hear the crescendo of the crowd, but he could begin to smell the blood of the ogre as Son of Farc began spitting it up all over him. The ogre's rock-hard ribs began to snap and crack like twigs and his energy was all but dissipated. Just as Son of Farc had become utterly defenseless, Venir's head got smacked from behind by the big fist of the once mighty Farc himself. Venir reeled from the blow and fell, but was quickly back on his feet, facing Son of Farc with his father between him.

"Stop!" Farc held out his hand.

Venir came at him.

"Stop!" Farc pleaded once more, louder.

His son, in a heap behind him, was struggling to regain his feet. It was all Venir needed to realize that his job still wasn't finished. Angered beyond all reason, he charged and leapt into Farc, crushing his last good eye socket with a mighty punch and then shattering his jaw with a knockout. In the meantime, Son of Farc had regained his feet as well as some of his lost vitality at the sight of his fallen father. He charged Venir in a vain attempt to bowl him over and grapple him down once more, but Venir didn't care. He braced himself and latched onto the ogre's large head and neck, locked on and squeezed so hard that the ogre made a loud choking sound.

Venir held on until his head was purple, and he wasn't letting go. Son of Farc kept trying to run and flip Venir off, but to no avail. Venir had full control of the ogre this time, and finally the ogre dropped to his knees. The crowd watched as the smaller man cranked it up, squeezing harder and harder, his muscles popping from his sweaty and bloodied body with the tremendous effort. No one imagined that he could possibly choke the ogre out, for it had never been known to happen. Nor did it. Instead, something else that had never happened, happened. As Son of Farc roared, his roar was cut off with a sudden, thunderous crack as his neck broke in the arms of the berserk human warrior. It was a sound no one had ever heard before at the pit. So far as anyone remembered, an ogre's back had never before been broken.

It was over. A huge, stunned silence overcame the crowd. Before their eyes, the man who had pulled off the improbable five years earlier had, this day, pulled off the impossible. When the cage was opened again and the warrior climbed out, a frenzied chant erupted.

"Vee . . . VEE . . . VEE!"

#

CHAPTER 12

Eep, flying in low and ignoring Oran's loud protests, did not fully anticipate the skill of the humans he assumed were Oran's assailants. He targeted the lower legs of the larger human who was brandishing a gleaming long sword. Tonio, however, parried his sword deeply into the imp's flight path, nearly cleaving the imp in two, but for the imp's incredible agility in the air. But Eep did not anticipate the two daggers, hurled like streaks of lightening, that caught him mid-air as he turned right into their path. One dagger lodged in a wing, while the other found the imp's large and now oozing eye. He fell to the ground in a heap.

"Charlonock!" Oran bellowed as Tonio leapt to finish off the imp.

Instantly the grass and foliage grasped Tonio's lower legs, halting him in his tracks, and Tonio let out a raging howl.

"Oran!" fumed McKnight. "You had better not be double cross-ing me." He pointed a wicked-looking double-shot hand crossbow at the underling.

Oran waved his hands frantically about his head. "I'm not!" he yelled back over Tonio's clamor. "Just don't kill the stupid imp. He must have thought you were attacking me!"

While he spoke, Eep managed to dislodge the daggers from his eye and wing, and prepared to attack McKnight.

"Eep," Oran commanded. "Stay still!"

The imp froze; not a muscle moved. McKnight and Oran then tried to calm Tonio, who had to be restrained from hacking off his own legs in his determination to escape his entanglement. It took about an hour of patience and explanation until Oran's spell finally began to wear off. However, with the immediate drama resolved, the natural tension among underling, imp, and humans resurfaced.

McKnight got them back to subject of their journey. "So," he asked, "exactly how is this awful imp going to help us, Oran?"

Oran paused, nodding his head long-sufferingly. "Eep can travel from our dimension to his own, the magical dimension. But imps are not ordinary magical creatures. From their dimension they can see into ours, as if looking into a crystal ball."

"So," McKnight asked coolly, "are you are planning for the imp to find the people we're tracking?" He seemed to grasp the situation easily. Meanwhile Tonio stood listlessly, showing no interest.

"Unless he has already found who we are looking for."

McKnight looked surprised.

"Eep, catch us up on what you've found out so far."

Eep began leading the small, miserable party south, playing question-and-answer with Oran and McKnight, while Tonio strode somberly at the rear.

"Two humans and a donkey, you say, entered Two-Ten City?" repeated McKnight. "Did this donkey seem capable of killing Tonio? Was it a rare, killer donkey, perhaps, distinguishable from a normal donkey?" He was making light of Tonio's recent demise at the teeth of Chongo; he cared little for the spoiled Royal warrior, and especially disliked being forced to his aid.

Eep eked out a few more details, but they had little to go on, except that the people they sought might be in Two-Ten City along with hundreds of other humanoids that traveled in and out of the city each day. They were not confident that they had the right people, and time was short.

Frustrated, Oran reluctantly made a proposal. "I shall send Eep ahead to find who he is talking about, and I will cast a spell that allows us all to see what he sees. This will have to do. It would have helped if Tonio could have given a better description than just 'Vee man'. Go, Eep!"

In a violent buzz, the imp disappeared.

"Now, McKnight, I need your word that you will not interfere with my spell casting."

"My word, underling. Anything to get this over with."

Oran decided that this would have to do, for there was no time to waste. He closed his eyes and began muttering his incantation. Several minutes passed, and then his spell began to take form. Colors began to explode before the men's eyes, sparkling, fading, swirling, and popping in and out like the crackling of hot embers in a fireplace. McKnight was enthralled; he would be much more mindful of Oran's abilities from now on.

Then the collage of colors began to take on a shape in the thin air before them, forming an oval boundary enclosing a black space. Suddenly a picture formed, a picture of the imp's single eye, now fully healed. Then the eye vanished, and in its place, everything the eye could see, they could see.

From high above trees and hills they watched, streaking towards the ground below, then hovering above a city where they could see people and humanoids coming and going. Then through the city they zipped, viewing sight after sight in an instant. Flashing before their eyes were humanoids of all kinds doing all sorts of things—many of which were indecent or inhumane. Now their gaze passed straight through beasts and buildings, and after many moments the images began to slow and settle, causing McKnight a tinge of nausea. The image settled inside an old tavern that appeared deserted, except for a band of dwarfs playing music.

Now they were looking down a stairwell, then into a corridor that opened into a wide arena where all types of humanoids were gathered with excited faces. It was odd to watch such a lively sight and not hear a sound. McKnight tried to read the lips of those he saw. The people were chanting, but not one among Oran, McKnight, and Tonio could find a familiar face among them.

"Nice try, Oran," said a disgruntled McKnight as the spell seemed to fade and the image pale.

Then the picture went toward the inside of an iron cage. A large, hairy ogre had a muscled, longhaired man pinned face down on the floor, and was forcing his neck back. A big V-shaped tattoo was visible on the man's back.

"Vee man!" screamed Tonio, diving straight through the image and into a tree with a tremendous thud.

The spell blinked out in a flash. Oran gave a deep sigh.

"Like I was saying, Oran, nice job!" McKnight chuckled. "Bone of a good job! I think we've found who we're looking for. And it would appear that this Vee man is practically dead already." With relief, Mc Knight could see his mission nearing its end.

Lefty Lightfoot had moved fast, very fast for a halfling. But halflings were known for their speed. To have survived on Bish with such feeble bodies, there clearly had to be magic in the feet of the halfling race. No matter how dire their situation, somehow they managed to move fast enough to survive their fate. But other than being quick and hardy, halflings were merely an occasional inconvenience. They were amusing little people who were usually only seen at carnivals or in small traveling packs fetching supplies as needed. Then they would not leave a person alone until they had traded whatever it was they had. People would take what they neither wanted nor needed just to see them gone; it was as if halflings could talk people into letting themselves be robbed. Yet there was much more to these little people, as young Georgio was about to find out.

The lively young Georgio, bored at home since parting ways with Venir, had abandoned his usual chores and was now in the woods, heedless of his parents' warnings. He was deep in his own fantasy in the forest, imitating his hero Venir, the Darkslayer. Equipped with his own hand axe, Georgio tossed it with surprising accuracy and skill into a tree, when suddenly he heard a rustle. He turned just as a little blonde head slammed into his chest.

"Help! Help! Help!" Lefty Lightfoot yelled, hopping in panic. "They're coming this way!"

Georgio, now sitting as a result of the impact, studied the halfling in puzzlement. He had never seen one up close before. The sight of this little blonde halfling in a panic made him giggle.

"Human, what you are laughing at?"

Realizing that the halfling was actually talking to him elicited even more giggles.

Frustrated, Lefty Lightfoot began to run on. Georgio scrambled up, still laughing. Not wanting to see the halfling go, he began to follow, but was unable to catch up.

"Stop!" called Georgio.

For whatever reason, Lefty turned.

"I'm sorry for laughing, I've never met a halfling before. I'm Georgio!"

"Lefty Lightfoot. I need help. We all do! There's great danger!" At that Lefty slumped to the ground, weeping.

Bewildered, Georgio sat down beside him.

Few living things survived in the wake of the Vicious-led Badoon brigade, as exposure to their overwhelmingly evil presence tended to stifle the life force in many lesser living things. But despite the path of devastation, where most vegetation and smaller vermin such as chipmunks lay brittle and dead, the Badoons did not manage to kill every living thing along their route. The strong life forces on Bish sent many creatures fleeing, and their unusual and untimely migration sparked alarm across the Outlands. The alarm reached a little known place that was as ancient as Bish itself. The Dwarven Hole was home to the giant dwarfs and to the red-bearded Mood himself, the largest and greatest of all hunters, who had lived there for what may have been forever. The ancient civilization was little more than myth, and the tiny hold was buried deep in the mountains of Bish— but not underground like the underlings. Few other races, if any, had ever seen the Dwarven Hole, and the giant dwarfs liked to keep it that way.

Though more than ten miles from the Vicious and the Badoon brigade, the giant dwarf rangers knew their activity and exact movements within hours of their departure from the Underland caves. And though they most often stayed in seclusion, the giant dwarfs had often been involved in the fate of Bish and its peoples. This was to be one of those times.

Despite being beaten within an inch of his life, the mighty Venir mustered more than enough energy to entertain himself with the bodacious part-orc woman he had flirted with minutes before stepping into the cage with Son of Farc. His animal instincts had been awakened, and Dolly, the part-orc entertainer, was eager to oblige.

The rest of his evening was spent within the stone walls of Dolly's private chambers. All Dolly wore was a tight black dress with a deep slit to show off her muscular thighs and a deep V in the front that amply showed off her full chest. As Venir lay down amid the fluffy pillows on her extremely large wooden bed, Dolly blew out the candles and slowly undressed. Her long straw locks fell across her wide blue eyes, piggish nose and snaggle-toothed smile. It wasn't the worst face he'd seen, nor the prettiest either, but Dolly's body could make even an old dwarf cry, Venir thought, as he crushed her into his arms and ravished her all night long.

Early the next morning, Melegal and Venir met Mikkel and Nikkel for breakfast in the tavern. The aroma of hot rolls, eggs, and bacon filled the air, and they all ate heartily after the big night. All were quiet, even the usual patrons of the tavern. The buzz of the battle had dissipated, yet the lingering silence seemed unnatural. Finally, the bruised Venir broke the solemn silence.

"Why is everyone acting like they're eating with a ghost?"

"I thought you were dead," Melegal answered somberly. "The fact that you aren't isn't easy to understand. Don't get me wrong, Vee, but I don't quite follow how you survived last night."

Venir took a deep breath and winced from the pain of his bruised ribs. He sipped his coffee and chewed on some more bread and eggs.

Mikkel smiled widely. "You must have wanted Dolly pretty bad, huh, Vee?"

They all chuckled.

"Venir?" Nikkel asked, his blue eyes staring in wonder at the man who had beaten the great orc. "How come you're bigger now?"

"What do you mean, Nikkel?" his father asked.

"Why, he's bigger, he's taller. How come?"

"You know," said Melegal, looking perplexed, "when you came down here I thought something was off. I figured it was all the swelling, but. . . Stand up, Vee. I think Nikkel's onto something."

Venir shrugged, pushed himself back from the table, and stood up.

"Mikkel, stand back to back with Vee."

Mikkel obliged. "Don't tell me he's taller than me now, Melegal."

"Well, no, but he's the same height!"

"What!? Turn around, Vee."

Venir turned, and met Mikkel eye to eye.

"Venir, you have grown. I think I saw it!" said Melegal. "I mean, when you were in the ring making your escape from Son of Farc . . . I thought you grew that moment, the moment you came back from blacking out, but in the chaos I forgot. But you are bigger, no doubt about it!"

"Never heard of anything like that before," said Mikkel.

Venir grinned, "It's happened to me before actually, when I was a little kid." They were all ears, waiting to hear what happened to him then. He continued, "When I was a boy, I caught a rare silver fish. I was hungry and instead of taking it home with the rest, I ate it. It was the most wonderful thing I ever tasted. I told my grandfather about it and he said such fish were magic and things might happen to me. The next day, I was bigger. I grew overnight."

"Man, that's cool!" said Nikkel

Melegal then asked, "So did Chongo eat some too?"

"Yep, but he didn't grow his second head until a long time after that."

"Are you pulling our legs Vee?" asked Mikkel.

Still grinning he replied, "Maybe."

They rolled their eyes then, and as if nothing had happened, they finished their meal without another word about it.

It was still early morning as the small group of friends began to part ways. Nikkel fetched Quickster and the two adventurers headed north out of Two-Ten City, back the way they had come. To Venir's embarrassment, Dolly came running out, begging him to take her with him, causing a scene that woke everyone within a hundred yards, but somehow Venir managed to break away, whispering, "I'll be back for you one day." Dolly fell for it long enough for them to speed off out of sight, while Venir secretly vowed never to return to Two-Ten City. Mikkel's laughter was audible all the way out of the city, while Nikkel waved sadly.

Melegal was still chuckling when he came upon the same smart-aleck orc boy he had encountered on the way in. Melegal locked eyes on the boy and scowled, and the boy trembled and ran off.

"Is there any chance," Melegal broke the silence from atop Quickster, "that that could be Dolly's boy?"

Venir didn't reply, as the shameful events of Two-Ten City begin to sink in. In the past he had never given such things a moment's thought. But, today, for some reason, he began to ask himself some searching questions.

Unbeknown to the two companions, another party of adventurers was spying on them at that moment. From high above, Eep's eye stared down on them, through which underling Oran and McKnight were keeping a close watch, having distracted Tonio into gathering firewood.

"I can't believe that big, tiresome human is still alive," hissed Oran as the swirling, scintillating colors at the edge of the vision began to fade.

"He must have had help," said McKnight.

The two paused, trying to imagine what they might be up against.

"Did you see that ugly orc woman? I find it hard to imagine that he. . ." He stopped with a grimace as if to remove the thought.

"Clearly you do not get around Bish much, human. You are rather sheltered in your City of Bone. Two-Ten is a normal city. You should visit it," said Oran wickedly. "You will be a changed man."

"No thanks! Unlike your kind I see no need to maintain sub-human standards."

"The human heart is as wicked as the rest. Even yours."

"Maybe so, but at least it's human. Now let's cut the politics. We have about a day to wait until they show up. In the meantime, let's go over our plans again, because getting that over-sized menace back to Bone alive won't be easy. Are you sure you and Tonio can handle it?" McKnight slung one of his knives, impaling a distant squirrel on a tree. "I'm quite sure I can dispatch his friend."

"I have Eep, remember? He will tip the scales in our favor."

"Good," said McKnight with satisfaction.

CHAPTER 13

JARLA'S ARMY

Many dark memories were stirring in the warrior's mind as they traveled further from the clutches of Two-Ten City. Just five years earlier, Venir and Melegal had been living comfortably with their comrades in this multi-cultural border city in the upper south. Back then, Venir spent most of his time outside the city as a mercenary scout, tracker, and hunter, while Melegal enjoyed finding new ways to profit from the over-indulgent locals.

Things were good for both of them then. The thief kept mostly to himself, while his friend's reputation made him well received and respected in Two-Ten City. Being the champion of the pit exacerbated his popularity, of course, but not to the liking of all. The resentment among other humans was apparent. For the time being, though, the Farc family had left them alone.

Venir remembered how he had enjoyed those outdoors days, hunting and tracking all over Bish. Despite the tragedy during his boyhood in the village of Hohm and his time in the orphanages of the City of Bone, his strong young spirit was never broken. His freedom among the forests and drylands kept a smile on his face most of the time. His blonde hair, bright blue eyes, deep tan, and handsome face gave the women in all provinces plenty to talk about, and his exploits and willingness to recount them left an impression on all he came upon. Unlike most mercenaries, Venir did not expect much in return from those who benefited from his deeds; a good meal and a comfortable place to sleep was more than enough to satisfy him. And so, without trying, Venir earned people's trust.

His transformation from that lean young hunter into a hulking warrior had been rapid. He could still remember the exact moment that it happened. Riding along on Chongo's back, the sudden memory caused him to shake his head in wonder. He could remember the weather and the sight of the red and orange suns just rising on that day when his life had suddenly opened up like a black cave and almost swallowed him like a drop of water. He didn't regret it, for somehow he had survived, just as he always did.

The underlings had not played the greatest part in his life until then, although they were still a big part, and his hatred for them was already certain. The trauma of his youth had served him well as a mercenary scout. Having already survived the worst the underlings could offer, where most were terrified to face them, Venir was fearless. Battles, raids, and skirmishes always kept soldiers like him busy, and Venir's ability to get the jump on the underlings made him especially sought after. The underlings were the enemy of almost all on the surface of Bish, and their surprising and unusual tactics left no one safe. Venir was hired primarily to keep track of underling activity, and with Chongo's aid he did this well. Back then the long-haired mastiff was just a normal dog, but his nose for underlings made him an unrivaled tracker.

The crafty young Venir often faced underlings with nothing more than a short bow, a quiver full of arrows, a long sword, and his grandfather's hunting knife—recovered by chance almost a decade after the slaughter at Hohm. Venir wore a dark red leather tunic and brown leather pants, high leather boots, a backpack, and a small belt pouch. He liked traveling light, to keep up with Chongo when the dog was on a scent. Venir was a fleet-footed hunter. With no axe, shield, or helmet to slow him down, he relied more on speed and cunning to bait and evade his enemies, with a skill well beyond his age and experience.

Underling hunting parties could crop up any time and any place, and although there had not been all-out war with the underlings in decades, they probed continuously for weakness and advantage on the surface. Their increasing frequency and boldness suggested that they were gearing up for something, but those willing to deal with them became few and far between. The people on the surface of Bish were losing confidence, and Venir was determined to remain a step ahead of the enemy by any means at his disposal. It was a risky business, but he was as passionate as he was successful.

Typically, the underlings sent their own scouts in pairs at night to seek out small villages to terrorize and destroy. Venir liked to trap them with snares, pits, and traps. He would then kill one, but scalp and remove an appendage from the other as a warning to the rest. He would then secure or evacuate the threatened village or town, leaving the dead underling's head on a spike, with his torso buried and the legs protruding, to warn the underlings. Then he would let the scalped underling escape, who would often lead Venir and Chongo right to his group.

Sometimes Venir's temper got the better of him and he would track and kill underlings on the spot. His tactics were successful and saved countless lives, but he could only be in one place at a time. He wished he could take the fight to the underlings more directly, but there was not enough manpower or willingness to take the risk.

One day a surprising menace revealed itself near Two-Ten City, and Venir's comrades called for his services. He met them at a tavern called the Orc's Elbow, as unimpressive a tavern as any in the city. It was a typical oaken tavern with grimy gray-brown walls, in a two-storey building with few support walls to keep the second storey from tumbling down on top of the first. And despite its name, no orcs were to be found inside. The tavern's previous owner, a full orc, had wagered the Orc's Elbow on the fight between Venir and Farc, and lost it to a human gambler named Billip; since then not a single orc had entered it. But Venir and Billip had been comrades ever since.

"So Billip, what's the wager tonight?" asked Venir, striding up to the barkeep, who sent a fresh mug of mead his way.

"Ah, wouldn't you like in on the action! Well, I'll tell you. I got ten good golds against Melegal's dirty donkey that he can't throw a bulls-eye blindfolded from ten paces." He cracked his knuckles and grinned. Melegal looked up and rolled his eyes.

Billip was not only the owner of the Orc's Elbow, but also a mercenary in Venir's scouting party, and he seemed always to be calculating under his mop of short black hair. Nothing appeared extraordinary about his stout, wiry frame or his weathered skin as he moved fluidly about the bar, but he was a tireless tracker and an unrivaled archer, and as loyal a man as could be found on Bish. Older than Venir, he had much experience as a soldier, a trader, and a gambler, which was partly what led to him to live in Two-Ten City in the first place. Though Billip kept his thoughts to himself and never confirmed it, Venir gathered that his friend had got in over his head somewhere along the line, and found the security of this undesirable multi-humanoid city as good a place to hide as any.

Melegal readied himself for the challenge while his challenger found him a fitting blindfold. Venir sat on a barstool and sipped his mead in amusement. Melegal stood still while Billip blindfolded him with a thick black cloth, then handed the thief a mug full to the brim, which Melegal deftly placed on his head. An X had already been in place where he stood, and Billip then walked over to the target wall and outlined a gold talent with a piece of white chalk.

The grey thief listened intently to the sounds of the man among the tavern noises while spectators began to gather. With keen ears, always concerned for his own safety, Melegal also counted the separate breaths of almost a dozen people. Even he had enemies, and no one was ever safe, even in Two-Ten City.

"Okay, Me, let me remind you of the rules. You can't spill a drop off your head, and," he emphasized, "your hit has to be inside the mark, not touching it. Not even close to touching it."

Melegal smirked and drew his throwing dagger. The crowd quieted to a hush. Then, with a whip, his dagger sliced the air and landed with a heavy thunk, dead in the center of the circle, before Billip had even had time to pull his finger away.

"I didn't say go, yet!"

Venir laughed out loud. When the others got over their amazement they began laughing, too. Billip snatched the dagger out of the wall and threw it to the floor.

"You wait until I say go, and you don't get to use your dagger. That's cheating. You didn't let me finish the rules. Don't move!"

Melegal waited patiently, hands on hips, sighing while his friend hunted about to find something less adequate for him to throw. Billip returned from the bar and handed him something for his new attempt.

Melegal felt and weighed the object. "Are you expecting me to throw a wood-handled steak knife into that wall?"

"Yep."

"Are you kidding me?"

"Nope. House rules. My house. My rules."

"It doesn't even have a point. It's round on the end. I'm surprised you didn't give me a spoon. This is ridiculous."

"Too bad. Double or nothing. No, triple! Make your throw or give me your donkey."

Billip well knew that calling Quickster a donkey always got a rise out of Melegal, and the argument lasted nearly five minutes. All the while Melegal spilt not a drop of his mead. Finally, someone from the crowd told them to shut up and get it over with or they would all leave. The two men then got back to business.

"Wait until I say go."

"I'm waiting," the thief replied.

Billip paced about, checking the settings until he was satisfied that Melegal could not possibly make the throw.

"Okay. Go!"

The knife flicked out of Melegal's hand like a snake's tongue and lodged itself inside the circle, the handle hanging at a forty-five degree angle. Even with the velocity of that near-impossible throw, he still had not spilt a drop.

"No! How did he do that?" seethed Billip through clenched teeth. "He does it every time. He's gotta miss one of these days."

Everyone clapped and cheered at the feat, and Billip finally conceded and paid Melegal his wager. Billip's mild temper rarely flared for long before he was back to his usual self and ready for the next challenge. Meanwhile, Venir and Melegal joined him at a more discrete booth near the back end of the bar to see what was so important to have summoned Venir.

"All right, so what's the big news?" Venir asked cheerfully, while Melegal counted his winnings over and over to rile his friend. Billip tried to ignore him.

"You know, I love the Outlands and the forests and all, but I don't see how you live out there as long as you do and survive. Don't you miss the comforts of the city? The food and companionship? The girls keep asking me where my muscled blonde friend is. I ain't got time to answer to your whereabouts all the time. I'm not your keeper, you know."

"Yeah, me neither," Melegal agreed.

"Anyway, things are stirring up around here. I'm not used to it. A detestable bunch of mercenaries, not at all like us, are doing a lot of recruiting here in Two-Ten. Some of our fellows say they're paying well, extremely well, and some have even joined up."

The gambler cracked his knuckles repeatedly as he spoke.

Just then a warm meal of steak, potatoes, and strong coffee arrived to help them unwind, as they typically did at this time of day. The powerful aroma of coffee roused Venir's senses; he hadn't had any in weeks. He loved the spring it put in his step. He took a few welcome gulps of his fresh brew.

"That's it? More mercenaries for hire? Just Royals up to their dirty tricks, somewhere. I don't see the big deal..."

" I'm not finished. Mind your elder, blondie. I've been chatting them up as they ask for people, and Melegal's been listening in, too. The keep pretty hush-hush about their purposes, but we're pretty sure we've figured it out."

He leaned back in his chair.

"Well, what?" Venir asked.

"You sure you wanna know?'

"Yes, big brother. What is it?"

"They're raising a brigand army of the likes never before seen on Bish. I'm talking almost three hundred brigands. And they ain't all human, either. They send humans to recruit, but it's the orcs that are leaving in their masses, more so than men.

"Great! The fewer orcs in Two-Ten, the better. What's the problem?"

"They're being led by a human woman."

"A woman? That can't be. I'll believe that when I see it."

"It's true, Vee," Melegal interjected. They call her Jarla, the Brigand Queen. They revere her. She started with a small band near the White Blaze Pass beyond the Underland, and she's been slowly carving her way through Bish for years. According to her men, they've been devastating merchant trains, human settlements, even

Royal outposts. Now, that's not normal protocol for brigands. They might rob men, but now they've been slaughtering them too, and their families as well."

Venir's brows creased over his blue eyes as he took in this news. He and his mercenaries had seen and done much that very few would understand, but they always drew the line at what had to be done. As for brigands, they tended to scare rather than harm their own kind, and normally there were no more than a dozen or so. The thought of a brigand army that plundered, killed, and apparently battled and overran garrisons didn't make sense. He hadn't been far south lately, but maybe it was time he went and checked on some old friends.

"What are you thinking, Vee? You wanna go check if the rumors are true? I'm ready when you are," Billip offered. "And Mikkel's keen, too."

"Count me in," said Melegal. "I need to get out as well."

"All right, but let's have some fun first," said Venir. "We'll figure something out tomorrow. I need to unwind. Say, where are they keeping the pretty women these days? Clearly they still aren't coming in here."

"Melegal runs them off every time. He offers them a ride on his donkey."

With that they laughed and began their revels, which lasted well into the long, hot night.

Two days later, the small band of men and beasts began the journey south towards the camp of Jarla, the Brigand Queen, and her army. The land they traveled was far more hospitable than the vast wasteland south of the City of Bone, as vegetation and water became increasingly available. The southern lands contained less marsh and more small, blue-green forests, which provided vast oases with large streams that ran endlessly in their midst, and the terrain was anything but flat. Unforgiving hills and valleys made for slower travel as it forced the travelers to wind through passes rather than straight over the hilltops. The high ground was good ground, as small outposts could be seen with the flags of their people or of Royal soldiers who kept watch over this lush land. Farms and villages thrived in the rich soil, and food, water, and timber were valuable commodities among the world's rulers. They protected their investments well, yet the southlands of Bish were just as treacherous as those of the north. Brigands, orcs, dog-faced gnolls, and kobolds thrived and raised their kind in this land. Most of the time they fought one another, but they also raided and pillaged the more peaceful inhabitants as a natural part of their own survival, and so it had been for as long as they remembered.

As the men passed quietly through the villages they happened upon during their trek, the tales of Jarla's brigand army became more intriguing. They could not tell if what they heard was truth or rumor, but there were repeated claims of a large army of orcs, kobolds, humans, and gnolls all functioning as a single unit under a woman's command. It was a hard story for the men to swallow. In their experience two races rarely fought cohesively together, let alone four. That a woman led it compelled them to see for themselves. Even Melegal was curious, as female warriors were rare in the world of Bish. Most races did not have fighting women, and for such races to follow a female leader, let alone one of another race, was astonishing. As for female soldiers, the men had known plenty among human ranks, but ultimately they never ventured together too long, as the men tended to want the women as more than just fellow soldiers, and those men often suffered dire injuries as a result. So how had this one woman created an army that threatened the southern lands of Bish? They were about to find out.

"Man, I can't believe there are kobolds in that army. That's stupid!" complained Mikkel in his deep, rumbling voice.

"Yeah, I'm not so sure we need to get too curious about all this," Billip added.

"Let's just get a quick look. It's hard to imagine the stories are true, but who knows," answered Venir.

The small band of four were all traveling on foot, as it made them more difficult to follow. They had traveled like this dozens of times over the years, and they all knew how to handle things if they ever got into a pinch. They were lightly dressed in tunics and leather armor, except for Melegal who wore clothes of his own design. Backpacks, canteens, belt pouches, and weapons of choice made up the rest of their personal gear. The south was a more humid climate, which was apparent from the sweat that rolled off the men's heads. Mikkel and Venir had beads of sweat not only their brows but also on their bulging biceps revealed by the sleeveless tunics. Billip did not sweat as much, and Melegal hardly at all.

There was no apparent danger, so the men did not brandish their arms as they navigated the difficult terrain. Billip carried a short composite bow across his back, and Mikkel had a heavy crossbow strapped across his. Venir carried a short bow, and each had a quiver, while Billip also carried a spare. Swords, daggers, and knives could be seen at their hips. Whatever Melegal carried was not readily apparent.

"So what's the plan, Vee?" Mikkel asked. "I know you have one. Do we take a look? Spy. . . attack. . . join?"

"I thought we'd just rob them. I'm sure we can take them all on since you're with us, Mikkel."

"Well, I'm the only true fighter in this gang. I've no idea why you brought these other two sandbags along; they never fight closer than thirty feet."

"Hey, don't talk like that," said Billip. "I do my fair share, unlike Me. Just look at him, he even avoids his own sweat."

"Hey, you can say all you like, but someone's gonna have to dig your graves one of these days, so be grateful. And just to be clear, I won't do the digging, I'll use Billip's money to pay his urchins to dig."

"Man, Melegal you are cold. But I like it! You're my man!" Mikkel flashed his big white teeth in the sun. Billip nodded.

Chongo reappeared at Venir's side after scouting far up ahead. The shaggy brown bull mastiff licked his master's face, while Venir poured water from his canteen into his meaty palm, and Chongo quickly lapped it up. Then Chongo began scurrying back and forth, signaling them to follow.

"All right, Chongo's found something. Let's step it up. I got a feeling we're about to happen upon the brigand army."

"Great, so when you gonna share your plan, Vee?" said Mikkel. "Or do I have to come up with one myself?"

"Bad idea. We know how your plans turn out," Billip said.

"What you talking about, Billip?"

"Oh, well, how 'bout the time you wanted to…"

"Shut up Billip," Mikkel cut in. "Vee, what's the plan?"

"I say we just act like we're interested, is all. Hopefully we won't arouse any problems. I figure we can get a closer look first, though."

"Well, don't expect me to act too friendly with the kobolds," said Mikkel. "If they get too close, I'll crack their stupid little skulls."

"We know!" they all replied, and Mikkel's blue eyes widened in his black face.

Then like seasoned scouts they flowed after Chongo, deep into one of the southern forests.

Lost in his memories, Venir was in a daze on Chongo's back, and had all but forgotten that Melegal was behind him when Quickster sneezed, jolting Venir back to the present.

"Ah. . . did Quickster startle the deep-thinking lout of a warrior?" Melegal snickered. "You're not even humming a tune. What's going on in that thick skull of yours, Venir?" There was concern in his voice as he rode up closer.

"Ah, just thinking back to when things were different, is all."

"You mean, before Brool?"

"Yeah. But not just that."

Melegal remembered those days too. But that had all come and gone, and he was able to move on, as most people did in Bish. Few dwelled upon the past, although long journeys could cause a man to reflect from time to time.

"Two-Ten City stirred you up, didn't it. But I think we've had as much good luck as bad there. I mean, you wrestled an ogre and lived—you should be happy. Well, I'm glad for you. Besides, I made a killing on that bout," he said wryly.

"Bet you did, thief. And by the way," Venir smiled, "where's my share?"

"In due course, Vee. You gotta get me back to Bone, first. Now, quit thinking so much, you're gonna hurt yourself."

Their spirits brightened as they continued across the dusty plains, but Venir soon slipped back into his memories.

———

It had taken almost thirty minutes for Venir and his fellow mercenaries to catch up with Chongo, who finally reappeared, issuing a low, excited yelp of warning. The clash of steel could be heard not far in the distance. Although the trees and broad foliage muted the battle sounds, the seasoned scouts knew it was not far off. The men glanced at one another, not expecting to hear the clang of steel this deep in the forest.

Using hand signals, Venir positioned Billip behind Chongo, followed by Venir and Melegal, with Mikkel guarding the rear. They moved like big grey foxes through the terrain, then all but Billip and Chongo stopped in a clearing, close enough to distinguish the voices of men crying out in battle.

Venir gestured to Melegal, asking how many he heard up ahead.

Melegal flashed ten digits.

We can take them, Mikkel signaled back.

Venir almost laughed while Melegal scowled. He had no intention of engaging anyone, even if his companions liked to attack first and think later. In nervous anticipation they waited for Billip to return and report. Ten men was a lot to take on, and they would need to be ready to fight at a second's notice—or flee if necessary. As trained scouts they didn't always take things head on; sometimes it paid to just watch and report. The seconds dragged on and still Billip and Chongo did not return. Concern showed on their brows. Finally Chongo appeared with Billip running behind.

"It's safe to talk low," Billip said, slightly out of breath. "Ten Royal foot soldiers are already dead, and about six are left, heavily armed and battling four gnolls and an armored woman. The soldiers have their hands full. They're below this ridge; looks like they got trapped."

"Any others?" Venir asked.

"I took a good look. No signs. But that woman fights better than two gnolls together. Never seen anything like it. What do we do? You want to go around?"

Venir didn't want to risk anyone unnecessarily, but he couldn't stand the thought of men falling to gnolls: tall, fanged, wolf-faced humanoids who were dreaded warriors that killed for pleasure and were known for their lengthy torture of prisoners. Despite their hairy, wolf-like appearance, gnolls spoke like most other the races. They were not vast in number but were extremely well trained, armed, and formidable warriors. And the fact that a woman fought with them suggested to Venir that he was about to encounter the brigand army.

Curiosity got the better of him. He would see for himself and then decide what action to take.

"Let's take a look. I have a feeling this is what we came to see."

Billip led as they ran ahead. They crept to the edge of the ridge, flat on their bellies with weapons drawn, bolts locked, and arrows knocked. Below, the battle scene was furious and bloody. The seasoned Royal soldiers battled valiantly with long swords and shields, wearing breastplates and battle helmets. They were bloodied and most of their comrades had fallen. It was only a matter of time until the others fell too. But at times like this, the inhabitants of Bish had to weigh their own odds of survival before getting involved.

What was striking was that the female warrior seemed to be carving up the soldiers almost singlehandedly, as if they were just boys. The impression she made on Venir and his men was unforgettable. She wore only a sleeveless chainmail dress of bronze that ended high above her knees. Her long, sinewy arms and legs were blood-splattered, and long, jet-black hair flowed from beneath an ornate-looking spiked black iron helmet. The only other protection she wore were iron-banded bracers around her forearms. The men had never seen the likes of her before. But most impressive were the weapons she used so ferociously. She commanded unique matching weapons, one in each hand; each a battle-axe head with a long serrated spikes on the back side. With precision and fluidity she wielded them, as easily as a jester juggling apples. Her strikes were viper-like, powerful, and devastating.

The men watched in awe from above, uncertain how to react. Seeing men die under the banner of a good Royal house was not easy to watch without action, even more so as the evil gnolls were taking part. Anticipation and the passion to act built up in the men, except for Melegal, who watched coolly from Venir's side, holding his friend's shoulder to keep him from doing anything impulsive and foolish. They maintained their discipline and continued to watch the battle unfold.

Jarla's haymaker axe blades felled her opponents one by one. Her axe spikes penetrated their shields and ripped them from their grasp, leaving the men to fight with their long swords. The gnolls cut off the others from her path, allowing her to fight them one at a time. It was clear that she relished what she was doing. One soldier managed to get his hands on another long sword and fight her two-handedly, but he was not fast enough to counter her attacks. A spike in his skull finished his valiant efforts, and she was on to her next victim. Despite the demoralizing situation, the Royal foot soldiers did not cower; they faced her bravely, one by one.

Now the soldiers were down to just two, fighting back to back, pinned in by the brigand Queen and the remaining three gnoll warriors, who surrounded them and backed off from their attacks. From above, the men could see that Jarla was agitated; these soldiers were proving more formidable than expected. She decided upon a truce and demanded their surrender. But the exhausted men did not yield; they preferred to rather fight and die. One was bleeding heavily and on the brink of death. Two gnolls pounced on him first. The soldier commander had time to kill one of the gnolls, cutting him heavily on the back of the neck. Now his comrade was dead, and it was just him left.

Two gnolls moved to his left and right, leaving the commander to face Jarla alone. But he was ready. He took his chances against her, and faced his fate head on. Mikkel could not restrain himself any longer. He fired on the first gnoll that moved, striking a bull's eye into the gnoll's forehead. Though the Royal commander did not even notice, Jarla did. The other gnoll fell with two arrows in his chest from Billip, and Venir charged down the ridge in aid of the soldier.

Uncertain of who and how many surrounded her, Jarla fearlessly attacked the Royal soldier, moving in like a panther, swinging low to tear out his armored left knee with one axe-blade. The soldier cut back with a powerful two-handed blow, which Jarla caught and deflected with her banded bracer. Then she countered with a crunching blow, through his breastplate and deep into his clavicle. He dropped his sword and fell to one knee. Her finishing blow was too fast for Venir to stop. The soldier was dead. She turned just in time to see the young warrior coming for her, and laughed.

"It seems you are too late to save this man, blonde warrior. Can you save yourself, now?"

Venir paused ten steps from her, brandishing his long sword and hunting knife. Beside him, Chongo barked loudly at her. He measured his next move carefully, knowing that he had more support than she. She did not seem worried about the likes of him, though, or the rest of them. She stood patiently before him, tall and proud. Now he was so close her features captured his imagination. Her bright blue eyes burned from behind the eyelets of her helmet, intelligent and cunning. He yearned to know more. Blood dripped from the axes that hung loosely at her side.

"Hey blondie," she taunted. "If you see something you like, why not just come and get it."

Venir's bright white smile caught her off guard.

"Why would a woman like you run around with these filthy gnolls? Surely you can keep better company?"

Now it was her turn to stare back and take better measure of the man she faced. Her battle-raged mind was calming slightly, and the images of faceless enemies began to leave her. As she took a closer look at her new adversary, she liked what she saw, and removed her helmet in a gesture of truce.

Venir remained wary after all he had just witnessed. They

continued to size one another up. Jarla's face was beautiful, slender yet strong, her dark blue eyes looking him seductively up and down. Her skin was browned by the suns, her cheekbones high and noble, and her cheeks scarred and somewhat disfigured; but Venir kept his gaze on her eyes alone. She noticed that. Slowly she came closer. Venir seemed to fall under her shadow, for she was taller than him. If this woman isn't the brigand queen, he thought, she is queen of something. Jarla stopped just out of striking range. Chongo had stopped barking, and now sat on his haunches. Danger still prickled the air, but it could wait.

"So tell me, blondie," she continued, "why did you kill my men? They had no quarrel with you or yours." She looked around, but there were no signs of his companions.

"My name is Venir. And gnolls are not men, they are wretched beasts that we like to kill. Luckily for you, you are not a gnoll, and we don't like to kill women, or you too would be dead."

Jarla laughed. "Even if I were a gnoll woman, you wouldn't be able to kill me," she replied, waving her battle axes in front of his face. Their craftsmanship was of the likes he had never seen. He found them almost as fascinating as her.

A few more moments passed, and the tension in the forest seemed to ease.

"I tell you what, Venir. I'll spare you and your men if you tell me what business you have in my forest."

"Spare us? Hah!" smirked Venir. "Anyway, we are looking for some people."

"What kind of people?'

"Ones who follow a brigand queen named Jarla. If she lives in your forests you may have heard of her," he said sarcastically. "I hear she runs around with gnolls. Know anything about that?"

"You are a witty one, Venir, I will give you that. It is obvious to you now, hmm?"

"Yep. And it looks like the queen needs a new escort as well."

"I suggest you watch your tongue with the queen, blondie. I think you see what I can do when I want something done."

He nodded. "So why did you take them down? Royal houses are not often trifled with."

Jarla's face darkened suddenly. "It was payback," she answered coldly.

Feeling the shift in her voice, Venir backed off the topic.

"So, now what?"

"Tell your two men to come on in. I'll take you back to camp and feed you. But, don't kill any more of my gnolls. Got it?"

"I'm not promising anything."

⌒

Billip and Mikkel were quiet and uncomfortable as they accompanied Jarla back to her camp. It was unsettling. Marching a more-than-capable warrior back to her own camp containing natural enemies among the ranks was not the best idea for survival. Chongo was also uneasy. But Venir reassured them that it would not be a problem. Their friend seemed to have little idea what he was getting into, but if he went, they would watch his back, regardless. He would have done the same for them. Melegal, however, managed to evade the situation. Jarla had given no indication that she knew of his presence, and none of the men tipped her off. Billip felt Melegal had made the intelligent decision, but that was Melegal. Billip was relieved to know that the thief could tend the Orc's Elbow in his absence.

Jarla led them a few miles deeper, to the end of a wide ravine-like pass that came into a massive hill with a flat top, where they were encamped. It was a location where one could hold out as long as needed, as the well-guarded pass would ward off any pursuers trying to hunt them down. The camp, however, was unlike the army camps they had served in over the years. Most noticeable was the variety of races that grouped together and the slaves they had acquired to serve them—a cruel and despairing life, Venir thought.

The majority of the army were human, but it was clear that their time in the brigand army had worn down their humanity to the point where they didn't seem to care what happened to their own kind at the hands of the gnolls, orcs, or kobold bandits. Human slaves were even used as bartering chips for sport among the ranks when they weren't busy raiding.

It was Jarla who kept things under control, and it seemed that she didn't get involved so long as her soldiers didn't become too distracted. Her commanders were expected to handle such matters, and if they didn't, they did not last long in her army.

It was evident that Venir and his men were not welcome. Billip and Mikkel clearly didn't want to be there, either, but their arrival with Jarla had an impact, and no one dared approach them. For the first few days they kept to themselves and did not settle in. Jarla stayed busy and spent a little time with Venir, but ignored his companions. They could not follow why he was so caught up with Jarla, but he was. He convinced them that he was still figuring things out, so they trusted him and waited.

Mikkel spent his time describing to Billip all the different ways he'd like to kill every kobold he saw. These small humanoids looked a bit like halflings, with ruddy, snakelike skins and two tiny horns on their heads. Mikkel did not explain why he hated them so much, but Billip let it be, for there were things he hated, too.

Venir knew his friends were concerned, but he assured himself he had things under control. He told himself he really wanted to find out what this brigand army was all about, but in truth he was infatuated with Jarla. The powerful warrior woman had captivated him in ways he did not understand. He was uncomfortable with it, but wanted to discover what she was about and why he was drawn to her. Indeed, she might be his enemy, and it seemed only prudent to keep a close eye on her—a task he truly enjoyed.

The three men and Chongo slept near the edge of the hilltop, off to one side by themselves. In the late hours one night when their campfire was burning low, a ferocious growl from Chongo alerted them to the approach of two of Jarla's personal armed escorts. The men leapt awake, weapons to the ready, but one of the escorts spoke.

"Jarla wants to see the one called Venir," he said gruffly. "Come with us."

Venir shrugged, grinned at his men, and followed her escorts. Mikkel and Billip looked at each other and rolled their eyes, then lay back in their grassy beds.

"Venir's a dog!" groaned Mikkel. "He has all the luck. I was just dreaming about being in the sack with my woman right now."

"Yeah, your woman is something!" said Billip.

"What?!"

"Go back to sleep, I'm just messing with you. Don't get me thinking about it. Things are bad enough. Even that one orc woman brigand is starting to look attractive to me."

"Well just you dream about her then, not about my woman, got it?" Mikkel gave his friend the eye.

"Got it. Go to sleep," Billip said with a grin.

Mikkel rolled over and was fast asleep, but Billip kept churning the whole night. He was ready to leave, and determined to convince Venir to do the same.

The escorts left Venir at the entrance to Jarla's extravagant tent. His nerves were on edge with anticipation as dozens of favorable scenarios inside her quarters raced through his mind. He pulled his blonde hair back from his eyes, took a deep breath, and entered with a smile.

Her tent was plush inside with purple and red pillows, carpets, and curtains, softened even further by glimmering candlelight. The fragrance was overwhelming but soothing. Venir saw no sign of Jarla as he walked casually toward the center. From behind one of the many curtained sections she spoke.

"I'll be with you in a moment, Venir." Her voice was playful and sultry.

He was all anticipation for what awaited him behind the purple and gold curtain. His temples began to pound as if he were entering the battlefield to face an enemy he had never seen nor prepared for.

After a few more seconds, Jarla emerged from behind the curtain wearing thick gold hoop earrings and a sleeveless black silk gown that stopped mid thigh. Her dark blue eyes were magnetic, drawing into his as she approached him. Her jet-black hair was pulled into a pony tail that lay over her broad shoulders, and her thick red lips revealed a small white smile, letting Venir know how glad she was to see him.

She brushed her chest against his and looked down into his blazing blue eyes. "Come," she whispered. Taking his eager hand in hers, she led him further back into her tent.

No other words were needed between them that long night.

The relationship Venir established with Jarla made things easier for Billip and Mikkel. They were given a decent tent within the camp that was supplied with better rations. Jarla and Venir were not often together, but it was clear that she favored him over all others, and she gradually began bringing him in deeper, sharing her plans for the brigand army. Venir's friends still wanted to leave, but could not talk him into leaving, despite numerous arguments: the brigand camp was rotten; no amenities could make it any better; and they wanted to go, and go now. Regardless of Venir's assurances that they would soon depart, they knew that Jarla was calling the shots. She made both Mikkel and Billip uncomfortable. They had never met a woman like her, but they were not beguiled like Venir, despite her impressive looks. Venir was a good judge of character, and it was against his normal cunning to take up so tightly with a woman like her. Clearly he should be able to see that Jarla was not the company to keep, but he did not, and that really worried Billip.

In the meantime, the two companions worked with Venir and the harsh, unpleasant brigand queen. Before they knew it, days had become weeks, and they were in it thicker than thieves. They moved with the brigand army on raid after raid, mostly of merchant caravans that ran commerce north and south. The brigand army and its queen's reputation had clearly been spreading, as merchants began bringing along more men-at-arms on their travels. The merchants were angry at their losses and although they lacked the forces to take out the brigand army, they could at least start to deter them and take a few with them in the meantime.

Jarla was a brilliant bandit. She planned her raids using resources and preparations unrivaled by the best war generals on Bish. Venir was learning much from her, and was impressed by her knowledge of the field. She would locate the caravans and exploit their weaknesses with uncanny precision. Venir could not work out how she did it. In addition, she charged into every melee that came their way on her large dapple-grey steed named Nightmare. Nightmare was lightly armored and a force unto himself. They watched the horse trample body after body under powerful hooves that seemed to crush bones to powder. Jarla could fight with both spiked battle axes on horseback as if on her own feet. The carnage she wrought was a spectacle to any observer, but to Venir it was an inspiration. Though even he could not match Jarla's body count in battle, he and his steed were the only ones to come close. Jarla was impressed by his fighting skills, and so his acceptance among her ranks grew. But Billip and Mikkel weren't comfortable with the bloodlust, for it seemed unwarranted. Instead they relied on their wits and their range weapons—and no one complained, as they were the best shots among the brigands.

Venir spent most of his time with Jarla before and after each caravan raid. Over the past months Jarla's army had had great success and grown to over five hundred strong. Her leadership and battle skills allowed her to control the various races of her army well. When she was occasionally challenged by one of her commanders, she would make him pay by a fight to the death. Her victories were often quick.

Venir had the pleasure of watching her dress for battle, although his favorite was to help her undress afterwards. She had her own sequence for putting everything on or taking it off. First she put on her iron-toed boots, then a sleeveless white cotton shirt, followed by her sleeveless bronze chainmail dress. The sight of the magnificent warrior woman never failed to please Venir's blazing eyes. Then she would grab an unusual leather sack, kneel down, and remove an iron-banded bracer for her left arm, followed by another for her right arm. Then she would reach in with her left hand to pull out the first spiked battle axe, and follow with the right. The axes drew Venir's attention. They did not stand out as extraordinary, but they were special in design, each about three feet in length. Their dark steel blades and serrated spikes seemed forged from an unfamiliar metal, and their thick oaken handles shod with iron. Having set them at her sides, she would then pull out the helmet of the same design and construction as the axe and bracers, with a small iron spike on top.

When she returned from battle she would shake the blood from her axe blades, kneel down, and put them back in the leather sack, right first and left last, then toss it casually beside her bed with a clank. The sack never clanked except when she did that, and it never appeared big enough to hold all its contents. The sack must hold the magic, he thought, but never saw reason to ask her. For the time being he was just enjoying being there, and she would surely tell him if there were anything she wanted him to know.

Venir continued to assure his friends that he was busy gaining Jarla's trust, but Billip had doubts. The pay of a few silver coins a week plus some of the additional booty from their raids certainly appealed to the men, but the company they kept failed to grow on them. Mikkel's overbearing hatred of the kobolds had expanded to include the gnolls and orcs as well. Even Billip, who didn't really hate much, found himself disliking these other races more and more. The two passed their time finding ways to accidentally wound or kill the kobolds, particularly during raids, being careful to use arrows and bolts that were not from their own quivers. This had become a contest between the two. Mikkel would then argue that his marksmanship was superior to Billip's, which was not true, impressive though it was. The sight of a screaming kobold impaled to a tree by one of his heavy crossbow bolts made great target practice for Billip, who shot on horseback. Billip was surprised to find this amusing, while Mikkel took his own sort of pride in it; while the kobolds simply did not care enough about there own to suspect foul play.

Even though their exploits had gained them respect among many of their fellow human brigands, Billip felt that Jarla's longest-standing fighters still held too much too close to the chest. More than once he had felt the snickers of gnoll and orcen commanders, and it was more prevalent when Venir was around. His gut told him something was not right, and it was in his nosey nature to find out exactly what it was.

Late nights on the hilltop provided the best conditions for

snooping around. The cloudless sky left the campground pitch black except for the flicker from dozens of burning campfire embers. Any mercenaries who were not sleeping were drinking and not paying much attention to anything else. Boredom was the most dangerous element in the brigand camp, but the commanders kept it under control with the occasional painful punishment. Billip made himself a little scruffier to try to blend in better with the common soldiers. It wasn't hard for him to saunter around as if moving from one group to another without really engaging with any of them. His goal was to reach the centre of the camp where Jarla's tent was surrounded by the four smaller tents of her commanders. As far as Billip knew, only she and Venir occupied her tent most nights, but occasionally Venir did not get the comfort of her quarters. Billip chuckled at the thought of his spoilt friend being kicked out during one of Jarla's searing moods.

He spent several nights within range of these tents, watching the commanders—gnoll, human, and part-orc— come and go. Typically, they would meet late evening or early morning at one of the four tents, and Jarla would attend from time to time, but always without Venir, which surprised Billip. There was normally an armored guard with a spear at both the entrance and the rear of each commander's tent, but during meetings an additional guard was stationed at each side of the tent.

Late one evening Billip watched Venir stroll into Jarla's tent, and not long afterwards the remaining commanders gathered in the tent directly behind Jarla's. It seemed sudden and uncharacteristic, and in their haste they had not doubled the guards, leaving right and left sides unguarded. Billip felt nervousness set in. This might be his only opening for days; he had to take it; and being a gambler, he did.

Luckily the red moon was casting a shadow over the right side of the tent, leaving it pitch black, even to his keen eyes. Smoothly and silently he crept into its shadow and lay flat on his back. His heart was pounding in his temples so that he could hear almost nothing else, but after a few minutes in his prone position he became composed enough to listen in. For thirty minutes he did not learn much. Then the orc guarding the front of the tent stepped into view and mumbled something in orcen. Shortly thereafter the other orc guarding the rear stepped around. If either of them came his way he would be caught, he knew. He kept his eyes closed lest the whites of his give him away. They were speaking low in orcen, but not moving any closer. If they saw him and sounded the alarm he would have to run and try to blend in elsewhere, but the whole camp would surely be interrogated, and he and his men would be the likely suspects. He heard the guard in front take a step his way and then another, while the one at the rear also seemed to be getting more comfortable out of his immediate area of responsibility. Regret flooded through Billip's mind. He should have gotten the Bone out of this camp long ago! His heart was thundering so hard the guards would surely hear it. He thought about where he would run first, and then awaited his fate.

Then a loud orcen voice sounded, not from the guards but from within the tent; someone was on his way out. The guards hastily retreated to their posts, and the front guard was reprimanded for not maintaining his position. In defense, the guard pointed out to his commander that the tent was not properly secured with additional guards at the sides. That only complicated Billip's problem, for now the commander took it upon himself to check both sides, peering intently around their corners. After many long seconds, Billip squinted to see what was happening. He thought he saw the commander shrug, then walk back into the tent. No one seemed to be dispatched to find more guards. Despite his better judgment, Billip chose to wait it out again, guessing that there was little likelihood of anyone coming in his direction again.

Inside the tent the meeting was heating up. It was being

conducted in common human language, presumably Jarla's prefer-ence. The tones were low to prevent the guards from listening in, but Billip could hear clearly through the thick canvas of the tent. Excitement was rising in the voices of the commanders, and cruel laughter, as Billip listened in on a conversation he could never have anticipated. The ambition and evil plans of Jarla and her command-ers did not bode well for humans, but it was what was behind all of these exploits that Billip found so utterly incomprehensible.

The meeting was almost over; the savvy scout had no time to waste. He rolled out of the shadow and made his way back to the camp.

———

"Mikkel!" Billip whispered urgently, prodding him in the ribs. "Wake up!"

Mikkel sat up quickly, his bearded black face groggy but clearly perturbed. Chongo stirred and greeted Billip with a few licks.

"You'd better have a good reason, Billip. I was dreaming of my woman and those dreams don't come often in this stinkin' camp. What's going on?"

"Listen to me; we're in danger."

"Me? Why's Me in danger?"

"Not Melegal. You, me, and especially Venir. Now get your gear ready and don't make it obvious."

Mikkel pondered the sudden news. Then, knowing that Billip was a cautious man who never fooled around with such matters, he followed instructions. The look in Billip's face and his chronic crack-ing of his bony white knuckles told all. Mikkel had never seen his comrade so edgy. His own nervousness began to rise as he rounded up his gear.

"Billip, tell me what you heard, brother. You're worrying the crap out of me."

"Okay, but keep calm; I know how you get. Hear me out."
Mikkel nodded reluctantly.

"I just listened in on one of the commanders' tent meetings. They're planning to attack Outpost Thirty-One in the next few days. . ."

"There ain't no way! Outpost Thirty-One has a thousand well-armed soldiers of the Royal house legion."

"Let me finish. They already have help; over two thousand strong are waiting to help sack the outpost. . ."

"Even with that many it'll be hard to take. They'll have to starve them out, and by then help will have arrived. Besides, no one just attacks a Royal army outpost. It would be suicide, an act of war. Even gnolls and orcs don't have the numbers to face the humans when you come down to it."

Billip was nodding. "Let me finish again; it's not orcs or gnolls or humans or dwarfs or striders. . . or even halflings for that matter." He paused as if unable to go on, which gave his confused friend a moment to think about it.

Then Mikkel's eyes widened. "Ogres!"

"No Mikkel, not ogres. Worse. Worse than all of them combined."

"Will you just tell me?"

"If you'd just let me finish you'd know by now."

"Well, if you'd quit arguing, maybe I'd let you finish."

"We got more important things to do now than have another stupid argument."

"Since when?" Mikkel was chuckling now and Billip grew agitated.

"Underlings, you idiot! Jarla's brigand army is in league with the underlings! And has been for quite some time. No wonder she's been so successful. And we've been helping her!"

"Bone," was all the dumbfounded Mikkel could say. He sat back against a log near their tent. "We gotta tell Venir. He's gonna freak.

Man, he hates underlings more than I hate kobolds."

"That's the other thing. I'm glad you're sitting down for this next bit of news."

Mikkel looked up, at a loss for what could possibly come next.

"It seems Jarla has no more need of Venir's services. I assume that includes us, too. And I think the last guy that slept with her is dead. And the guy before him. And so on. You catch my drift?"

"Man, she is one evil lady! No wonder those guys always chuckle when he walks by. Glad it wasn't me after all. I guess dreamin's better than dyin'. "

"Except you're the one get's to save him."

"What? I'm not gonna run in there and pull him out of her bed! He might as well go happy, I guess."

"That's not the plan. And shame on you!"

"Sorry, just kidding. I knew she was evil. It's like she hates everything. I never saw that woman smile, but still she looks good. Tough break for Vee, though. So what's the plan?"

"First off, I gotta warn Outpost Thirty-One. Before that I need to clear a hole through the wretched ravine watch for you and Vee to follow. There are five guards on each side of the ravine, spaced out over a mile. They use bird pipes to signal. I'm gonna cut off of the west side of the ravine. That's the side you and Venir will have to take to get out of the camp and past the brigand squadron at the end of the ravine. They're only orcs and usually sleep between the whistles, especially right before dawn, so I shouldn't have much trouble taking them out. If I have time, I'll take out the other side as well, and you guys will hopefully be able to disappear from camp altogether. Got it?"

"I'm with you."

"It should be dawn before long. Hopefully Venir will make his way back here as usual to tell us his exploits. Break the news to him and get the bone out of here! Meet me at Outpost Thirty-One. Got it? I'm going on foot, so have my horse ready for Venir. His horse is stabled so don't fool with it, it might draw suspicion. And you, Chongo, you make sure he doesn't screw this up."

"Good luck, Billip. You're gonna need it."

"I like my chances better than yours, so hang on to that luck," he smiled grimly and slipped over the edge into the ravine forest, hoping to use its cover to eliminate the ravine watch before dawn cracked on the horizons. He had to be at his best and not miss a single shot in the blackness; if he had to he would sneak up and cut their throats. This do-or-die mission was as frightening and exciting as any he had ever faced, but he was determined not to let down his friends—or the rest of his race, for that matter. They all had friends in that outpost, and it was a key stronghold that helped keep the underlings from gaining control in the north. Without it the tide would quickly turn, and underlings had already been gaining ground for some time.

Mikkel's forehead was beaded with sweat as he prowled their campsite, waiting for Venir. Dawn was long past and Billip had been gone hours. His friend should arrive any minute, he thought, but the minutes passed slowly. It was agonizing; he felt like a dead duck among the now awakening army. Chongo's ears kept perking up as if Venir was coming, but they were all false alarms. The big brown dog sniffed and snuffled continuously, adding to Mikkel's frustration. Only the horses remained calm, but they were well-trained, and ready to be ridden out of camp at a second's notice.

"Where is he, Chongo? He should be back by now!"

Chongo looked up but gave only a low yelp in reply. Mikkel began to worry that his friend was already done for. If Venir took much longer, he would have to leave without him. The thought was disturbing, but no more so than the thought of what might be happening to Venir in Jarla's tent.

———

Venir awakened from his slumber in the brigand queen's tent just like any ordinary morning. Jarla was always up first and busy with all the tasks of maintaining command of her army, or her "hapless horde" as Venir liked to call them. He never understood how she kept company with such an assortment of races rather than a full company of her own; but if she could live with it, so could he, he thought, for a while anyway. Clearly she was capable enough to command any army, so why she chose this one he could not figure. In the meantime, he would make the most of it. He was confident that he had a good handle on his situation, and it would not be long before he gained her total trust.

In fact, this very morning it would all come together for him; not as he anticipated, but certainly in a way he would never forget.

There was not the usual activity in the tent. Usually Jarla could be heard busily muttering to herself, but not this morning. He was about to dress when he decided to look around the large tent to see if Jarla was possibly reading or recording her plans. She was very thorough with the details of her business. The tent was the same as always, yet something seemed amiss. He couldn't figure out why his gut told him something was wrong. But he wasn't one to be paranoid and he was sure that whatever might be going on had nothing to do with him. After all, Jarla was rather fond of his prowess—both on and off the battlefield—so if anything important was up, he'd be the first to know.

He wandered back towards the bed to dress himself when he heard her footsteps approaching the tent's entrance, so he turned to wait. In came the brigand queen, and he greeted her with a smile. Clothed in her typical attire, she smiled ruefully at him, nodding strangely as she looked his unclothed body up and down. He responded, and was about to greet her in his typical fashion when two gnoll commanders, Throk and Keel, entered behind her, fully armed for battle. Brazen though he was, Venir was embarrassed.

"Don't you two ever enter the queens tent uninvited! Now get out of here!"

Throk and Keel chuckled disrespectfully from behind their queen's back. Venir looked at her, expecting her to deal them a sharp reprimand for their indiscretion. But she did not, and he turned back toward the two gnolls, quickly regaining his composure.

"So, I guess you two want a closer look at the best looking man, and I emphasize man, in the camp?" He stood proudly before them, arms wide. "Well, here I am." Again there were surly chuckles, and Venir started to feel uneasy.

"Jarla, what in bone are these two doing in here? What's going on?"

"They're here to help me take care of some business."

"I'm sure I can help. Let me get some clothes on."

"No, stay right there, my pet. I like you as you are."

Venir's dander started to rise. "Pet? I am not your pet, Jarla."

"Pah! You've been my pet all along, buffoon. You're no different from all the other fools I've had before. You aren't the first and you won't be the last. But I'll give you credit; you were one of the best."

The uneasiness that had crept in turned into something he had never dealt with before: uncertainty. Jarla's beautiful eyes burned hatefully now, her features twisted into a persona he had never encountered. This was not the woman he knew. She looked at him like he was just another man among a hundred who had wronged or spurned her in some horrible way.

"What are your plans for me then? Am I to be expelled from your army? I wouldn't miss it. I'd be happy to leave."

"It's not that simple, Venir. No man who shares my bed ever lives to tell about it."

His body went cold and his mind numb at the heartlessness of her statement. He knew she meant it and was prepared to end his life with a single command. He felt a fool as he stood flat-footed and naked with no means to defend himself. He was about to be slaughtered and he felt the fear and sweat break on his brow. But fear began to trigger anger.

"Are you going to at least give me a fighting chance?" he asked, almost in defeat.

"No. I've seen you fight. Giving you a chance is too dangerous."

"So what then?" he shrugged.

"Throk and Keel normally eliminate my pets while they're sleeping. Or sometimes as they try to escape. They've been begging to kill you and your men as payback for the loss of their comrades and one of my best commanders, Durn. But that's in the past."

A sudden guilt for the danger he had created for his comrades began to subdue his anger. He was a fool whose folly would lead to the death of two good friends as well. Yet despite the news Jarla had shared with him, he still found her magnificent. To her surprise, he even managed a grin.

"Well, that's a first. A fool grinning in the face of the death. You are something, I'll give you that."

"Oh, I know you think at least that much of me, and more," he answered with a wink.

Throk and Keel chuckled, agitating her so that she decided to continue with the bad news.

"But in your case, my pet, there's a pretty steep bounty on your head."

"What bounty?"

"The one my army's outside interest have put on you."

"You have me at a loss, again. Who is this outside interest?

"Actually, I'll tell you. I was careful not to disclose anything to you before, because I know how you feel about them. But there's been a war going on for a long time, a secret war. I'm part of it—a distraction for the most part—but I'm very well paid, as we all are. And I don't mind carving into the supporters and forces of the Royals who lead the humans. They put me through great pain long ago, so it satisfies my thirst for revenge. The truth is, I don't feel much for any race, I just enjoy what I do. I could do it for either side in this war. But right now, I'm on the side that's gaining on the humans."

Venir sensed that she was about to say something he dearly hoped she wouldn't. She mustn't. He simply could not believe it to be true, and that he, too, may have become a part of it.

"The bottom line is, it doesn't matter to me who wins or loses. But when it comes to tendering for my services, the underlings pay better."

Rage exploded inside the big man's chest at the realization that this woman he had been sharing a bed with for months had been in league with his most despised enemies, had even known how he felt, and had used him anyway. The betrayal was as enlightening as it was overwhelming. It was a cruel twist, but an awakening as well.

Still helpless and almost shaking, he replied, "I'll make you pay, woman! You'd better kill me now if you ever want to sleep again! I will hunt you down!"

Jarla laughed lightly.

"I've survived bigger threats. Don't worry, the underlings have agreed to let me be present when they put you through it. Apparently, some of the underlings you've allowed to escape would like to apply your own methods to you. We're going to watch them scalp you and put your head on a spike. They're even going to let you lead their army as we take Outpost Thirty-One."

Venir didn't wince at her words. He stared at her with hate. "They won't take me alive. You'll have to kill me. I won't give you a choice."

"I assure you, that won't happen. Give yourself up, man. You're unarmed and the whole tent is surrounded. It won't be hard to wrestle you down. Be good, and I'll try to make your suffering quick."

With the desperation of a cornered tiger, Venir eyed his surroundings for a weapon of some sort. The only object close to him was Jarla's leather sack, lying on the map table she used to store her weapons and armor. He had looked in the sack several times before, unbeknown to her, and never found a thing. He knew it was futile to try it again, but he felt compelled to; he had nothing to lose.

"Well?" she said. "What's it going to be? Do you give yourself up or do my men wrestle you down?"

He sprang like a deer, grabbing the leather sack off the table and reaching down deep inside it. Throk, Keel, and Jarla laughed loudly.

"They do that every time," Jarla sneered. "These poor brutes just can't come up with anything better."

Venir turned slowly to face them, with the same look of surprise they had come to expect.

"Now, put my sack down, Venir. It's time to end this game."

"Why would I do that," Venir smiled, "when I have this?"

He pulled out an object and their eyes widened, none more than Jarla's. For she was not gazing upon either of her twin battle axes, but a much larger one that looked like both of hers put together. Venir was amazed too.

"Bone!"

Jarla's eyes locked on his for a moment and then returned to the great axe he now wielded.

"Put that back, Venir. Put that back in the sack now! Do it, Venir!" she began to scream in rage. "Do it! Do it! Do it now!"

He had never seen a woman so angry in his life, and he had seen plenty. Her frenzy almost persuaded him, but he caught himself, realizing that he no longer cared any more for her than for a marsh witch. He flashed them all a deadly grin.

"I think I might just cut you all down instead!"

In that instant Jarla knew her time was up, but her instinct to survive prevailed. Without her weapons she could not maintain control of her army, but she was still in command, so she gave her final order, hoping to regain what she had just lost.

"Kill him!" she screamed at the top of her lungs. "Kill him!" It was the last Venir ever heard from her.

Throk and Keel drew their bastard swords in time to attempt to parry his vengeful attack, but he was all over them like lightening in a rainstorm, shattering their blades and their bones with his hand-and-a-half axe Brool. Venir's new weapon felt alive in his hands and power seemed to course through his body. It felt good, very good indeed. The gnolls were dead and their bulky bodies blocked the entry of the other brigand soldiers, who hesitated at the sight just long enough for Venir to pull the shield and helmet from the sack and prepare himself for a stand. It suddenly struck him that the back of Jarla's tent faced the entrance to the ravine and the path to Billip and Mikkel's tent. As the guards charged in he slit the tent canvas and ran through it as fast as he could.

Mikkel had been on tenterhooks for what felt like an agonizing eternity. Through his small spyglass he had been surveying the rear of Jarla's tent. He had watched her leave it, seen the brigand soldiers quietly surround it, and watched her re-enter it with two gnoll commanders. He knew that he was about to witness the assassination of his old friend. No one seemed to have noticed Billip's departure, and no one seemed concerned with him either, so he waited, keeping watch for a few more minutes.

He was about to pack it in and go when he saw Jarla bolt from the tent and start barking commands. All the guards converged on her tent's entrance. The camp was still in a slumber, but many were now alert and sounding the alarm. Then he saw a figure emerge through a slit in the back of the tent; a naked man with a great axe, a shield, and what looked like the brigand queen's helmet came running out of the opening straight in Mikkel's direction. Two orc brigands intercepted his path and as the naked warrior cut them down, Mikkel saw a big V-shaped tattoo on the man's broad back. He snapped his spyglass closed in surprise.

"Man, it's Vee!"

Chongo bolted to his master's aid while Mikkel jumped on his horse and led the other mount quickly into his friend's path. Two more brigand soldiers cut off Venir's path, but Mikkel shot one clean through his skull and Venir practically severed the other in two with a wide swipe through his belly.

"Come Vee! Let's go!"

Jarla's men were coming. The whole brigand army seemed to be awake and on the move, but Mikkel and Venir had the jump on them for the moment. Venir leapt onto Billip's readied horse and they raced down the hillside and into the ravine, with Chongo leading. Hard and fast they rode, and to their surprise nothing seemed to stand in there way. Billip had done his job. They even passed clear of the ravine squadron at the end of the pass. Billip must have led them all on a fox hunt.

As they galloped clear of the ravine, Mikkel shouted to Venir, "Good thing Billip left his horse for you!"

"Why?"

"There's no way I'd let you ride with me looking like that!"

Venir had forgotten all about his nakedness.

"We'd better get you into some of my clothes. If Billip or anyone else sees us now, we'll never live it down! "

"Thanks. Let's keep it between ourselves. I'm just happy to be alive, either way!"

"I heard that!"

They laughed, and rode on toward Outpost Thirty-One.

From that day on, things were never the same for Venir or the others. Another layer of innocence had been lost in the ruthless world of Bish. That day, Venir became something other than himself. Unknowingly, he had become reborn as the Darkslayer.

And as he remembered those times with Mikkel, Billip, and Melegal, Venir realized that he had changed more than he even had been aware. But he had no regrets, and as he and Melegal continued their ride north from Two-Ten City, he put the past firmly behind him.

He was determined to see his life through now as the Darkslayer—right to the bitter end.

CHAPTER 14

TRAPPING THE DARKSLAYER

The omnipotent Scorch had existed in the infinite universe longer than most eternal beings. But to Scorch it did not matter how long he had been there; it mattered only that he existed. Unlike many of his counterparts in the universe, he had no assigned realm of responsibility, for he pre-existed even that. Having dealt with his eternal frustration long before most infinite beings arrived. he told them, "There is no end," but they did not listen. So he made the most of his situation by doing whatever he wished. Time and time again, his meddling led to the demise or the enlightenment of planets and their civilizations. And now Bish was to become his latest exploit as he tossed one additional ingredient into the secret stew that Trinos had created.

The winds on Bish were brisker and cooler than normal for this time of year. It was typically a warm, dry season, but things had become rather strange. Venir and Melegal had been traveling steadily since leaving Two-Ten City with hardly a word between them, when Melegal finally broke the silence.

"Why are we heading back towards Bone, Venir?"

After a pause that seemed to last forever, Venir answered, "I don't think it makes much difference which way we go. I just think we need to start heading back towards home."

"It's barely a week since we left home, but if we're going back, shouldn't we go straight? Why northwest instead of north? Surely there are other northward paths we can take that aren't the same as the one we took southward?"

"I don't know, Melegal, but this way we'll catch Mood and Chongo quicker. Mood usually stays east of Dwarven Hole and I have a feeling he's gonna be there. He won't be expecting us so soon, so he's unlikely to be at our original rendezvous north of Two-Ten City."

"Well that was a mouthful, considering you're not drunk," Melegal said, attempting to lighten the dour mood. Things hadn't felt right to Melegal since they had left. Venir seemed different; even the weather and the trees seemed different. The thief had never felt such a grimness all about him like this. It was not an overwhelming feeling, but just enough to make him aware of it.

The mighty Venir was jogging quickly and with determination, although he too did not quite understand his pressing need to move in this direction. But he did, and with little thought. And as fast as Quickster was on his furry, quick-pony legs, Venir was always ahead. A large patch of thickened forest lay ahead. The sight of tall tree-tops bunched together for miles across from east to west was new to the city-bred thief, but appealing nonetheless to Venir's less-traveled partner. Dark clouds seemed to roll slowly over the gray-green tree-tops with rays of sunlight breaking through the clouds to brighten the green. Flocks of birds swooped in and out by the hundreds, and dived in and out of the clouds. This did not cause Melegal to suspect anything odd, but Venir seemed to know better and slowed.

"Something's ahead. I can't quite say what, but I feel it might be waiting for us," he added somberly.

"Well, Vee, should we venture in, or find another way?"

"I think whatever it is will find us anyway, so let's take the fight to it."

"Or them?" the skinny thief added. "What's this forest ahead of us, anyway?"

"That, my friend, is the Great Forest of Bish. Its trees are triple the girth and height of any other trees on Bish. It's spectacular. It's actually twice as far away as it appears. And those birds you see are pretty large too. Don't get spooked though. Travelers make it through on the whole. Well, in most cases." The warrior gave a slight smile.

"Man, all this yakking is strange, coming from you."

"Maybe you should write this stuff down."

"Maybe you should start acting like the brute you are and stop blathering. That ogre must've squeezed something loose in you. Did he finally get the blood to flow to your head?"

Maybe he did, thought Venir, but Melegal was clearly irritated at the thought of facing another encounter. Venir picked up the pace toward the Great Forest of Bish, and Melegal was relieved to see him in action rather than talking. But the great forest ahead left him uneasy, more so than the Red Clay Forest. Melegal was a city man, and being too long in the woods no longer appealed to the thief. Suddenly, dodging the authorities in the City of Bone seemed the more pleasant option after all.

Lord Almen's methods quickly bore fruit. He was now busy witnessing the torture of another Royal family member from a discreet location far outside his palace walls. Two others also bore witness to the incarceration and torture of the man who had assisted in Tonio's fall. The first, who was also the torturer, was the unattractively flabby and half-naked Sefron. The other witness was a newcomer far more mysterious even than the discreet Detective McKnight. His name was Teku, and he stood even taller than Lord Almen. He was a pale black man, dressed from head to toe in loose, nondescript white attire, a sort of sleeveless robe or kimono that seemed to have a mysterious significance. Even Sefron was struck by the man's appearance, and was even more surprised when Almen smiled at the man from time to time. For Almen truly valued this man's service. Teku spoke to Almen in deeply respectful, rumbling tones, and smiled, and his long white teeth glistened in the strange torchlight as he and Almen mumbled and nodded to each other. The leather-bound prisoner was from the Royal House of Agenta, a house that was moving quickly into the upper ranks of the hierarchy in the City of Bone. This man's deeds had finally caught up with him, and he was to be the sacrificial son for his family, for he was one of many. The man's name did not matter, and he laughed at the sight of Sefron approaching. But his laughter subsided abruptly as drops of acid were slowly sprinkled all over his body. His screams would last for hours, but only four men would ever hear them at all.

Mood and Chongo had been spending some time in the Great Forest of Bish. But recently the giant red-bearded dwarf had become uneasy and grown concerned about his human friends. Chongo, however, was mellow, and was now sleeping quietly at Mood's feet, while the big dwarf himself sat with his back against a vast tree and his legs propped up on Chongo. All the while, he was smoking a mellow, sweet rolled-leaf cigar of the dwarven kind. The red clay leaves burned slowly around the tobacco that was harvested unseen in the caves of the giant dwarfs back home. The smoke from his bearded lips was light blue and non-aromatic, but cooling to the environment of the Great Forest. It was at times such as this that Mood enjoy the peace on Bish as his great escape. But today, neither the powerful narcotic of his dwarven cigar nor the rich green, mossy forest with its gentle plant life and blooms were able to take the edge off his mind. At length, the ears of the double-headed mastiff ears perked up; one pair anyway, while the other remained asleep. Mood's blurry eyes showed a sliver of blue beneath his brows, for he too sensed that something—nothing dangerous—was amiss.

"Let's go, Chongo." At Mood's prompting, the two quietly began to move along the forest paths like ghosts of the night. Despite his size and stature, Mood easily negotiated the forest because of its equally enormous plant life. That was one reason he liked it there. Chongo, being a large beast himself, experienced the same benefit. They felt at home in the Great Forest of Bish and the forest was never disturbed by them. But sometimes the wrong creature would bother the forest, intentionally or not, and Mood had a feeling this was about to happen. Mood sat astride Chongo in his ranger gear: thick canvas-like robes of brown and green, two giant-hand axes forming an X across his back, high, soft leather boots, and a large belt pouch containing various requirements. Mood was still smoking his cigar in the saddle when the muscled mountain of a dog caught the scent of something. Although the scent was far off, the dog could track anything from many miles away. Leaving virtually no tracks, the two made their way unnoticed by any except the forest itself. Or so they thought.

"Run! Run! Run!" screamed Lefty Lightfoot, who was running at full speed towards young Georgio who had stopped to pee at the edge of the Great Forest.

"Wait! What's going on?" Georgio hollered, trying his best to cut off in midstream, and getting splashed as he ran in Lefty's direction. "See what you've made me do again!" he hollered, running towards the sounds of the panicked halfling.

"What are we running from, Lefty? We need to keep westward."

"No! Come, or we'll be eaten!"

Georgio had seen the little halfling panic several times over nothing. The poor little man could barely sleep and Georgio pitied him, but it was becoming annoying. "Will you stop a second and tell me what you're talking about?" Any creature seemed to spook the halfling, but the curly-headed Georgio was beginning to gain Lefty's trust that he could take care of him. Finally, Lefty stopped to explain.

"It's a gigantic two-headed dog with a huge red man-thing! Run!"

The poor halfling's ashen face almost broke Georgio's heart, and he had to bite his tongue to keep back the giggles that had offended Lefty earlier.

"I'll handle the beast, don't fear, Lefty. I'll protect you." Georgio patted his shoulder, turned and pulled out his hand axe. Lefty stood frozen in his tracks, for these past few days had left the poor halfling not knowing what to expect any more.

Georgio's wait among the mighty trees seemed prolonged. The boy had only meant to be playful, but as the moments passed and the forest became quiet, Georgio began to have doubts. His hands grew clammy. Was he wrong about what Lefty had seen? Then he thought he heard something, and his hairs stood on end.

Lefty, too, was frozen with fear in his hiding place among the great trees. The forest seemed so still and quiet that their heartbeats were all they heard. He saw Georgio's once brave shoulders begin to slouch. Then Georgio turned and began walking casually back toward him, his hand axe swinging lightly by his side. The big boy had a look of disappointment on his face. As Georgio came towards him, the little halfling suddenly knew something was about to happen to the boy. Sweat broke out on Lefty's forehead as he waited, until he could stand it no more. He wanted to scream for Georgio to run, but the boy kept walking, slowly, his eyes to the ground. Oh, look up, stupid boy, thought Lefty. He's going to die and so am I, he thought over and over. Finally, Georgio looked up and around; their eyes met and Georgio smiled. Lefty felt momentary relief, but it was short lived. Georgio's smile turned to surprise, and he froze in his tracks. Just then Lefty felt the hot breath of something in the nape of his neck, and turned.

Facing him were four huge eyes, two heads, and two massive sets of teeth, and above these a giant hairy red man-thing. Lefty's normally fleet feet were immobilized, and he knew he would be dead soon enough.

"Eat me," said the stricken halfling. "Please get it over with." Lefty squeezed his eyes shut and awaited his fate.

His fate came in the form of two giant wet licks and an uproarious laugh. Certain that he was being slowly consumed by a giant mocking beast, it took the constant shaking of his shoulders by Georgio to get him to open his eyes.

"Are we dead, Georgio?" the little halfling asked, shivering.

"No, Lefty!" Georgio answered cheerfully. "We're saved!" And at that unexpected answer, the light-footed halfling fainted before his new friends.

Venir had been jogging along effortlessly as one setting sun dipped toward the western horizon, while the other began to sink to the north, behind the treetops of the Great Forest of Bish. Neither warrior nor thief noticed this incongruity or wondered why it was, but it did make for a strange light, as the treetops were much higher than average, making the dusk set in far sooner than normal. Rugged and still running, Venir suddenly picked up his pace. Except for his spiked helm, he had emptied his arsenal from his sack so that his large iron-banded shield was now strapped to his mighty back, and his menacing battle axe, Brool, whistled sharply as it cut the wind. Melegal made a point of keeping up but avoiding the axe, the only inanimate object that ever made him feel uncomfortable.

Abruptly, the big warrior came to a halt and dropped to his knees in the tall grass. To Melegal's surprise, Quickster took no notice and sped past. Gritting his teeth, Melegal yanked the reins to stop the pony and turn back to Venir. But Quickster kept right on, despite Melegal's efforts. As he neared the forest, dread overcame the skinny thief and he abandoned his saddle in a quick hop, duck, and roll. Then he looked about, retrieved his floppy hat that had fallen from his head, and put it on before looking around for Quickster. But the beast was already out of sight.

With a sigh and a grimace, Melegal began marching back to where he had passed Venir. In the dimming light, his eyes caught Venir running toward the forest in full battle gear, the spiked helm strapped to his chin, his large shield on his back and Brool swinging in cadence from his right hand. The helm's iron eyelets glowed menacingly, but the man he knew as Venir was not there. No, this was the Darkslayer, running fleet and quiet as a forest stag.

The city thief stood alone in the dusk before the looming forest. Should he follow the Darkslayer or try to find Quickster? There was no time to waste. Deciding that the Darkslayer was more capable of taking care of himself than Quickster, the thief set off in the direction Quickster had gone, running as fast as he could. But the Great Forest of Bish was further than he had anticipated, due to its sheer enormity. All his judgments that were based on what he had learned in the City of Bone seemed wholly inadequate now. With great caution and misgiving, the thief entered the forest after his beloved but dimwitted mount.

Oran used his spell once again to help the evil party plan their surprise attack. Through the eye of Eep, Oran and McKnight viewed the swirling image of Venir the Darkslayer as he approached the Great Forest of Bish.

"I must say," said McKnight to Oran, "I'm rather glad you and Tonio have chosen to tackle the big fellow; I can't say I have any desire to be in your boots. He looks rather menacing. Good luck to you."

"It should be you, in fact, city man," said Oran without looking up from his mirage. "But I shall do what I must. Be thankful I have set you an easy prey. In a few moments that pony will deliver into your lap the other resident of your filthy city."

"Rather a shame, really," said McKnight, "to lose another fine citizen of Bone. I suspect we need every sneaky human we have to keep your underling lot under control." He wagged his finger at Oran. "Tsk, tsk, such decisions as to which lives to take and which to let be!" McKnight looked surprised at his own comments. "I ought to note that down," he added, "it sounds rather profound!" As left, McKnight turned. "I shall try to be quick and return to help you. I rather think you may need it."

Staring at the fading image, Oran thought how good it would be to be forever rid of this impudent human. As the image died, Oran caught a faint glimpse of what was coming his way: a man with a spiked helm glowing brightly around the eyes. Oran gave a slight gasp.

"Tonio! Take your position. He comes!" Then he closed his eyes. "Eep," he commanded through thought, "you know what to do!"

CHAPTER 15

BOLT CATCHER

In the southwest corner of the Red Clay Forest, several piles of hot ash lay smoking. They were the remains of the forest magi, whose lust for magic had drawn them toward a great magic presence in the forest. There they had come upon two intruders. The two great underling lords, Verbard and Catten, did not stop to introduce themselves to the forest magi before cruelly snuffing out their lives in a flash of lightening. Surprised to find themselves surrounded by ten floating forest magi, they were hardly alarmed. The leader of the forest magi came closest, enough to get a sense of the danger the two underling lords represented. He began to back off, but it was too late. Verbard struck the first bolt of chained lightening into his retreating form, while Catten sent a second bolt into one floating opposite the leader. The silver-blue bolts shot counter-clockwise, gaining speed, spinning like grinding stones and growing brighter and brighter as they passed through each of the forest magi, until just ten piles of ash remained.

"Didn't even have time to even scream," Catten noted in disappointment. Verbard chuckled.

The Darkslayer charged into the Great Forest of Bish like a human juggernaut shot from a cannon. He grew angrier with every stride as the scent of underling consumed him. Though wary of a trap, the Darkslayer always took things head on and relied on his battle instincts to take care of the rest. His blue eyes flashed beneath his spiked helm as Brool slashed through the foliage intercepting their path. The Great Forest of Bish had darkened a great deal since he had entered from the more open plains, but the lack of light did not affect the Darkslayer. He knew the Great Forest like the back of his hand and his feet guided him as if it were daylight in the desert.

He was about two hundred yards in when trouble became apparent. Spider webs, giant spider webs, suddenly engulfed the trees from the ground to as high as the eye could see. The Darkslayer slowed his pace slightly and began to weave his way among them, for not all the gaps between trees were covered. The recesses of his enraged mind, meanwhile, asked a question whose answer he already knew. For this reminded him of the fish traps he had set as a boy in the silver streams of Hohm. But this was a crueler version, designed by underling hunters to trap their prey. The labyrinth of webs let you find your way through, but at the end, if you succeeded without getting stuck, you were trapped and then quickly killed. This he knew. He and Brool had been in this situation a few times, and the trap had failed a few times. The first time was the hardest to survive, of course. The labyrinth had finally opened into a cove fully laced with webs around all its vast trees. Rather than wait like a victim, Venir had tried an unexpected tactic. Running straight, he had charged forward at full speed, and Brool had cut with ease through the thick webs that curled away and dissipated at the slightest touch of its deadly sharp edge.

The forest had opened wide again, but was darker still. Venir expected to quickly encounter his enemy, but to his surprise, he found nothing. His helm warned that an underling was near, but now a new sound came to his keen ears, a high buzzing that zipped toward him. In the total blackness the Darkslayer quickly swung Brool up, just in time to stop the talons of the demonic imp from slashing his throat. Fighting blind was nothing new to the warrior, but this was a new flying opponent. Eep zipped in and out, and his evil mocking seemed to echo from all sides. More webs began to coat the trees and the Darkslayer had to monitor his surroundings while under attack. Eep was unhindered by the webs, giving him a clear advantage, but Brool chopped off Eep's path at every last second before he could deliver the lethal blow. Brool's deadly spike jabbed and poked at the imp, who was beginning to grow frustrated. The Darkslayer could feel that he was gaining control of the trap Oran had set for him. The real trap, however, had yet to be sprung.

Although Brool had cut through the spider webs with devastating effect, the axe could only do so much, and the webs were closing in faster than the Darkslayer could contain the imp's attacks. Over and over the imp rushed in and out, just beyond Brool's reach. Then, very suddenly, the imp flew away.

Silence fell. Peaceful moments passed in the forest, but the wary warrior kept cutting away at the thick webs, and used the time to move his shield from his back to his left arm. Then with a buzz and a swoosh the imp was back, flying in and out again, just out of range. Then more moments of silence, while the sweat rolled off Venir's chiseled face in large drops. And now a distant hum rattled the high branches of the forest. Swooping up and down and in and out from a very safe distance, the imp began playing another game. Not waiting for the next series of strikes, the brawny warrior pressed on cautiously through the forest at a trot, cutting through the webs, knowing full well that that imp was not alone. For he could sense the presence of an underling. The mere thought refueled his anger, and with that, the beating of the imp's bat-like wings was suddenly shrill behind him. He whirled to his left and cut high with his battle axe, but nothing was there. It seemed nothing had ever been there. Tricked, his senses screamed and he whirled back to the right, this time with shield raised. He just caught the powerful blow from Tonio's flashing long sword with a bone-jarring clang.

Melegal had had more than enough of this misadventure. Both Venir and Quickster had frustrated him to his limit. He stomped through the Great Forest, peering about for Quickster's tracks and doing his best imitation of a ranger as he ran his hands through the dirt and leaves. He followed a straight line as best he could, guessing where a pony might go, but to no avail.

The darkness was settling in fast, and as Quickster had most of Melegal's gear, Melegal was growing uneasy. Muttering and cursing under his breath, he finally heard a familiar sound not far ahead: the neighs and munching sounds of his ever-hungry quick-pony.

Relaxing a bit, Melegal strolled to the side of his shaggy mount. Sorely tempted to choke the stupid beast, he stroked his mane instead.

"Whatever made you drag me into this cursed forest better have been worth it," he huffed, glancing around and preparing to remount. "Now let this be the end of it."

"I should say it was worth it," said Detective McKnight, "and this will be the end of it, for yourself, at any rate." He aimed his double-hand crossbow at Melegal's exposed back. "No sudden moves now, I'm pretty good with this crossbow at twelve or so paces, my fellow."

A shiver of shock ran up the thief's spine. It was a long time since he had been caught off guard like this, but then forest was not his habitual terrain. Melegal recovered enough to reply coolly, "I was figuring you'd swallowed your tongue, city man. In that gaudy black attire and hat I thought you'd be too embarrassed to open your mouth."

"Hah! Fine guess, Melegal, but compared to that filthy sock on your head my hat is simply glorious. My, my, but you've certainly grown since I last saw you living like a rat in Bone. You must be rather uncomfortable outside the city, I should think."

"No more than you, McKnight. It's not the first time I've been here, and far from the last."

Melegal stood coolly with his hands open wide, palms outward and in the air, as McKnight came around in front of him. The two men from the City of Bone—the thief and the former thief turned detective—stood eye to eye, while between them Quickster continued to munch happily. A few quiet seconds passed.

"Why exactly are you looking for me, McKnight?"

"Well, now," McKnight mused. "I could offer you an explanation, or I could just shoot this bolt through your eye socket and go and get paid. No hard feelings, of course." He took aim through his sight at Melegal's eye socket. Noticing the wry look in the thief's eye, McKnight eased off and continued. "You knew you were being pursued by the Royals, which is why you and your large companion, the Darkslayer or whatever, fled Bone. Myself, I'm merely the hired help of the Royal Almen House. This situation is rather unusual, in that it's taken me out of the city. Somehow you fellows managed to tangle with that Royal Almen brat Tonio, who—you may wish to know before you die—is alive and present with me. As a matter of fact, he's just preparing to dispatch your brutish friend once and for all, with some additional assistance from an underling and a foul magical creature called an imp."

"Boy, McKnight, all this trouble over little ol' us? Seems a bit much. So how much is this gig supposed to pay you?" enquired the thief. "I'd hate to think you went to all this effort for nothing. I mean, what if you don't achieve your objective?" And in the dimming light McKnight thought he noticed a small flicker of a wink.

Somewhat perplexed, he regained his composure and refocused his crossbow on Melegal's eye. "Goodbye, Melegal." He slowly squeezed the trigger until it clicked, but no bolt fired. Alarmed, he pulled the second trigger.

The unexpected click of the misfired crossbow seemed to echo in the shocked silence. Melegal chuckled. Then, mockingly he twirled the crossbow bolts in and out of his fingers in a blur.

"How...?!" McKnight dropped his crossbow and reached for his daggers and short sword. They, too, were missing.

Two silvery flashes caught the red moonlight as they sliced through the air and went thunk into McKnight's chest. McKnight clutched at them, trying to remove his cherished daggers, but the poison he had tipped them with stopped any further movement. His own former student had turned the tables on him. Melegal strolled over calmly with McKnight's short sword and pointed its tip into McKnight's bloodied throat. The hireling of the House of Almen, on his knees vomiting blood, asked his final question through blood-splattered lips. "How did you do that?"

"Not sure, exactly. I think it's this hideous hat of mine that allows me to hypnotize my victims," said Melegal, "or whatever you consider yourself to be." Then he leaned in to stare directly into McKnight's watering eyes. "I never liked you when I was a kid, and I still remember why. I think it's time you know what you'll be remembered for." Melegal stood straight up and examined the fine short sword he had removed from McKnight moments earlier. The blade was light as a dagger and sharp as a razor, and Melegal's eyes and hands caressed its fine craftsmanship. "Thanks, McKnight. Nice to have it back after all these years."

Then he gathered Quickster and departed. The detective from the City of Bone lay on his back on the hard, slowly bloodying ground, staring at the sky between the treetops, and wondered what would happen when he died.

⌒

Heavy clangs were ringing down on the Darkslayer's iron-banded shield. The forceful blows of Tonio's long sword could have shattered a far larger shield as the deranged half-dead Royal swung heavy two-handed blows as if trying to hack through it to reach the man he hated so violently. The Darkslayer could not engage his demented foe as Eep kept buzzing in, high and low, jabbing at his exposed limbs with thick, sharp talons. The flanking tactic forced him to keep shifting awkwardly to avoid falling prey to the attacks, but Brool's spike did well to parry the swift imp, time after time. The situation wasn't entirely new to the warrior; he knew what was required, but the opportunity was not presenting itself as easily as in the past.

The underling cleric stood within a short distance of the melee. Oran was fascinated that the human was somehow withstanding Tonio's attacks, blow after blow. Never had Oran witnessed either man or underling withstand such heightened ferocity, but Oran knew that the Darkslayer was no mere man. Now he saw why he had become the scourge of the underlings. As fast as Eep was, he had managed only a few good cuts to the sinewy arms and legs of the great human, and though they bled freely and looked bad, they were superficial wounds at best. After many centuries of life experience, Oran knew that the longer his pawns went on struggling to dispose of the big warrior, the more likely they were to fall prey to a trap. Oran decided it was time to put an end to what should long since have ended. From his thin, purplish lips the cleric began to mutter an incantation in a low, barely audible tone. Yet to the keen ears of the Darkslayer, and with the aid of his helm, it was audible enough.

The Darkslayer knew the sound of an underling spellcaster as well as he knew the cry of the wind. The cleric had done what the big blonde warrior been waiting for, and with the location of his last enemy revealed, the flanking game he played with Tonio and Eep could finally end. With Tonio's tireless blows still hammering in a steady rhythm on his shield, and the imp still flying endlessly in and out, he was ready to act. And act he did. Brool parried as Eep zipped in with a low slash, and while the imp retreated for another attack the Darkslayer quickly turned on the unsuspecting Tonio. Tonio's sword clanged one more time off the Darkslayer's shield and then no more. He did not see it coming; no man could. Brool's return swing from parrying the imp caught both Tonio's elbows and severed them cleanly with its razor-sharp edge. Tonio's fresh stumps went on chopping the air with vigor, and the astonishment and anguish in his eyes reflected his last remaining shred of humanity, before the Darkslayer brought Brool down to cleave his head and body in two. One half of Tonio fell to the left and the other to the right.

Not pausing to savor the moment, the Darkslayer whirled, impaling the bewildered imp on Brool's spike, and as Eep squealed in agony, he rushed in the direction of the underling cleric. Eep dangled screaming on the serrated spike and struggled vainly to pull himself free. But the imp's screeching could not distract the meditative Oran from his spell, for his deep concentration could not be broken. Oran was feeling a renewed sense of confidence and power. Time seemed to be at his will, and everything seemed to take place in slow motion; he had never felt such magic within him. It was as if the gates that held the magic of Bish had burst open for him. Coolly he waited for the Darkslayer to enter his path so he could wipe this brutish human from the face of Bish forever.

Eep's big eye saw Oran first. "Now you will die, human!" the imp hissed. "Drop your axe and surrender, fool!"

But the sight of the underling cleric only made the Darkslayer's eyelets glow brighter.

"No, you all die today!" he growled.

The imp laughed scornfully as the Darkslayer hoisted Brool high above his head and charged into Oran's path a mere thirty strides away. Oran was screaming aloud now, his spell fully prepared, and his triumph imminent.

"Die now, Darkslayer, at the hand of the great underling Oran!"

A narrow bolt of red-blue fire shot straight at the Darkslayer as he swung Brool down.

"No!" screamed Eep as Brool caught the deadly bolt and the imp was instantly fried to blackened char.

Oran howled in rage and astonishment. The bolt that should have shattered the axe and destroyed the man had not, although its blast had knocked the warrior flat onto his back. Brool's astonishing power was now evident to the evil cleric, for the Darkslayer was still intact and moving with the great axe still firm in his grasp, smoking.

Quickly Oran readied another powerful blasting spell, fully prepared to destroy everything that lived and breathed within a mile, so intent was his rage.

The Darkslayer was shaken but able to move slowly, despite the pain that coursed through his hardened body. The jolt had stunned not only his body but also his mind. Fighting through the pain was not easy as he lay on his back, longing to rest. But his survival instincts would not let him give in, not until he was dead. Slowly he rose to one knee and caught sight of the underling preparing another spell. He dropped his shield and breathed in deep as he stared at his opponent, letting all his fury and hatred for the underling kind quickly rebuild in him.

Now the pain was erased from his mind and only the urge to destroy the underling remained. Like a cat he was on both feet, springing at full speed back into the path of the last blast, Brool raised high in both hands. Oran could not believe that the human could be so stupid. He let loose the next spell prematurely at the angry juggernaut approaching at a mere twenty paces. But the Dark-slayer was ready. He dived to the ground as the lightening cracked red-blue over his back, singeing the hairs on his neck and leaving his clothing burnt and smoldering. This time he was not stunned, just maddened, yet closer still to the underling. Then Oran's scream could be heard for miles as it carried through the giant trees of the Great Forest like a siren. It was the most powerful of underling spells that he now used as a last resort to save his own life. It's hideous shriek was destined to shatter the Darkslayer's eardrums. And so it would have, if not for the helm he wore. Unfazed by the ear-splitting screech, the Darkslayer rose from the ground once more and charged the final twenty strides in an instant, leapt into the air, and came down swinging Brool at full force into the side of Oran's screaming head. Oran's head was sliced off clean below his black eyes, and his screaming spell was silenced as his body collapsed on the forest floor.

The Darkslayer stood still, breathing heavily, still shaking with rage. Only his boots and his shorts remained, for his clothing had burned away, but among the scorch marks on the rippling muscles of his torso the giant V remained, spread across the breadth of his shoulder blades. His thick purple veins pulsated, and blood and gore was burned red and black all over him as if he had just crawled out of the mouth of a volcano. He was the picture of every raw, wild, and powerful element on Bish. Brool hung in his right hand, and his eyes still blazed through the eyelets of his spiked helm, still held by the leather chinstrap under his grizzled chin. Casually he banged Brool's spike onto the heel of his boot, knocking the charred remains of the imp to the forest floor. He inhaled deeply, filling his powerful chest with the cool night air, and then let out a bellowing battle cry so loud and deep that time seemed to stop until it was finished.

Invigorated, and with his battle rage calmed, he picked up his shield and turned to look for Melegal.

Chongo's four ears perked up just an instant before the unbearable inhuman shriek of some powerful being pierced the forest. None had ever before heard a sound that so stabbed and seared their ears and each prayed never to hear it again, for long after it had passed their ears still rang and their stomachs remained curdled.

"What was that?!" Georgio gasped and then gagged.

"Turn back!" Lefty wailed, panic-stricken, with one hand over his eyes and a finger in his ear. "I can't take it, make this dog turn around!" But Georgio held him tight. "Don't worry, Mood and Chongo won't let anything happen to us!"

The grizzle-faced Mood just grunted through his red beard and then bellowed back in joy. The battle couldn't be far off and he was tired of babysitting and ready to act. Soon a human-like roar reached Chongo's ears, and though Mood, Georgio, and Lefty were not sure of its source, Chongo's keen ears recognized his master. His two heads began to howl like puppies in love, and Mood and Georgio realized its meaning with relief.

Grinning, Georgio proudly yelled, "Lefty, you're gonna meet my big buddy!"

"Oh. . ." said the halfling weakly, still clinging on for his life.

Melegal and Quickster cut through the forest straight towards the cracks, screams, and howls they were hearing. Melegal knew it was Venir, and he knew he was very close despite the unfamiliar dark forest, for that battle howl could only have come from the lungs of the Darkslayer. Cheerful thoughts of returning to Bone began to dance in his head. It was the simple things about the City of Bone that Melegal enjoyed so much, like skimming in the bars, breaking and entering a wealthy family's home, and taking jewels on an as-needed basis. Certainly, great perils lurked within the walls of the City of Bone, some greater than he had encountered on this trip, but at least in Bone there were always pleasantries nearby, and it was home after all.

Quickster slowed, interrupting his daydreams. There were cobwebs all around. His homesickness intensified, but Quickster continued his trot, slowly and carefully weaving among the web-covered trees. For whatever reason he felt no danger, even though he was freaked out. Whatever made the cobwebs must be dead or gone, because the webs were disintegrating as they passed. Now a clearing lay ahead. His gray eyes made out a hulking silhouette coming slowly his way; a familiar figure with a spiked helm and a mighty axe, but what most gave him away was the great smile that shone in the moonlight when he saw Melegal and Quickster approaching.

"Hah!" roared the silhouette. "Great night in the forest, Me!"

"Humph?" Melegal was unimpressed. "You go berserk and run off. . . my donkey does the same. . . I get totally lost, then I get trapped and attacked by McKnight from Bone. . . I have to kill him and then come and try to save your butt. . .great night!"

"You killed someone from Bone? Then I guess that's the last of them. Don't figure anyone else it still looking for us. But it's not time to run back home just yet, Me," Venir added with a slap on his shoulder.

Melegal rolled his eyes. "Great," he muttered.

"Come take a look at who I killed here. It's that Tonio guy from the bar and the stables."

"Shouldn't he have been dead already? You almost beat him to death, then Chongo chewed him to death. How does that work?"

"Magic, Me. Good ol' evil magic. Take a look."

Melegal looked at the corpse, split down the middle with arms cut off at the elbows. As horrible as it appeared, Tonio had not bled at all. A chill ran up Melegal's spine.

"Vee, that is some serious magic. He was already dead when you killed him—or killed him again, that is. Who has that kind of power?"

"Well, did you hear that battle earlier?"

Melegal nodded.

"That's who, is my guess." He pointed. "That was an underling cleric, very powerful. Certainly the most powerful I've ever crossed, and I've crossed plenty. He's dead as a rock now, though. I'm more concerned that an underling and a human were both coming after us."

"Or after the Darkslayer."

"It's strange. This Tonio character must be way up among the Royals and have one powerful family. But these three that are dead are the only ones who know what we look like. So maybe we'll be safe now."

"So now what?" Melegal was almost smiling.

"We make a fire and find something to eat. How's that sound?"

"Good."

The sounds around them in the Great Forest of Bish had returned to normal. The forest owls hooted and the crickets chirped in unison while the orange fire glowed. It was only a small camp fire, but its warmth and light soothed Melegal's soul. Relaxed, the pale, skinny man from the City of Bone lay back against the belly of Quickster, who was also enjoying the warmth of the fire. All was well in the forest. It was the most peace they had known in weeks. The Great Forest harbored very little evil, siding rather with the better nature of Bish. Its animals lived in a sanctuary that was neither questioned nor explained. The Great Forest of Bish was just what its name implied, and for a moment Melegal could vaguely understand why Venir preferred this to the city life. He quickly dozed off as Venir, stoking the fire with a stick, stand up abruptly, peered about, and then moved silently past Melegal and Quickster and back into the Great Forest.

All too quickly the morning crept up upon Melegal, and the sounds of the awakening forest became louder with every moment. Unlike the sounds of the city, these sounds couldn't be quashed by closing a window or a thick oaken door. Groggily, Melegal could hear loud snoring on the far side of Quickster. Then he heard Venir's voice talking quietly somewhere in front of him as sunlight began to shine into the forest. The thief was starting to stretch, when his hand brushed against something humanoid.

"Agh!" Melegal yelled, jumping clear over the smoldering fire in one bound. With McKnight's daggers drawn, Melegal peered at a small humanoid disappearing behind Quickster.

"Hey, get off me, Lefty. I'm trying to sleep."

It was the familiar voice of Georgio. There was a loud laugh from Venir and Mood, who were as bright-eyed and bushy-tailed as could be this early in the morning.

"What's the matter, Melegal? Got a bed bug?" piped the grizzly giant red dwarf.

"What was that creature, Venir?"

"That's Georgio's new halfling friend, Lefty," Venir laughed.

"Hey, Me, it's me!" beamed Georgio. "Meet my buddy, Lefty Lightfoot. He's a halfling! See? Look!" Georgio was just pulling Lefty over when the halfling bounded from his grasp and ran almost right onto Melegal's toes, stopping short when Melegal's drawn daggers nearly pierced his tiny neck.

"Easy Melegal, he's just greeting you. Haven't you met a halfling before?" asked Venir.

"No." Melegal said flatly, and walked off.

Georgio put his hand on Lefty's shoulder. "It's not you. He's not a morning person."

Then Georgio and Lefty smelled something good and their stomachs began growling. "What's for breakfast?" they asked, almost in unison. Lefty was stamping his little feet and clapping in excitement.

"Mood's been cooking up a young stag. Big as a deer but tastier. That'll hold your hunger for most of the day," said Venir, as Mood presented their breakfasts.

'Delicious, don't you think, Lefty?" said Georgio, chewing the steaming hot meat happily.

Lefty could only stare in bewilderment. The food was so hot, he had to wait patiently for it to cool while his burnt tongue recovered. As he waited, his hand strayed to his pocket, where he had quietly tucked something that had him smiling widely for the first time in many days. After meeting Venir the previous night, and hearing his account of the battle, the curious halfling had gone to explore the battle site, and among the robes of the dead underling cleric he had found two red, bullet-sized gemstones that shone mysteriously.

When they had all eaten their stag meat, Venir decided to present Georgio with Tonio's long sword. The boy was thrilled almost beyond words.

"Wow, Venir! This is the best gift ever!" He twirled it awkwardly, pretending to slay everything in sight. "Are you going to teach me to use it?" he asked.

"You bet. It's one of the finest swords I've come by. I couldn't believe it didn't break against my shield. It came down with force on every blow, but there isn't a nick on it. It's big but it's light, and one of the finest of its kind. Those Royals must have one mighty good weaponsmith. It's a keeper, Georgio. You take good care of it and I'm sure it'll take care of you." He gave the boy's shoulder a firm slap, and Georgio grinned in speechless thanks. Venir was clearly his hero.

"All right, already, can we go home now?" asked Melegal, now fully awake and full, and more than ready to get back to a real bed in his own bedroom.

"We're gonna try," said Venir. "But things could get tough. Mood has word of many more underlings about. No one knows why, but we can only hope they don't get too close before I get you home," he answered.

"Well, if anyone's still looking for us, I'd rather take my chances back in Bone. At least there are no witnesses left to bother us there. And there no one can find me if I don't want them to. So get me back. I need a hot bath. And so do you. Look at you, letting your dog lick the muck off you. It's disgusting!"

They all chuckled, broke camp, and saddled up. Then they headed northeast out of the Great Forest of Bish.

CHAPTER 16

WELCOME TO THE WARFIELD

The two orange suns had risen as usual from the east and the west, and they blazed now upon the open Outlands, making the ground hazy to the naked eye. The sparse vegetation yielded little for the humanoid appetite, although enormous green cacti, bone trees, fire bushes, red toads, leather lizards, palm trees, and even sunflowers survived without oases, although they were hard to come by. This particular section of the Outlands was a bit more climatic, though. It was far to the southeast of the City of Bone, east of the Red Clay Forest, northwest of the Great Forest of Bish and just northeast of Dwarven Hole, and it was the most dangerous place in the whole of this barren land. It had been home to more battles, wars, and acts of terror than any other place in the world of Bish. This dry and dusty area had come to be known as the Warfield.

The Warfield lay in the center of the most productive land in the world of Bish, where the majority of the tiny world's population lived and thrived. The small villages surrounding it had distanced themselves as far as possible from the Warfield, which was inhospitable for occupancy or commerce. The Warfield was always the hottest and most humid spot on the planet at any time of day, and only the toughest creatures occupied it. It was also the place where all the chest beating of the races of Bish began and ended. For no skirmish, battle, or war was worth recalling that did not take place at the Warfield. As with so many other things in Bish, no one knew or cared why they battled in that place; they simply did. It was where true warriors came to earn their badges of honor.

For centuries the Warfield had been devouring the bones and armor of the greatest warriors and wizards that ever lived, but all traces of these events quickly dissipated in the hard and bitter land and were only too quickly forgotten. No one ever cared to visit the final resting place of the Warfield's fallen heroes and villains. It was an unyieldingly loathsome place where tempers would flare between even the best of friends and the closest of family members. The survivors of the battles that broke out here never returned for the fallen; they took whoever they could and left the rest to the impossible climate.

There were survivors, though; many had survived battles at the Warfield, and they became renowned throughout the land. The toughest of each and every race were Warfield veterans and their names were revered among their kin, but those who had survived more than once, whether twice or even a dozen times, were undoubtedly the toughest men and women on Bish. One would know it at a glance, sometimes, for the Warfield always left its mark, a mark on their persona that was indescribable yet always discernable. Some boasted of their excursions, while others kept silent about their personal horrors, but the quiet ones always seemed to revisit their restless war demons in the hope of putting them to rest forever.

One man and one woman who had survived, but had never been able to erase their demons, had remained there. And now they were once again to witness a great battle in the history of Bish unfold. Unfit for society, they were the Nameless Two, sandaled, clothed in dull white robes from head to toe, and insane. They lived in a cave behind a rocky crag on a gargantuan hill in the Warfield. With nothing left to live for, these grizzled veterans practiced their fighting and survival skills over and over, tempering themselves into perfect Warfield warriors. They were known as nothing more than ghosts, and they showed up whenever they chose to and fought whoever they wished, but mostly they mercy killed those who could not make it home after a battle—though usually not without some kind of fight, of course.

Today the Nameless Two stood outside on their craggy stoop high above their cave, watching a strange event unfolding far away. An underling Badoon brigade had ventured into the Warfield to block the passage northwards, or so it seemed. A squadron of giant red dwarf rangers appeared to be flanking the Badoon brigade from the west. The Nameless Two had learnt how to harness the powerful magic deep within the cave they occupied, which they used now to assist their sight. It gave them the vision they needed for all things occurring within the Warfield. It was this secret that had allowed them to survive for so long, and a secret they would never risk losing to another. It was a secret that came at a price, but it was a price they were willing to pay.

Venir was leading the venturing party as they headed north towards the lower rim of the Outlands. Melegal was clearly perplexed and agitated by a decision that had been made without consulting him, and it did not help that he was at the mercy of his friends to return home.

"Why are we heading north again, and not back through the Red

Clay Forest? I have absolutely no desire to try to pass through the Warfield."

"We're just going to the rim, Me, take it easy," Venir replied grimly.

"If you're going anywhere near the Warfield, count me out." Melegal announced defiantly. "I know you'll go in and I want nothing to do with that dreadful place. I've heard enough of your stupid barroom bragging to know that you'll never pass up the chance of another story to brag about. And if even half the bull crap you say is true, it's more than enough reason to know that the Warfield's clearly no place I ever want to be. So *I* am heading west to the Red Clay Forest, with or without you. I'll take my own chances."

Even Georgio and Lefty seemed to agree with Melegal in this case, and they edged a little closer to the unpleasant thief, who plainly did not care for either of them.

"Whatcha think, Mood?" Venir asked the bushy-faced giant dwarf.

"Trap," he replied cautiously. "If it ain't all a trap, I'm a halfling's uncle."

"North?"

"North, south, east, anywhere but west. They're waiting, Vee. Exactly where, I don't know."

"Who's waiting, and who's setting traps?" Georgio asked.

"Underlings," answered Mood.

"More underlings?" shivered Lefty, his nightmare revived. "Not the ones that killed my village?"

"I'm afraid, Lefty," Venir answered from Chongo's back, "those *are* the ones. To get home we're gonna have to cut through 'em. Them or something else."

Silence fell on the party as each contemplated what might be their next—and possibly final—move.

Melegal broke the silence. "Well, I don't care. I'm going back through the Red Clay Forest, with or without the rest of you." He patted Quickster dourly. "Whatever's looking for you, probably isn't looking for us." Then hung his head, somewhat ashamed.

"Melegal, we're not splitting up now!" said Venir. "They want us to head to the Red Clay Forest; it wouldn't be so wide open if they didn't. They know enough about where we are. If you want to get home alive, stick with us. And that means *all* of you!" With a low roar Venir nudged Chongo forward, and Mood followed. Melegal and the other two hesitated. Then they sighed in unison and followed, despite their ever-growing dread of what might befall them next.

Mood trotted up to Venir and Chongo. "Wait. Let's head west towards my dwarven kin. We can maybe slip around these underlings, or at worst, perhaps I can slip our friends around the underlings and back home. Whatcha say?"

"That's as good a plan as we've got, I guess. I hate to drag 'em into all this. You'll have to look out for them in case I can't," the brawny slayer answered somberly.

"Just don't go any further north, and let's see what happens when it happens," the dwarf finished with a wink, and lit up another sweet-leafed cigar. Its mellow smoke carried slowly back and soothed the minds of the boy, the halfling, and the gaunt thief who rode quietly at the back.

"It seems they are on to us, brother Catten," Verbard commented in the midst of their long meditation on the edge of the Red Clay Forest. "Shall we wait, or shall we depart for the Warfield?" They had sensed that the Darkslayer and his companions had not taken the bait of a clear and easy path through the Red Clay Forest on their way to the City of Bone.

"Oh, I say we have waited enough. It is such a long time since I witnessed a lengthy battle. And a Vicious-led Badoon brigade does promise a salivating new amusement." He licked his lips, silver eyes flashing in anticipation. "I would think the risk worth taking, brother. I don't know about you, but I feel our day has come to finish off the Darkslayer. I am not boasting when I say that I feel more powerful than ever?"

"Quite so, I feel just the same." Verbard's golden eyes shone with elation. "I feel ready for anything."

"I wonder, is it just us, or do all of our kind feel this way, Verbard."

"Well, if it is all of us—underlings, that is—then the Darkslayer is doomed, and Master Sinway will be very pleased."

"Ah, I had almost forgotten that Master Sinway had set us this charge. Perhaps he does not feel as we do, brother," he hissed.

"Yes," Verbard answered in an even lower hiss.

The two top underling lords longed to remove Master Sinway at some time during their lengthy existence, but neither could hope to achieve it without the other. Though they never spoke of it, both brothers thought constantly of usurping the rule of the underlings from Master Sinway. Each plotted for the two of them to team up against the long-tenured underling Master and put him to death; then at some future point, to kill his brother. But for now, first things first. They had waited centuries, so a few more decades of planning could not be too much to endure. With these thoughts in mind, the two underling lords cast a spell upon one another that took them sailing quickly through the sky, unaided by wings, from the Red Clay Forest to the edge of the Warfield, where battle sounds were in full cry somewhere in the distance.

One lone forest mage, who had arrived too late to partake in the deadly encounter with Catten and Verbard, had witnessed the whole terrifying spectacle, yet survived. Fortunately, he had escaped the notice of the two underlings, and had watched them depart like ghosts into the sky and out of sight. Morty, floating in the same brown robes as his comrades, was now trying to gather their ashes for storage in a makeshift wooden urn. Although they had been prematurely cremated, he could still feel the magic from within their ashes. He had managed to gather most of their ashes into various pouches when he came upon a peculiar-looking silver coin. Picking it up to study it, Morty saw the face of the underling Lord Verbard staring back at him. Terrified, the forest mage tried in vain to throw the coin away, but it would not leave his hand.

"No! Get away!" Morty screamed at the coin, squirming and wriggling as he tried to brush the coin from his hand against the ground and branches. But it was futile. Finally, he looked at Verbard's face on the gleaming coin and pleaded, "Please, be gone!"

But the evil image looked back, winked a golden eye, and hissed, "Goodbye!"

Thunder crackled in the air. Morty lifted his hooded head. Looking in horror into the darkening sky he saw a blinding white flash as he was blown to smithereens. The coin dropped to the ground to await its next victim, and somewhere far away Lord Verbard chuckled.

⁓

The Warfield was living up to its name this day under the blazing suns of Bish. From the west two squadrons of giant dwarven rangers had flanked and fully surprised the underling Badoon brigade. On Bish, the giant dwarfs were also known as the bloodrangers. There were less than a hundred of these bloodrangers on Bish, making them among the rarest of races. They were direct kin to the dwarfs, and were sometimes born to that short, stocky race. Every decade or so, a new bloodranger would be born among the thousands of dwarfs, and were immediately distinguishable by their size as well as their bright red—sometimes blood red—hair. The bloodranger babies stayed with their mother and father for less than a year before being turned over to be raised and fully trained by the bloodranger clan until they were men. Only they knew what went on deep within the mountains at Dwarven Hole, and this they did not share. When a new one emerged, he was a fully fledged bloodranger ready to take on any and all comers on Bish. The bloodrangers were the pride and joy of the dwarfs.

A dozen hardened underling hunters had already fallen before the expert aim of the heavy crossbow bolts fired by the bloodranger's unanticipated onslaught. As stunned as the underlings were, it was not long before they were fighting in full force, especially with the Vicious leading the Badoon brigade. Soon the fight was being taken back to the bloodrangers and one of the most violent skirmishes ever to take place in the Warfield had begun.

One squadron of bloodrangers, dressed in red and brown leather armor, squared up against the remaining five squadrons of the Badoon brigade. Six powerful dwarven warriors fought hard, wielding their famous giant hand axes, while the remaining six fired their heavy crossbow bolts at the underlings with bull's eye precision. Heavily armored dwarven women did the reloading of the crossbows, while several other dwarven women clerics prepared healing and protection spells for casting. The female dwarfs wore chainmail dresses and small metal helmets over their thick black hair, framing their pleasant round faces as they worked, intently and diligently, to make sure their men were fully prepared for battle. Each giant dwarven man was supported in all things by at least five hardworking women, who were charged to take care of him always. The fortune of being a bloodranger was that women outnumbered them by over a thousand to one, which gave them plenty to choose from and the certainty of courting whoever they chose. These sweet, yet hardened dwarven women took excellent care of their giant men folk, and saw to it that they were prepared for days such as this. Yet for this day they could not possibly have prepared, for what was about to come from above they had never before witnessed or heard of; nor would they ever forget it.

Just as the next squadron of Badoon underlings was about to clash with the six bloodrangers, a giant wall of flame leapt eight feet into the air, running north–south continuously to prevent any underling from flanking the giant dwarfs and their female support teams. Screeching to a halt in abject rage at the flames, the underling hunters came as close as they could and then switched their short swords and daggers for light crossbows and poisoned bolts. This infuriated the Vicious, who ordered small groups to run through the flames and attack their foes at a single point. The bloodrangers stood among the flames, waiting for them, protected from burning by the magic their women provided. With their short swords drawn again, a dozen Badoons charged into the flames to attack a single bloodranger among the front six. As they tried to overwhelm him he chopped hard with both axes, each hitting its mark and dropping two underlings in the flames. The underlings' discipline and hatred drove them on in the scorching inferno, but as they continued to assault him they fell to his axes one by one. The bloodranger was more than a match for several burning Badoons, but the underlings used their own magic to counter some of the fire's effects, and the next wave of dark bodies started to slow down bloodranger's efforts. They pinned themselves to his arms so that he could swing no more, and finally he was overwhelmed and slain. Screaming in glee at their triumph, they turned to find more prey, and some broke through the flames to the other side, where they were cut down under the relentless fire of the rear rank of bloodrangers with their repeating heavy crossbow bolts. Scrambling to escape the attack, the underlings had either to retreat through the flames or stand and fight. They decided to turn and fight rather than cross back to face the Vicious, but their hesitation cost them heavily as the bolts pierced their temples, throats, eye-sockets, and black hearts. Falling, bleeding, and burning, another dozen underlings died quickly at the hands of the bloodrangers. Two dozen Badoons were now defeated, and four dozen more remained. The odds seemed to favor the dwarven ranks as all the men and women on the western side of the flames maintained their positions and prepared for their next course of action. The bloodrangers were patient and seasoned warriors who did not rush into anything without careful thought. The remaining members of the Badoon brigade maintained their position to the east of the flames and lined up their remaining squadrons north to south. The Warfield was quiet, but for the crackling wall of flame. The Vicious stood boldly in front of the ranks, their hardened black bodies glistening under the two hot red suns without a single drop of sweat. Long, clawed hands opened and closed in unison with the gnashing of their teeth. The savvy dwarven bloodrangers did not fall for this provocation, although provocation was not the deliberate intent of the evil and burly Vicious—it was merely their wicked nature. As the two suns blazed on the Warfield, the morale on both sides remained high, but suddenly the underlings received a dramatic boost as the two powerful magi lords, Verbard and Catten, walked up beside the two Vicious. With barely a whisper, Lord Catten extinguished the wall of flame.

Traveling mostly westward from the Great Forest of Bish, but also slightly north, Venir led the way on foot, shoulder to shoulder with Mood and with Chongo in tow. They were still set on joining Mood's people west of the Warfield. The other three miserable adventurers kept pace behind, with Melegal finding renewed strength to complain with every passing minute. Georgio giggled at Melegal's profanities, many of which he had never heard before.

Lefty took note of all this, but his knowledge of the common language was not enough to follow most of the gutter-mouthed squalor that passed Melegal's lips, much of it probably being made up as he went along. Lefty tried asking Georgio, who just shrugged and giggled, for he had little clue himself what Melegal meant by most of it. Lefty took a keen interest, however, assuming that these strange words were some sort of thieves cant. But Melegal's discontent was evident, and soon they both covered their ears and tried to think of other things. Melegal's caustic mutterings were only making the trip seem longer, and finally Lefty could take no more.

"Please, human," he said loudly, "shut up!"

"You can walk if you like, halfling," Melegal retorted.

"Fine, I can keep up," Lefty answered grimly, and hopped off.

Lefty chose to catch up to Venir and Mood, leaving Georgio unfazed with his bad-tempered friend. Lefty came up beside Chongo, whose left head stared at him and snorted while the right tried to lick him.

The halfling tried not to cringe away from the beastly dog. "Okay, big fella, don't eat me and I'll pet you," he said, putting out a tiny hand for the heads to sniff, which they did. Then they licked it. "Whew, can I ride you?"

To Lefty's surprise, Chongo flopped down. Lefty hopped on, and quickly Chongo was on the move again. Lefty found the big dog's company much more pleasant than Melegal's, and enjoyed scratching his four big floppy ears. Lefty Lightfoot had another new friend, and Chongo looked equally pleased.

The party moved quickly through the plains between the mountain caves of Dwarven Hole and the Great Forest of Bish, but they were still several miles south of the Outlands. Mood hoped they would not get to close to the skirmish that was happening or bound to happen just north of them. But hope was always scarce on Bish, and things had been mysteriously changing over the past days, so that the big dwarf was feeling edgy. Concern for his kin was praying on his mind, and the safety of his friends concerned him as well. Mood tried to focus on getting back to Dwarven Hole and then on to the battle if need be. Clearly his brethren should not have trouble with the underling brood, but the air was different this day.

Then Venir halted. Coincidentally, at that same moment, Lord Catten whispered in the distance. The big warrior quickly jammed on his helmet, brandished his great axe Brool, strapped his shield onto his back, and howled like a hundred warriors gone mad.

Chongo howled too as he caught sight of the Darkslayer, who peered back towards his friends through the now glowing eyelets of his helm, and then took off in a dead sprint due north.

Mood caught Chongo quickly by the reigns and hopped on before the big dog could run after him.

"Who was that?" Lefty exclaimed in fear.

"That was Vee," answered Mood, puzzled by the question.

"It was? It didn't look like him."

"I suppose not, but he's on our side, you know."

"I'd hate not to be on his side."

"Me too."

"Melegal," the dwarf asked quickly, "what do you want to do? Follow Vee or keep going west?"

"Follow Vee!" screamed Georgio like a battle cry, hoisting his new long sword high into the air and howling like his hero, Venir.

Melegal rolled his eyes. "If I have to fight underlings to get home, so be it!"

"Can Quickster keep up with Chongo, then?" asked Mood.

"Now you're ticking me off," huffed Melegal, spurring his quick-pony. The shaggy mount shot off like a race horse, almost losing Georgio, who howled in glee. Passing Chongo in a breeze, the pony's little legs pumped rapidly and Chongo jumped right in behind, with Mood and Lefty still on his back. Lefty hung onto Mood and closed his eyes, while Mood grasped Chongo's reigns, amazed at the speed of the thief's quick-pony. But could they catch up with Venir? That was another matter entirely, as the possessed man was nowhere in sight. But Chongo knew where to go, and so did Mood.

"Yer've made yer point, man," Mood bellowed to Melegal. "Now let me lead so we don't get lost."

As Melegal began to slow, Mood came up beside him. The city thief smiled broadly. "Pretty fast, eh?" He lifted his eyebrows proudly, awaiting a compliment.

"Guess so," Mood answered gruffly. "Now let's get after him."

The party galloped over the plains, mile after mile, without coming anywhere close to the Darkslayer. Clearly the Darkslayer could run full speed for miles, though they could not. Their quick pace would have to do, and they hoped to catch up with the Dark-slayer in time to be of some aid before it was all over. It wouldn't be long, that much was certain to both Melegal and Mood, for the Warfield evidently awaited them all.

Something in the universe was raging, but then again, there were always things raging in the universe. Time and again, chance or manipulation would cause such an event to occur. Scorch had recently manipulated an event on Bish, as he had done elsewhere many times before. And now Bish was quickly coming to an end; but Trinos arrived. She was just in time to limit the havoc Scorch had wrought. Damage had been done, however, to her tiny world of Bish. The ripple effects could not be reversed, for a door had been opened and innocence lost. Trinos implemented some hasty pro-tection to her world to mend this catastrophe, and it would have to hold, because Scorch had not stayed long enough to see it through, nor did not have to. Her pet project was done for, though. She seethed, something that should never have happened, but it felt good. Her search for Scorch through infinity had begun, and Trinos would not stop until she had found him and received and explanation for his actions.

~

As Catten extinguished the wall of fire, the veteran bloodrangers repositioned themselves as if they had been in this same situation a dozen times before, though they had not. The closest Badoon squadron was almost upon them before they could fully retreat, but instead, most of the underlings found themselves falling into a massive hidden pit set up ages ago by the dwarfs of Dwarven Hole. Thick dwarven bolts pierced the Badoon underlings trapped in the pit while the other underlings fired back with poisoned, but mostly harmless, light crossbows. The Vicious were furious, but Catten and Verbard merely cackled. Invigorated, the two magi lords began pushing back the bloodrangers with their own brand of firepower. Bolts of energy shot like missiles from their hands, blasting their targets with deadly accuracy. The dwarfs were roasted by the powerful magic but they did not die or fall, although they were forced into a rapid retreat. The underling brothers laughed.

Doom was upon all the fighting giants of Dwarven Hole; they were outmaneuvered and clearly overpowered by the underling lords. The remaining eleven bloodrangers circled their women and fought valiantly as the remaining underlings attacked them at all points with spells, bolts, arrows, and swords. The intensity was indescribable. The long-bearded bloodrangers with their bushy faces began singing in thunderous voices in complete defiance of the siege now befalling them. Chopping axes carved deep into black underling bone and heavy bolts impaled underlings left and right, but the sheer numbers of underling hunters and the superior magic of their magi lords were overwhelming the brave fighters. They sang and bled from wounds that weakened them by the second, but their women, their wonderful working women, shouted encouragement and stayed within their men's protective circle, casting spells of healing, strength, and vitality to help get them through each and every critical second. And the bloodrangers held their own as their blood and sweat formed pools on the dusty ground of the Warfield.

From their crag not far away, the Nameless Two saw it all, and the battle they were witnessing was a beautiful thing to them; so beautiful that it spurred them to thoughts of action. But the two troublesome underling lords caused them to hesitate.

Then Verbard looked at Catten, and Catten looked back at Verbard. "Are we being watched?" said Verbard.

"I believe so."

"How can that be?"

"I don't know. We should find out."

"I think so, Catten. Let us take the initiative. The Vicious will finish things off if these dwarfs hold out much longer. But I would have expected the Darkslayer to be here by now. I can't bear the thought that he might have flanked us, yet it may be so. Now, let us go and see what lies behind that crag."

Catten nodded, and like two ghosts they sailed through the air to the crag, cruising fearlessly towards the powerful source of magic they sensed from this out-of-the-way landmark, which looked like a mountain but was in fact merely a rocky hill with a large cave opening. Inside the cave they noted little, but a glance showed that it was occupied, although the source of the magic was not evident. They paced about trying to find something, but the all-seeing source they knew was there was not revealed. Finally they stepped out of the cave mouth and looked around.

"Do you see what I see, Catten?"

"I see it all, my brother."

"This is new, completely new and fascinating. I can see the whole area for miles just as plain as the nose on your face. I am stunned!" There was excitement in his voice.

"Stunning it is. But even more stunning is that those stubborn dwarfs are still fighting and the Vicious have still not acted. This whole thing should be over by now. I hate to think that we might have to go back to clean up when we could be enjoying the victory from here." Catten's silver eyes flashed in rage.

"Perhaps we can do what we must from here, if need be, brother," piped Verbard. "It is certainly worth a try." He sounded almost cheerful.

"Ooh. . . a good idea, indeed. Let's wait until the suns start to set; the moment is almost upon us. I like doing such things at night rather than in blazing sunlight."

"Certainly. Do you happen to notice something coming from the south at the moment? It's rather faint, but coming this way."

"Hmm, I don't see it, Verbard. Ah, now I do. Is this who I think it is? Finally?"

In silence the two peered into the path of two searing eyes running toward the Warfield from the south. They might not normally have observed his presence, but magic aided them. Just as they hoped, the Darkslayer was finally coming. As robust as Catten and Verbard had been feeling, neither relished the thought of possibly having to battle the scourge of the underlings themselves. But their hatred ran deep for this human who had managed to slay hundreds, possibly thousands, of underlings over the years to their great embarrassment. The underling lords never knew for sure how many deaths of their kind the Darkslayer was personally accountable for, but they secretly assumed he was behind the many unexplained deaths as well as the known ones. The toll had grown high over the years. The stories they had heard and the variety of descriptions of the man had never seemed entirely believable until now. But as he approached, the brothers made an uncharacteristic decision.

"Let us see if we can take him out from here, right now, Verbard."

"What shall it be, then? I suggest we slow him down, smother him, and burn him alive with all means at our disposal."

"After which we shall walk down there, skin him, and take his head from his shoulders forever," Catten finished.

The two stepped back and began preparing their spells. So consumed were they with this opportunity and confident in their power that they never gave another thought to whose den they were in or who may have been watching them. Whoever it was had fled upon their arrival, and they felt no further concern. Quickly they set about their spell making. So well trained were the two underling lords in the art of magic that they did not even utter a word; they needed only to think the thoughts uninterrupted and focus upon their target. Only Master Sinway and a handful of others had mastered this sorcerer's art. The two magi brothers focused steadily, their eyes wide, staring at their target over a mile away. Powerful energy surged into both of them simultaneously, but they were not alone, and nor were their thoughts left to continue uninterrupted. For the Nameless Two were upon them, and their moment of triumph was over. The Darkslayer would have to wait.

In the world of Bish none cared about how or why things happened as they did. Things were as they were, and none gave this a single thought. The bloodranger dwarfs did not question why they were being obliterated by the Badoon brigade when in the past they had always defeated underling groups without a scratch. The underling warriors gave no thought to why they were succeeding against the dwarfs when they had never done so in battles past. In other worlds in the universe the creatures cared to keep such scores, but not on Bish. For that is how Trinos had created Bish. But Scorch had caused an imbalance, which Trinos had had to correct. There had always been an equalizer for good and evil on Bish, and as the battle between these two forces swung back and forth over decades, centuries, and millennia, the score remained eternally the same—until Scorch decided to change the score. Although Trinos had now changed it back, Bish would never be the same. And to get things back on course, the equalizer of Bish had work to do, whether he knew it or not. Perhaps the bloodranger dwarfs that survived this day might wonder why things had unfolded so uncharacteristically this day, and the underlings from the Badoon brigade might possibly wonder the same. But it was just possible that the underlings would not get the chance to wonder about anything at all. For the fury of the unstoppable Darkslayer was coming their way. He was coming to slay them all.

Like a galloping horse the Darkslayer came in from the south, charging directly towards the underling hunters that had surrounded the bloodranger dwarfs. Venir's mind could not comprehend why he had moved so far so fast, but it was beyond him to slow his pace. His body no longer seemed his own. The spiked helm was strapped to his iron jaw and the eyelets burned like black fire, more so than ever before, leaving streaks in the air behind him. No clothing was left on the brute of a man but for some grimy bloodied pants and boots of indistinguishable color. With white knuckles he gripped Brool in his right hand, while his iron-banded shield was strapped to his left arm. The remaining rear flanks of the Badoon brigade were so caught up in their battle that they failed to see the astonishing spectacle of the Darkslayer coming upon them.

Even the highly alert Vicious, the two brutes with pointed ears and wicked clawed hands who stood giving orders from the back, failed to notice the Darkslayer before he had almost passed them. They screeched as he passed as if to taunt him into battle with them, but this did not slow the burly man from his mission. In haste, the Vicious set out in pursuit.

The two underling predators were fast enough to catch a human in seconds, yet they could not close in on this charging man, although they were close enough to see the wide V-shaped tattoo that stretched across his thickly muscled back. Impassioned by the sight, the almost equally muscled Vicious could only scream and gnash their teeth as they pursued this human juggernaut who clearly showed no interest in them, if he had even noticed them at all.

He tore roughshod through the shocked rear Badoon ranks, leaving all in his path mangled or dead, and drawing the first pools of blood. He was closing in on the front lines, and as each stride became quicker and longer, the dark bodies continued to fall. Finally the moment for a direct melee with his most hated enemies had arrived. Leaping into the air from his long-running start and roaring his battle cry, the Darkslayer cleared several heads of the underlings before landing like a great boulder, crushing two or three beneath him and slamming others with his shield.

The dwarfs heard the sounds of crunched bones over the battle-field, and it fueled their own fury. Upon landing among the Badoons, the Darkslayer rolled across the hard dusty ground and sprang to his feet. Instantly Brool became a whirling razor-edge of death.

The veteran underling warriors were caught off guard by the Darkslayer's sudden appearance, and many fell helplessly to his fury before the rest became aware of the Darkslayer in their midst. Now the black blood of the underlings began spreading over the ground in pools like oil, streaming and showering as their limbs and heads fell upon the ground as easily as autumn leaves in the wind, at the mercy of the Darkslayer's whirling arm and Brool's wide-arc-ing twin blades. The bloodrangers found renewed strength in their lungs as the Darkslayer's arrival refilled their weakening hearts with vigor. The Vicious were struggling to reach the Darkslayer after his amazing leap into the midst of their brethren. Heartlessly, they began to carve a path through their own ranks to get to him.

In the ensuing chaos the underling ranks resembled rats in a whirlpool; the more they struggled and thrashed, the less progress they made against the relentless, swirling mayhem. The focus of the underling brigade had always been the killing of the Darkslayer, and that is what they all now tried to do, but their efforts were chaotic and uncoordinated. The surrounded bloodrangers, who moments earlier had been facing defeat, remained exhausted, bleeding, and dying, yet they did not hesitate to take advantage as the underlings tried to run blindly through them to reach the Darkslayer. Heavy crossbow bolts penetrated the heads of underling warriors with unfailing accuracy. The bloodrangers' green and brown garb was now soaked red and black. Their hand axes also chopped, slowing the underling pressure toward the Darkslayer, but the Badoon numbers were overwhelming the dwarfs, whose wounds took a toll on their efforts. The underlings were falling one by one rather than in heaps, not fast enough to save the Darkslayer, who was being swamped by a sudden onslaught that had come upon him.

Brool swung high and low in large arcing circles at such speed that the Badoon underlings had to hesitate before entering the melee, and those who entered paid dearly. Venir swooped his one-and-a-half-handed axe forward and backward in an unpredictable rhythm, making it difficult to jab a blade at him. One bold underling who timed it perfectly got close enough to slash at his legs only have his head crushed by the edge of Venir's iron shield, while another nipped in and out only to have the tip of Brool's spike tear out his throat. Several more fell in similar fashion. The poisoned bolts of the underling crossbows were ineffective, as the underlings could not see to shoot over their own, so the battle became short swords and daggers against Brool. Rage seemed to overcome reason for the underlings who ran into Brool's erratic path and died. The underlings arsenal was no match for the Darkslayer.

As galled as the Vicious were, they remained cool, and had enough presence of mind to try to reorganize their Badoons before they all fell at the hands of the bloodrangers and the great axe of the Dark-slayer. As the dwarfs began carving into the underling hunters with increasing success, the Vicious regained control of their troops and redirected them toward the bloodrangers. One moment the Dark-slayer seemed to be slaughtering at will, and the next moment there were none within striking distance, for the remaining underlings were more than willing to take their chances against the giant dwarfs rather than face the Darkslayer's unstoppable fury.

After a moment's confusion as the Darkslayer peered for his prey, he noticed the Vicious beginning to circle him and howled with rage. Managing to clear some of the battle rage from his head, he recognized that the Vicious were not like anything he had encoun-tered before, but deep in the back of his mind he knew what they were and became wary.

Covered in black gore from helm to toe, except for his blazing blue eyes and the glint of steel from Brool, the man in the spiked helm was breathing heavily, his body exhausted and being pushed now beyond human limits. It was enough than his hatred for the underlings would never allow him to rest, but his helm, axe, and shield would not relent, either. In unison, the armaments he had donned seemed to consume his whole body, driving him mercilessly onwards. His mind screamed, wanting it all to end, once and for all, but he knew there was only one way it could ever end, at least for today. He had to fight to the finish yet again. It was time to dish out more revenge.

Flanked by the Vicious on both sides, the Darkslayer saw no value in going on the defensive. He leapt into action. Charging toward one Vicious he was quickly pursued by the other. The first Vicious readied hungry claws and teeth for the oncoming human while

Brool swung accurately at its head, but barely missed as the hulking Vicious was too quick and agile a brute. The pursuing Vicious began attacking the Darkslayer, who was already parrying, and both Vicious were now engaged at close proximity. It was clear that the Vicious wanted to wrestle him down to tear him to shreds and eat him alive. The Darkslayer knew they were more than capable of it, for they were possibly the fastest and most agile creatures he had ever faced. Brool cut and whirled in offense and defense, in short and long arcs, keeping the Vicious constantly at bay. They, in turn, pressed in with slash after slash at every conceivable opening, while artfully avoiding impalement or decapitation from Brool's spike and blade. The claws of the Vicious left their marks, inflicting more severe cuts than all the other Badoon underlings together. The claw marks burned and bled freely—as was the nature of Vicious wounds—taking their toll and draining his blood. Even his anger could not overcome the dizzying loss of strength he was experiencing.

Somewhere in his mind he knew he was losing, but he hung on regardless, battling through the pain without any fear of dying, for death meant nothing to the Darkslayer. He could slowly bleed to death at their mercy, he surmised, or try to kill at least one of them before he died. It would give the bloodrangers one less adversary to deal with. Reaching deep within himself he summoned all the anger and hatred he had left for one more valiant onslaught. Choosing his final victim, he slung his shield into the fang-like teeth of the Vicious, who howled in pain and surprise; instantly the Darkslayer raised Brool two-handedly over his head and wrenched it down with such speed and accuracy that the air winced at the blow. The Vicious dodged but lost its entire left leg. Defiant, the dismembered Vicious regained its balance and prepared to fight back. The lost leg seemed not to hinder or even hurt it as the Vicious crouched to spring one last attack. Against any other warrior on Bish the Vicious might surely have won the battle, but not against the Darkslayer. As the

Vicious leapt, Brool was chopping too rapidly, and the mutilated creature could only watch as parts of its body were hacked off like chunks of wood, until its magical life force finally subsided forever.

But the final blows came at a great price to the Darkslayer, as the remaining Vicious grappled him from behind until his shredded, battle-weary arms could swing no more, and the great axe slipped from his bloodied grasp. The Vicious grasped the Darkslayer in a firm choke hold and wrenched off his helm with a powerful yank that should have torn though the chin strap, but did not. The Vicious hung on to the roaring brute like an enormous blood leach, while its deadly claws cut and bored more painful, bleeding holes into the great man's body. It was man versus Vicious now as the unarmed and unarmored Darkslayer began the most epic struggle for his life. But dying, bleeding, and choking were nothing new to the Darkslayer, whose blood-soaked blonde hair was now being ripped from his head, possibly as some act of humiliation. The unarmed warrior now fought his adversary on equal terms, flesh against flesh. Although Venir had nothing left in his gut, and his exhausted body could no longer respond to the demands of his angry mind, somehow he continued to fight back. The two thrashed about the barren rocky ground, entwined like pythons. Venir's hard head, powerful elbows, and honed instincts kept the Vicious from taking complete control. Unused to the frustration of failure, the powerful underling suddenly let go.

The two warriors of opposing races now faced each other at a short distance. The Vicious clicked his talon-like fingers together, beckoning the wounded man to attack. The Vicious knew that the Darkslayer had nothing left that could hurt it, but it did not want the man to just die without a fight. In his mind Venir knew that this was it for him, and he charged in hard to receive two clawed hands puncturing him deep into his bloodied chest. But he did not cry out. Instead he clutched the evil thing's throat in his powerful hands and squeezed with all his might. The eyes of the Vicious bulged from their sockets and its black tongue gagged soundlessly. Blood came from the Darkslayer's lips as their eyes locked. The eyes of both were full of hate, and then, mockingly, the Vicious smiled. Venir's grip slackened, his body became ashen, and his remaining strength was not enough to stop him from slumping to the ground. He was helpless to stop the Vicious from ripping him apart.

Luckily, the king of the bloodrangers, Mood himself, was there to help. He began bludgeoning the clinging Vicious with the back of both his big hand axes. The big dwarf could not stand by to see any creature kill his friend. But he was astonished that his pounding had so little effect in loosening its grip. The Vicious merely scowled at the great bushy-faced dwarf and hung onto the dying man like a giant black tick. Mood tried using the blades of his axes, but that too made no difference. The thick skin of the Vicious showed slashes, but no sign of blood.

"What in the seven cities of Bish is this *thing*?" Mood bellowed, and began pounding the evil thing on the head as hard as he could without injuring Venir. Chongo joined in with his snapping teeth, but to no avail.

At the sight of the dying Venir, Georgio was moved to action, and he took out his new sword and poked at the monster. The Vicious let out a terrific scream of pain, but still it held on to the Darkslayer.

"Gimme that, boy." Mood snatched the sword from the unwilling Georgio and began jabbing the Vicious further. Though the sword did not fully penetrate the monster's hide, it did enough to make the creature let go of the Darkslayer so it could defend itself.

Now Chongo and Mood were able to keep the Vicious at bay while Melegal tended to the Darkslayer. The bloodranger and the two-headed dog cut off any further attempts of the Vicious to get near the man it had come to kill. Chongo managed to bite deep into its leg and hold it, while Mood slashed it deeply in the chest. The

Vicious drove its claws into Chongo, and the dog had to release it. But the furious Vicious remained at bay, with the dog and dwarf in relentless attack.

"Vee, what do you need?" Melegal asked in shock; his friend was pale and on the brink of death.

"Helm." This single, almost inaudible word was all the warrior's cracked and bloodied lips could muster.

"Georgio, Lefty! Find his helmet *now!*" yelled Melegal, spurring them into action. It was Lefty who made it back with the helm. Georgio showed up with Brool, while Melegal blinked sadly and placed the helmet back onto the big man's head. There was no response from Venir, whose eyes were closed. His breathing appeared to have stopped.

"Is he going to die?" Georgio asked, tears welling in his eyes.

Melegal looked back silently in pity and compassion. Then the helm flashed with white light. Venir gasped in a huge gulp of air. His bleeding stopped, and his color quickly returned. And then the Darkslayer was rising back onto his feet, his blue eyes blazing for battle once again.

"Give me my axe, boy," he said in his deep, rich voice, extending his hand to Georgio. Grasping Brool, the Darkslayer turned back toward the Vicious, and Georgio, Lefty, and Melegal cheered.

———

Verbard and Catten had been careless in their arrogance. And the appearance of the Nameless Two could not have come at a better time for those engaged in battle at the Warfield. Together, the Nameless Two attacked Verbard first, piercing the mage's chest clean through the back of his robes even before the powerful underling had a chance to counter. Falling to his knees, Verbard managed a protection spell just in time to prevent any additional attacks. The

Nameless Two, thinking Verbard dead, moved immediately on to Catten. But Catten was ready. Uttering magic words as the Nameless Two approached, he watched their heads burst into flame. Yet still they came after him, not screaming nor hindered at all by the magical flames.

"Catten," croaked Verbard pleadingly, for his wounds were critical.

Catten waved his hands and the Nameless Two were hurled, flaming heads and all, out of the cave mouth and over the giant hillside. Then Catten quickly came to his brother's aid and managed to slow the severe bleeding, but only temporarily. The wounds were grave and his brother was still in great agony. The underling lords were not as savvy in healing as in harming, which made Verbard's situation more serious than they were accustomed to. He could take the opportunity to kill his brother, thought Catten, but the timing was not yet right. With a quick examination, Catten determined that they needed the help of an underling cleric. But before he took his brother back to the Underland for better care, he chose to make sure that the battle at the Warfield had been taken care of.

What he saw did not please him at all, and he let out a shriek of rage.

"What now? Is he not dead yet?" Verbard dragged himself up to look at the events of the Warfield. Aghast, their silver and gold eyes watched the events unfold after the first Vicious was killed by the Darkslayer.

"We have to kill him now, Verbard," Catten seethed. "We may not get another chance."

"I have nothing for you, brother," said Verbard grimly. "I need all my strength to get home. Do what you can, and do it now."

Silently, Catten began a new incantation.

Dusk was falling as the Darkslayer turned to finish off the wounded underling creature that was being kept at bay by Mood and Chongo. The Vicious was incredulous to see the warrior approaching, unfettered, fully healed, and determined to kill it. It hissed ferociously. As the Darkslayer went in for the attack, thunder cracked from a distant rocky hilltop, and lightening exploded beneath the Darkslayer's feet in a blinding flash that knocked them all off their feet. The Darkslayer went down, stunned momentarily, while thunder continued to roll and winds swirled about the battlefield. The others were also dazed and struggling to regain their feet, while Chongo howled amidst the continuous thunder. Unfazed, the Vicious seized its opportunity, snatched up the curly-locked Georgio by his neck, and waved him before the Darkslayer. Still staggering, the Darkslayer's eyesight recovered from the blinding flash to face the sight of Georgio's face going purple as he dangled from the neck. The Vicious hissed out an evil laugh and ran a clawed finger from its other hand across the boy's throat, cutting it wide open, then it dropped Georgio coldly to the ground, where he lay in a growing pool of his own blood.

As Melegal and Lefty screamed and Chongo and Mood howled, the Darkslayer moved in to kill the Vicious. Cackling mockingly, it ducked and dodged the Darkslayer and his friends, but Brool's keen edge got closer and closer with each swing. Venir was in control of the Darkslayer now. Despite his rage and anger, he had it under control and he was going to put an end to this menace once and for all, and somehow save young Georgio. The Vicious mocked and dodged but could not run, for Mood and Chongo kept him corralled so that it had no choice but to face Venir.

Then, quick as a cobra, the powerful creature leapt at the Darkslayer, its Vicious clawed hand slashing. Instantly Brool sliced off the hand. The other clawed hand followed even faster, and Brool lopped it off at the wrist. Now the evil Vicious howled and screeched in rage and waved its bleeding stumps at its tormentor before leaping in again. In one swipe the great serrated spike of the axe ripped open its jaw, silencing it once and for all. The black thing fell to its knees, and stared hatefully as Venir looked into its merciless eyes and swept Brool down in a overhead two-handed chop that crunched deep into the marrow. He repeated the move several times, with one more for Georgio, and the final blow stopped its black heart.

It had all happened in seconds but it had seemed much longer. Nothing remained of the Vicious but a blackened heap and two severed clawed hands.

All the while, Melegal held Georgio's limp body in his arms, his head in his lap, with Lefty giving what aid or comfort he could. Tears were streaming down Lefty's face. His makeshift bandages were soaked red around Georgio's neck. Melegal had never experienced such a loss before.

As Venir came to kneel with his helm in his hand, Lefty cried, "The helm, let's use the helm!" Venir reached the helm down towards his young friend's head, his own face streaked from his eye sockets to his grimy cheeks, though not with tears but sweat. Yet his rugged face was torn with his own personal agony.

The boy coughed suddenly, and then again and again. Astonished, Melegal sat the boy up to help him from choking, and then Georgio screamed.

"Save me, Vee! Save me!" he cried, over and over again.

Venir dropped the helmet and grabbed the boy in his arms.

"Georgio, you're alive! Let me see your neck!" He removed the bandages. The boy's neck was bloodied but the nasty slash was closed and healed, almost as if nothing had happened. "You're a Regener! You're gonna be fine for a long, long time, boy!" Venir sat back, staring at the boy in rapture.

Then Georgio hugged him.

"He's a what?" asked Melegal, whose face shone with an emotion he had rarely felt before.

"He's a self-healer," Venir beamed. "He regenerates. I kinda suspected it long ago. Anyway, he's gonna be your friend for a long, long time, Melegal." The warrior winked. "I don't think we could get rid of Georgio if we tried! And I wouldn't want to, either!" He was still hugging the boy.

"Oh great." Melegal kept his head down, trying to hide his watery eyes. Even the grizzly Mood showed a smile, while Lefty jumped onto Georgio's back.

Chongo, meanwhile, was happily devouring the remains of the Vicious.

"I cannot believe this, Verbard. I cannot believe this."

"We had him, Catten. We had him. And now we have lost a brigade of our finest underling warriors and hunters, as well as Master Sinway's precious pets, the Vicious."

"My spell did not make a direct hit!" Catten spluttered, dumbfounded. "And that human boy appears to have revived!"

"Something has changed this day, brother," Verbard rasped weakly. "Something does not add up. Does that make sense to you?"

"Yes, I think it does. You have no time to spare, however. We must go now." Verbard did not object. In unison, the two brothers began concentrating, and blinked out of the cave. It was the first step of a strenuous journey back to the Underland.

Only six bloodrangers remained at the Warfield, plus their king, Mood. In no other battle had more than two bloodrangers ever died. But not a single underling hunter from the Badoon brigade remained. Upon the arrival of the Darkslayer, the bloodranger dwarfs had been able to rally and quickly carve up the underlings who foundered without the leadership of the Vicious. Still, the loss of six bloodrangers did not seem possible, and Mood was left wondering about this. The past few days had seen strange events, and many people of all races everywhere on Bish had begun to take note of this, especially the halfling Lefty Lightfoot.

Georgio was shaken, but the curvy dwarven ladies cleaned him up and calmed his young nerves with their healing and soothing touches. Melegal, Lefty, Mood, and Venir were all amazed that he lived and had not the slightest scar as evidence that he had almost died. Venir himself had scars all over, and those inflicted by the Vicious would prove the worst of them all. Venir's thoughts went back to the lightening.

"Did anyone notice where that lightening came from?" he asked.

"I saw it come from that mountain hill." Georgio pointed.

"I wonder if that's something we need to check out. Any ideas?"

"Yeah, let's get back to Bone," Melegal chimed in. "That's been my idea all along." He sounded more cheerful than usual.

"Well, I recall it was your idea to leave in the first place. And look at you, not a scratch on you anywhere!"

"It was your fault we had to leave. And I avoid booboos, unlike you."

"Come to think of it, I don't even remember why we left!"

"I'll refresh your memory on the way back, then."

"Thanks, Melegal. I'm looking forward to it already."

"Can I come?" Lefty Lightfoot had been so quiet he was all but forgotten; he had been busy writing something all along. Venir and Melegal looked at each other.

"Shall we let Georgio decide?" suggested Venir.

"He's definitely coming! But what about the mountain that

shoots lightening?"

"It doesn't appear to be shooting lightening right now, and I don't feel like fighting any mountains tonight," Venir answered.

"Me either," Georgio said. "And I really hate underlings now, Vee. I'm glad I'm not dead. I'd have missed you guys. What would've happened if I was dead?"

Venir shrugged. "Let's have no more close calls, Georgio, and let's get you home safe and sound. But we'll take a trip to the big city, first. Sound good?"

"Yeah!" Georgio, Lefty, and Melegal all agreed.

Mood returned to Dwarven Hole for the mourning of the lost bloodrangers in a battle that was to be remembered forever. The loss would be hard on his people, and they would need his help to get them through it.

The Nameless Two did not die below their hillside at the Warfield, but survived and returned to their cave. Their heads had long been extinguished, although they could no longer see one another. Blinded and disfigured by Catten's flames, they were still able to see the Warfield, but that was all they would ever see again.

Humiliated, Catten and his healed brother Verbard were given an audience with Master Sinway. If Master Sinway was disappointed or angered at their failure to slay the Darkslayer, he did not show it. He asked only one question.

"Do you have another plan?"

"Yes," said Verbard.

———

Royal Lord Almen had been busy with so many things that for days he had not given much thought to the absence of McKnight, Oran, or Tonio. But now he began to wonder if he would ever see them again. His son Tonio had been the pride of the House of Almen, and although his new condition did not bode well for Almen, Tonio was still useful. Detective McKnight had always been a resourceful ally and henchman, and his loss would indeed be a loss, something Almen did not need at the moment while he was under pressure from rival houses. He needed all the loyal bodies he could find, and his son and McKnight were two of them. Underling Oran he could do without, however, for he could not be trusted. It had occurred to Almen when they left that this might be the last time he saw any of them, but he hoped that he had not been right. In the meantime, he got back to his normal daily activities. He would find out about them soon enough, he decided.

McKnight's body, and the various parts of Tonio did not lie long on the ground after Venir and his company had departed. As night fell on their corpse-like figures, mysterious creatures came upon them. Several spider-like beings the size of large dogs surrounded each of them in the Great Forest. These strange creatures had never before been seen on Bish. They had the bodies of tarantulas but the torsos of humans, with arms and heads much like normal people, but not quite. The faces of these creatures were like those of other men on Bish, except that they had paired eyes like those of insects, and two small antenna protruded from their heads that were covered in jet-black hair. They carried small spears and had no need for clothing.

These creatures dragged McKnight alongside Tonio's parts, and laid them side by side. They communicated in whispers of high and low pitch like wind whipping through forests. They were mostly preoccupied with Tonio. A leader seemed to settle their discussion, and then two arachna-men lifted each body off of the ground, while two others stood before the men and began blowing at them. As the creatures opened their mouths, wide threads of spider silk emerged and began winding around Tonio and McKnight's bodies as the other two arachna-men spun them around. Soon each of them was enclosed in a cocoon. Then they gathered up the cocoons and carried them high into the giant tree tops of the great forest, before disappearing from sight on their tarantula legs.

Through the secret entrance and back into the stables in City of Bone passed a ragged party of four on two mounts, a shaggy quick-pony and a great, panting two-headed bull mastiff.

In the room above the Drunken Octopus, the four of them were comfortable enough, as Lefty and Georgio took up very little space. For days they slept and ate constantly, while Lefty's pen continuously chronicled all that they did. He asked question after question of Venir in particular, all of which Venir was more than happy to relate, especially while reveling; in fact, the warrior seemed to enjoy having his own personal scribe.

Still, Melegal could not help but notice that his friend had suffered more than he cared to let on. The wounds ran deep from the last battle, and the near loss of Georgio had frightened them all. The thief could see that Venir was content to remain in the City of Bone for the meantime, and so they made the most of it.

Georgio was not much the worse for wear. Indeed, he enjoyed cutting himself and watching his wounds heal. He also ate a lot. He did have bad nightmares, however, and would scream like a banshee in the middle of the night, clutching at his throat. Melegal took delight in complaining about the whole adventure, while Venir wondered how many underlings he had killed and how many more he still had to kill. Adventure beckoned, but for the moment it would have to wait. Recreation and relaxation were the priority for the small group right now. For the changed world of Bish would not wait long before thrusting its greatest hero, the Darkslayer, back into the field. In the meantime, its other heroes and villains had plenty to do.

The days ahead would all be different now, ever since that day at the Warfield when the ripple caused by Scorch had rapidly taken effect throughout the world of Bish. But for now, the Darkslayer's shield, his helm, and his great axe Brool lay quietly in their leather sack that served as their sanctuary in another dimension. Yet even inside that unique leather sack, their services were still needed, and someone who had been looking for them for a long, long time was on the brink of finding them once again.

ABOUT
THE AUTHOR

Craig Halloran resides with his family outside of his hometown Charleston, West Virginia. When he isn't writing stories he is seeking adventure, working out or watching sports. To learn more about him go to: www.thedarkslayer.com